MW00587370

"I think somebody nothing."

"Let's get clear about why you're here," I suggested. "You want me to decide if this threat is real or not. Is that it?"

"Yes."

"How do you imagine I can do that?"

"I don't know. Can't you recognize paranoia when you see it? Didn't they teach you that at therapist school?" Her tone was sharp, but not offensive.

"I must've been sick that day. And I'm afraid I don't have any business seeing someone I've been arrested with. It's not ethical to have a dual relationship, and there are good reasons for that."

"So what are you saying? You can't help me?" Her smooth voice went up in pitch at the end of both questions more than called for. It was a novel form of emphasis.

I thought about it for a while, and she let me. In hindsight, my decision-making was skewed by my attraction to Dizzy, so I made a leap to an even more inappropriate behavior than she was asking. "Do you know what I did for a living before this?"

"No, but let me guess. Pro football?"

I shook my head.

"Fireman?"

"No, but that's a good guess. It would explain the burn scars."

"I give up. Just don't tell me you were a serial murderer, okay?"

"I was a private investigator. And I still have a gun and a permit to carry it. Dizzy, you're looking at your new bodyguard."

Praise for Verlin Darrow

Finalist for Next Generation Indie Book Awards—best mystery of 2018 (Blood and Wisdom). This is the largest non-profit book award organization in the world.

"Verlin Darrow has a sense of plot and style that carries the reader forward into that special place of anxious expectation, the place where putting the book down is unthinkable. Darrow gets us into the minds of people you wouldn't want to invite for dinner. Fascinating."
~ Richard House, MD, author of Between Now and When.

"I am so engaged by Verlin Darrow's writing. He thinks outside the box, brings in-depth insights down to real-world behavior, provides constant introspection flavored w/philosophical truisms, superbly mixes the cosmic w/the comic."
~Steve Lawton, publisher, Otter B Books.

Murder for Liar

by

Verlin Darrow

This is a work of fiction. Names, characters, places, and incidents are either the product of the author's imagination or are used fictitiously, and any resemblance to actual persons living or dead, business establishments, events, or locales, is entirely coincidental.

Murder for Liar

COPYRIGHT © 2023 by Verlin Darrow

Cover Art by *Kim Mendoza*

The Wild Rose Press, Inc.
PO Box 708
Adams Basin, NY 14410-0708
Visit us at www.thewildrosepress.com

Publishing History
First Edition, 2023
Trade Paperback ISBN 978-1-5092-4897-1
Digital ISBN 978-1-5092-4898-8

Published in the United States of America

Dedication

To my loving, supportive wife Lusijah, who also helps me realize what doesn't make sense in my manuscripts (there's always a healthy quotient).

Chapter 1

Once I saw a male penguin courting on television. He selected a small black rock he imagined the female might like, transported it with his long, thin beak across a desolate shore, and then laid it gently at the feet of his beloved. The female, however, was fussy, and this first offering failed to warm her heart. Second and third efforts fared no better, and a pile of smooth black stones accumulated, each studiously chosen and painstakingly hauled into place. Finally, one of the gifts pleased the female, and the birds mated off-screen, their hot penguin love presumably too provocative for public viewing.

Did the rocks vary in any significant way? Not to my eye. Had the male proved his commitment by bringing a certain number of rocks? Was the female helping her future mate understand the essential capriciousness of intimate relationships? I don't know.

I feel as though this snippet of bird courtship lore is the core metaphor of my life, except that unlike the male penguin, I've never selected a rock that worked. I don't mean just with women. It's as though everyone else knows something I don't, or at least they all pretend they do, perhaps following a set of conventions no one's told me about.

So what profession does a confused-by-penguins kind of guy ultimately select? Psychotherapy. "It takes one to know one," my aunt liked to chant. She also was fond of declaring, "To each his own, said the lady as she kissed the cow," so I never relied too heavily on her folk wisdom. But there is certainly truth in the notion that therapists in all the standard flavors—psychiatrists, psychologists, social workers, and counselors (listed in descending order of average fee)—tend to be at least odd. I believe most practitioners are drawn to their livelihood by an unconscious understanding that healing is omnidirectional. The client and the therapist both reap the rewards of their sessions, and sometimes elderly psychologists are almost tolerable at cocktail parties.

As for me, at age forty-four after fifteen years in private practice, the process was still ongoing. I was nowhere near as depressed and anxious as when I began, yet no one would nominate me as a poster boy for American mental health.

It was difficult to ascertain how my open-door policy affected my long-term healing. Unlike virtually every other therapist in Santa Cruz, I saw absolutely any client, no matter how bizarre, obnoxious, or hopeless. By weathering the entire available continuum, I hoped to expose myself to the maximum dose of reciprocal healing. Sometimes, though, severe pathology and aberrant personality disorders functioned purely as corrosive solvents, attacking the structural integrity of anyone in the room.

It was rarely dull—that's one thing I can state with certainty. Northern California is simply a lively place to practice. It's chock full of offbeat psyches. Some of my all-time favorites: a man deathly afraid of spontaneous combustion, a couple who could only make satisfying love in the back of pickup trucks, and a young girl who believed she was the reincarnation of a rock star who wasn't dead. Usually I heard "I can't sleep," "I'm anxious at work," or "There's nothing wrong with me—I'm just here to make my wife/mom/boss happy." These generally serve as prologues to the actual work. The core task is uncovering what lies beneath such presentations. Being a therapist is like being a detective, except the suspect has already turned himself in.

Despite this advantage, clients can be even less cooperative than criminals. For one thing, they're often unaware of their hidden material. For another, most people work at least as hard at maintaining the status quo as they do on changing, regardless of whose office they've dragged themselves into. So a therapist is compelled to work with a client's unconscious psyche, which often embodies a completely alien agenda. Sometimes I felt as if there were a secret race from some other world that lived deep inside us all. An alliance between these strangers and our conscious selves was not a simple matter to negotiate.

At any rate, George Arundel was something new, and by now this was rare. I met him at my downtown Santa Cruz office on a Tuesday afternoon in late April. My first impression was of a tall, overweight fifty-year-old White man who couldn't accept his baldness. Arundel's combing-forward strategy lent his forehead a comic-strip-character effect, as if a lazy illustrator hadn't bothered to sketch in all the details. His facial features were reasonably regular, although his mouth was a bit oversized and his teeth were worn and rounded, as though his diet included rocks or something else much harder than ordinary food. He was pale and freckled, and he wore a white dress shirt and brown wool pants.

"Tom Dashiel?" he asked, extending a large pink

hand as he hovered in my doorway. The tone of his question implied an uncertainty beyond a first meeting's customary hesitancy. Could he be seriously wondering if I was an imposter?

"That's me," I responded. "And you're George Arundel?" I was conscious of an odd feeling as I strode forward and shook his meaty, moist hand—something tight in my gut. Before I could process it, my prospective client had nodded and asked another question.

"This is your office?"

"Yes. Please come in."

He hesitated, as if unsure whether to believe me or not.

"Is there a particular concern I can help you with right now?" I asked in my fragile-client voice.

"Well, I expected something rather different," he answered, still frozen in the doorway. His voice betrayed no anxiety, just mild surprise. Apparently, this was sufficient to immobilize him.

"Would you like to sit down and talk about it?"

"Of course, of course," Arundel sing-songed, surging past me with great energy. This behavior was completely incongruous with my sense of the man thus far. He plopped down in the green armchair that was obviously mine, sighed heavily, and peered around with no apparent interest. That is, his eyes surveyed the contents of the room—the antique wooden furniture, the floral watercolors on the walls, the one large window— yet there was no impression that anyone saw them. His face was a mask, and his eyes seemed to be sending signals that never reached Arundel Central.

So far, I'd observed enough pathology to justify a few different diagnoses. I tried to ignore all that and focus on the matter at hand as I seated myself across from Arundel. It was distracting, though, to see the room from the perspective of the client's chair. The desk and coffee table really didn't match the way they appeared to from my usual seat. And the gray carpet bulged in two spots in front of the window as though it covered some embarrassing secret. Dead rats? God knows why I thought of that.

"So you had particular expectations?" I began.

"Yes." The brain and the eyes were back on line.

I caught a faint whiff of body odor and realized the scent had been lingering in the air. It just hadn't registered yet as I focused in my customary way on visual input.

We stared at one another for a moment. All I knew about Arundel before that day was that he'd been referred by a local psychiatrist who had described him as "a substantial challenge." This was standard inter-clinician code for "a big pain in the ass."

"I had a dream," he told me. Now his voice was soft—a stage whisper.

"A dream?"

"Right. You were smaller and younger, and your office was like a washroom in an old train station."

"Are you disappointed?"

"No. Should I be?"

I shrugged in lieu of explaining my strong feelings about the word should. I wish we could just exorcise the concept from our language.

"I can feel myself adjusting," Arundel reported.

This struck me as worth investigating. "What does it feel like?"

"Like adjusting."

"I'm not sure I know what you mean."

"So?"

"You don't care?"

"Should I?"

Here we were again. I didn't respond. Arundel began cleaning one of his ears with his index finger. After a long pause I decided to start from scratch.

"What brings you here?" I asked, my standard opening line when I haven't been preempted by a client's idiosyncrasies.

"I need help," he announced, squinting his eyes as though I was emitting a strong glare.

"Why do you say that?"

"I cannot fulfill my mission without help." Arundel shifted in his chair.

I did likewise without thinking about it. Now we were both tilted to our left, with our legs crossed. "Your mission?"

"That's right." Arundel began cleaning his other ear.

"What do you mean?"

"Surely you know the meaning of the word 'mission'?" He was smiling now, but it was a cold, creepy smile.

"I'm interested in what your idea of the word is," I explained.

"My personal definition is no different than the one in a dictionary."

"And what would that be?"

"A series of tasks designed to achieve certain goals." Finished with his ears, he laid his hands on his expansive belly, one on top of the other.

I was struck by Arundel's ability to provide a concise, accurate definition of a fairly complex term. It's been my experience that the average person can't manage that.

"So you need my help, but you'd prefer not to tell me why at this point?" I tried.

"I have told you why."

"But how can I help you fulfill your mission if you won't tell me what the mission is?"

"Won't is not the proper word. Won't implies a willful disobedience over the course of time. As yet, I haven't told you what you want to know, but that doesn't mean I won't." He smiled briefly and then looked down at his hands.

For some reason, my gaze fell even lower, and I found myself studying his shoes. They were unremarkable low-tech white running shoes, except for a small, well-formed letter K scrawled across the toe of each one in black Magic Marker. A team insignia? Borrowed shoes? Was Arundel his real name?

I looked up quickly, expecting to be caught out; it seems as though clients always know when their therapist has become distracted. George Arundel, though, was still gazing serenely at the pile of fingers on his gut.

"So are you ready to tell me?" I asked.

"No. It will work out best if I don't go into that now. But the time will come when it will be appropriate."

I was struck, once again, by the formality of the man's language, and also by the literal quality of most of his responses. Technically, he always answered my questions, yet no information beyond the bare minimum was ever transmitted. What did I know so far? Practically nothing.

Belatedly, I was aware that Arundel had thoroughly

wrested control of the session away from me. By sitting in my chair, playing games instead of providing useful answers to my questions, and lecturing me on word usage, he had created a context in which he was comfortable. That it might have come at my expense didn't seem important to him. I was impressed by the efficacy of this feat but also disconcerted by the way this Arundel varied so drastically from the confused soul who had loitered in my doorway minutes before.

"Perhaps you'd like to tell me something else about yourself?" I suggested.

"What would you like to know?" He uncrossed his legs and stretched them toward me. A moment later, he retracted them and recrossed his legs, restoring his original position. Then he jiggled his foot arrhythmically. The movement implied both a restlessness and an urgency he hadn't exhibited thus far.

I was perversely pleased to see it. "What do you feel would be relevant to our work here?" I asked. I was trying hard to remain non-directive. On the one hand, continuing to ask him to supply an agenda was playing into his game of holding the power by refusing me, but on the other hand I wasn't ready to abandon one of my key principles yet. I firmly believe that session agendas need to emerge from the client, and what clients choose to share is a vital piece in the therapeutic jigsaw puzzle.

"I have no idea at this time," Arundel finally pronounced. "Do you?"

"Well, there are certain areas that are customarily discussed."

As soon as these words crossed my lips, I regretted them. They were nothing more than an announcement that I would indeed collude with Arundel in the business of my own manipulation. It was one thing to choose that course of action consciously, but I had simply spoken carelessly and now here we were.

Arundel frowned, perhaps disappointed that I didn't represent a more formidable challenge. "What?" he asked sweetly.

What the hell, I thought. "Let's see. Occupation, family of origin, current domestic situation—that sort of thing. I can't help you unless I understand your life context."

"Administrator, a mother, father, and brother, and I live alone," he reported.

"Are you uncomfortable letting me know you? Do you distrust me?"

"No. Not at all." He held his foot still and made an obvious, concerted effort to physically relax. "Do I look uncomfortable?" he asked.

"Not now," I replied, smiling.

He ignored this, waiting expectantly for me to continue. I thought about making a stand by remaining silent or saying something like "that's my answer," but I decided to raise the stakes even higher.

"Look," I began, "talking with you feels like pulling teeth. You've systematically refused to cooperate with me, and frankly, I'm feeling very frustrated. If we can't deal with any meaningful content in here today, then at least let's talk about why we can't. You must have some reason for your reticence."

I figured I'd either lose Arundel entirely or else jar him into loosening up. If he wouldn't give a little, I didn't care to work with him anyway. I didn't consider he'd find a way to deflect the substantive portion of my diatribe, rendering the choice irrelevant.

"So everything that happens has a reason?"

I sighed. "That's my belief. Yes."

"Such an attitude inevitably generates frustration," he told me.

"Do you have an alternate point of view?"

"Yes."

"Would you tell me about it?"

"No."

I wondered if he was this way with everyone. It would certainly explain why he had problems and needed therapy.

Suddenly, he stiffened. I can't think of any better way to describe it. He just became rigid. It wasn't a convulsion or a cramp or anything else I was familiar with. A second later, he was supple again, blinking furiously and poking his tongue out of his rounded mouth.

"Are you all right?" I asked, seriously concerned.

"I'm fine," he boomed. His voice was now low and loud. "But I have to go."

"But we haven't decided if we can work with each other," I pointed out.

"Yes!" he shouted.

I flinched as though I were being physically attacked—a first in a session. "Yes?" I mustered.

"Yes, we can!" he boomed.

"I'm not so sure. Why should I help you?"

"It's your job!" he roared.

My ears were beginning to hurt, and his verbal assault was churning my gut as well. "That doesn't mean I have to accept every potential client I meet. I don't have the impression you're interested in the sort of work I do."

After a pause, Arundel responded in a much quieter,

gentler voice. "I believe that a friend of mine is actually an angel."

I stared. "Is the same time next week convenient for you?"

"Yes." Arundel rose and clumped out of the room.

Chapter 2

There were still fifteen minutes remaining in the fifty-minute session. I sat and tried to make sense of my experience. An angel? Was that another ploy or a sincere belief? If it was just an attempt to ensure I'd see him again, it had certainly worked. My interest was piqued. Sincere or not, mentioning it the way he had, after all the verbal jousting, was strange. Strange enough to engage me long term? Perhaps. As far as I was concerned, though, the strangeness ran a great deal deeper than that.

Generally, people manifest a certain kind of internal integrity. That is, they may be composed of various parts and some of these parts might, at first glance, appear to be odd bedfellows or even paradoxical, but at a deeper level, the composite mosaic of personality traits makes sense. The sense may be idiosyncratic, bizarrely twisted, or hard to understand. But when I meet people, I can usually intuit that their way of being is in fact a way of being, not a random assortment of attributes.

I received no sense of this from George Arundel. For short stretches, his reactions had been consistent, but there seemed to be no unifying theme underlying the behaviors he'd demonstrated so far. It was more of an intuition than something I can describe well in words. I guess another way to say it is that I didn't experience the continuity I've come to associate with personhood.

Were I a fledgling therapist, I might have attributed

the phenomenon to a lack of perception on my part. After fifteen years, I interpreted it as evidence I had been chatting with a truly weird character.

I didn't have time to think about George Arundel for the rest of the week, but as the hour of his second session neared, I found myself eagerly anticipating the event. I was puzzled by this. Had I enjoyed the first session? No. Did I have some special interest in angels? No. Perhaps I'd developed a hitherto unknown fascination with delusional disorders? Another no.

I finally realized (on poor Alice Loomis' time) that I was looking forward to finding out what made Arundel tick. I use the vernacular since the attitude harkens back to my original, pre-jargon motivation for entering the field. I'm simply someone who wants to understand people. I guess I keep hoping that if I figure everybody else out, I might be able to help myself.

****

Arundel wore a black polo shirt and well-worn jeans this time. His belly bulged over a wide, black belt that gathered the waistband of the jeans. Perhaps he'd been heavier back when he'd purchased them. As he ambled through the doorway, he held his facial features markedly immobile. Even in default mode, he guarded against giving any clues about his inner experience.

I did find one. His gaze fell on a black and white photograph on the wall behind my desk, lingering for more than several beats. Apparently, Arundel's attention could be captured by landscape imagery—in this case, an undulating meadow studded with granite outcroppings. I'd taken it in New Zealand on a disastrous honeymoon. For some reason, it didn't remind me of my ex the way a lot of things did.

I nabbed my chair; he didn't seem to care. He opened his arms as he sat across from me, as if he were demonstrating how big a fish he'd caught.

"I'm prepared to answer more questions today," he told me.

"Great. Shall I get right to it, then?"

"By all means." This time he gestured with one arm, moving it horizontally across his body as though he were scattering seed. I couldn't discern any correlation between his words and his movements.

"You mentioned last week that you were an administrator. Who do you work for? What exactly do you do?"

"Once again, I'm afraid it would be best not to go into great detail. I am the number two man in an organization. I do what's needed, which varies a great deal."

"I'm getting an image of you smoking a cigar in an Italian restaurant, surrounded by burly men with machine guns."

Arundel held up a hand, although he presented the back of his hand rather than his palm. "Rest assured. It's not a criminal organization."

"I didn't think it actually was. I just wanted you to understand how my mind fills in the blanks you leave."

"That's fine. The way your mind works is a topic in which I have a great deal of interest."

"Why is that?"

"I'd rather not answer."

We were both silent then. A leaf blower whined in the yard next door as I watched Arundel survey the room carefully, never looking at me. After a few minutes he spoke. "I like the photograph," he said, pointing inaccurately over my shoulder.

"You do?"

"Yes."

"Why?" This is a question that therapists are taught to avoid. I break this rule regularly.

"I don't know. Perhaps because the pattern of the rocks resonates with something within me."

"That's an elegant thought," I commented. "I admire the way you use words."

"Thank you. At one time I was a professor of English literature."

"Really. Where was that?"

Arundel waved an arm vaguely toward the office window on his right, which faced west. "Back East," he replied.

I was encouraged; we were almost having a conversation. Perhaps if I could keep addressing the qualities embodied in his responses, instead of the stingy content itself, we could make some headway.

"That's an interesting phrase, isn't it?" I tried. "Back East. It seems to refer to more than geography."

Arundel nodded. "It definitely has cultural and sociological implications."

"There's a certain duality to it, too."

"There's no east without a west. That's true enough. But is that really duality?"

"What do you mean?"

"Is hot the opposite of cold or are they just arbitrary labels for certain ranges on a continuum of temperature? On our planet—and some say in the entire universe— traveling either east or west will eventually bring you to the same place. Where is the duality?"

"I don't know," I confessed. "Obviously you've put

a lot more thought into this than I have. Do you have an interest in philosophy?"

"In a way."

Back to silence. Apparently, that question had been too personal. I wanted to build on what we'd managed to eke out thus far, so I broke the silence this time.

"Is there anything else you're willing to tell me about yourself?" I asked.

"I am a careful man."

This cued me to study Arundel's face more closely. Could I discern caution? Dark stubble formed irregular patterns on his rounded cheeks. A horizontal indentation spanned the bridge of his long nose. Apparently, he sometimes wore glasses—or perhaps sunglasses—at least often enough to leave a mark. Dark semicircles sat under his deep set, brown eyes, which I'd never noticed before. I speculated that he'd slept poorly.

Sunlight filtered through leafy branches outside my window, casting dappled light on Arundel, highlighting a skin cancer scar on his temple, as well as a mostly closed hole in one earlobe. I could never remember which lobe was supposed to indicate someone was gay. If the hole was in the gay indicator lobe, perhaps he'd come out to the world with an earring and then retreated back in.

"What do you mean by careful?" I finally asked, foiled in my attempt to find wariness in his features.

"In this context, it means that there must be an exchange of information between us. I need to know who you are."

This interested me. In effect, he was saying "Let's reverse our roles," which provided me with a lovely opportunity to model behavior for him. Ordinarily, I wouldn't allow myself to abdicate the therapist role while in session. With Arundel, it felt perfectly appropriate to show him how to safely reveal himself. I couldn't resist one quick retaliatory response, though.

"What would you like to know?" I asked in true Arundel fashion.

"What theoretical school of therapy do you espouse?"

"None. My work is eclectic."

"Were you born with the last name of Dashiel?"

"Yes."

"Do you have a family?"

"I'm divorced, and we didn't have children. I'm in touch with my mother and an older sister, though." So far, so good. I was hoping he'd ask something inappropriate so I could demonstrate how to set limits.

"Are you right-handed?"

"Yes."

"Do you drive a foreign car?"

"Yes."

None of these questions were truly inappropriate, but they certainly didn't seem germane to our work, or even related to one another.

"Why is your face scarred?"

"An automobile accident. It didn't help my worn-out knees, either."

One of my cheeks had been badly burned, and a network of thin white scar tissue encircled the eye on the other side of my face. I was lucky to retain my vision, but unlucky in that I couldn't afford plastic surgery at the time, which my insurance company termed "elective." Later, when I had the money, I found that I'd become accustomed to my face. I'd always been a bit of a brute physically; now I had an obvious excuse to refrain from dating. That made things easier somehow. I hadn't had an urge to repair the damage in a long time.

"Have you ever traveled to Asia?" Arundel asked next.

"No. Just Hawaii."

"What did you do before you became a therapist?"

"A variety of things. Just before, I was a private detective, actually."

"Was it fun?"

"Fun? No, not really. It was usually boring and occasionally depressing. I mostly handled employee theft and divorce cases—accounts that my father passed on to me. And I wasn't particularly good at it."

"It's more exciting in the movies, eh?"

"Absolutely."

"Are you a picky eater?" Arundel asked next.

"No."

"Have house pets played an important role in your personal history?"

I had to think about that one. "I'd say yes," I replied.

"If you had to be an inanimate object, what would you be?"

"I can't imagine why you feel you need to know that, but in the interest of getting acquainted, I'll give it a try." I was obviously stalling. "Hmmm…you have to get into an odd frame of mind to even think about that. I'd say…Stonehenge."

"And what would your favorite color be?"

"Blue."

"Okay. That's it."

"It?"

"We're done. I'm satisfied." Arundel leaned back in

his chair and tried to assume a posture and expression of satisfaction. He looked constipated. He'd narrowed his eyes by pulling down his eyebrows, forming furrows above them, low on his forehead. His mouth tightened as well. Only his body language expressed a simulacrum of satisfaction. He'd slouched into a studied, more relaxed pose. The man had a lot to learn about congruent behavior. And once again, I belatedly smelled body odor emanating from him.

I still couldn't sense any pattern to the series of questions, which led me to doubt my client's sincerity. Could these really be the facts he needed to know to trust me? Had I misunderstood his motives? Was he toying with me again?

"Will you tell me about your friend now?" I asked. I reasoned this would serve as a gauge of the exercise's effectiveness.

"What friend?"

"Your friend who's an angel."

It was as if I'd goosed him. He jumped up, clearly alarmed. "Who told you that?" he demanded. "Have you been following me? There are laws against that, you know." His anger quickly gave way to fear, his eyes widening and his initial movement toward me morphing into stepping back and leaning away from me at such an extreme angle that I worried he'd topple over. His fists balled up, and his face was fire-engine red. Some of his plastered hair had even unplastered itself somehow.

"You told me, George. Last week."

"I did not!"

I felt like telling him, à la a five-year-old, to use his inside voice. "It was at the end of the session," I said instead. "That's why I agreed to meet again.

Remember?"

"Oh, I see." He sat down and replastered his hair. His movements were practiced—precise. I wondered how many times a day he had to enact the maneuver. "That's all right, then." His tone and volume had resumed for what passed for normal in the Arundel universe.

"I'm sorry I upset you," I said softly.

"I can see it was all a misunderstanding. Just one of those things. Don't mention it. It's fine, really." He was stringing all this together in an abstracted tone of voice as he studied my face. After a long moment in which he seemed to focus on my mouth, he abruptly stood again. "I have to go," he announced.

"Right now?"

"Yes. Right now."

"Will I see you next week?" I asked.

"Probably," he shouted. If anything, he was even louder than earlier.

Before I could say good-bye, he was gone.

This time I used the leftover time to buy a chocolate ice cream cone from the kiosk around the corner.

Chapter 3

Santa Cruz is situated on the northernmost tip of Monterey Bay, about seventy-five miles south of San Francisco. By virtue of the horseshoe shape of the bay, the Pacific Ocean is actually south of town instead of west, while inland lies to the north. For me, this is typical of the place; everything is rotated at least a quarter-turn sideways. Culturally, politically, artistically, and even sexually, Santa Cruz dances to its own drum ensemble, composed of motley, offbeat musicians. In a town of sixty-five thousand, there are eleven health-food restaurants, seven organic grocery stores, and eighteen coffee houses. Eateries specializing in Ethiopian, Brazilian, New Orleans, Caribbean, and Korean cuisine draw crowds.

A boardwalk and amusement park attract tourists, the University of California campus on the northeast edge of town attracts local and international students, and the beaches, redwood forests, and marvelous weather serve as a magnet to a variety of residents. By and large, this diverse cast of characters, while not electing to fraternize a great deal, interact amicably enough. Old-timers resent the university population, and everyone experiences the tourists as somewhat parasitical, but they maintain a balance in the economic sector that no one is anxious to upset by alienating them.

One unfortunate side effect of our demographic

seems to be a high crime rate, especially violent crime, and lately a serial killer had been stabbing his way into the headlines. The victims were an elderly retired man, a UC Santa Cruz coed, and now Denise Heilman, a colleague I knew quite well. At breakfast the morning before I was to see Arundel again, the local newspaper reported the details of this latest murder, along with an obituary.

Denise had been a wonderful person. I first met her at a workshop on narrative therapy, in which the therapist helps the client rewrite the story of his life. It was a fascinating weekend, all the more so for Denise's presence. By chance, we were paired off for a practice session, and despite very different backgrounds, we hit it off immediately.

Poor Stuart. Her husband had been completely devoted to her. He was the type of man who glowed when he was with his partner, becoming more than the sum of his parts. He must be devastated, I thought. I wrote myself a note to give him a call soon.

Denise had been a hypnotherapist with an office on the west side of town about a mile and a half from my own. After seeing her last client the evening before, she'd been stabbed seven times in the chest as she was unlocking her Volvo station wagon—the same type of car I own.

The parallels personalized the tragedy. I don't have a problem with death, per se. In fact, part of me looks forward to the whole messy business of life finally ending. But Denise was young and had a family. What purpose could such a sudden, horrible death serve? To warn us all to live as though this were our last day? To trust no one? To instruct us to park under streetlights? To move to Sweden?

This was how I tormented myself, this endless futile attempt to make sense out of everything. If I could've just thrown a switch and thought half—no, a third—as much, I would've been better off. Accepting reality without processing it—the very idea smacked of irresponsibility to my mind, which was always wrangling to become even more indispensable.

****

The next session with George Arundel began with silence. He'd wandered in as though he still wasn't sure if my office was where he was supposed to be. There was no eye contact, and all his movements were tentative. Eventually, he pursed his mouth, hinting at disapproval, and his wrinkled brow confirmed this interpretation.

Since the side of my nose itched, I took a moment to scratch it. I figured something meaningful to someone ought to happen.

Silence can be a powerful tool in therapy or a complete waste of time. I was curious to see what emerged out of this particular silence, speculating at various points that Arundel would erupt in anger, intellectualize about the silence itself, or never speak the entire session.

After five minutes, he spoke. "People pay you for this?" His voice was completely different this time—high-pitched, soft, younger-sounding.

I nodded, puzzling over the new voice and the disappearance of the disapproving guy. Now he seemed to be naively curious, his eyes wide and his mouth tentatively turned up at one corner.

"That doesn't bother you?" he asked.

"No. It's a hard job, believe me. I earn my fee."

23

"Oh, I guess I believe you, all right. Crazy people give me the heebie-jeebies," Arundel told me, rolling his eyes and flashing a broad, earthy grin.

I was beginning to understand. As I smiled back at him, he continued without prompting.

"Heck, I give myself the heebie-jeebies sometimes."

"How's that?"

"I don't know. I guess sometimes the way I am, or the things I do seem kinda drastic." He wrinkled his brow again and frowned.

"Drastic?"

"Yeah, the kinda thing you can't even say out loud 'cuz you know ahead of time that anyone hearing you would freak out."

"Can you give me an example?"

"Do you promise not to freak out?"

"I promise."

"Well, you already know one—the angel."

"Oh yes. Can you tell me more about that?"

"Of course I can. You mean will I?" The professor was back. The voice, the demeanor, even the cunning gleam in his eye was now familiar to me. It was a separate, distinct personality.

"May I speak with the other guy?" I asked.

"No," the professor replied. "I'm the one you'll deal with. That was a mistake."

I was facing my first client with a clearly defined multiple personality disorder, or dissociative identity disorder, as it was now called. I preferred the older, more descriptive name. I'd worked with several highly dissociated women who may or may not have split into actual personalities, as opposed to ego-states. And since, on the average, MPDs are in therapy for years before they're correctly diagnosed, I may have seen a few without knowing it. But here was one—a classic example—basically admitting his situation in the third session. This was an extremely rare event in the therapy world.

"How many of you are there?" I asked.

"Quite a few. Let's leave it at that."

I constructed my next question as carefully as I could. The exact wording seemed important. "Why are you the one who can best profit from this experience?" My chest tingled and my breath shallowed as I anticipated his response. I wasn't sure why his answer was important to me, but it was.

"Your inquiry is unanswerable due to several assumptions that are subsumed within it."

"Subsumed?" My breathing returned to normal, but the tingling increased, spreading down my arms to my hands.

He nodded primly, and I heard his teeth click.

"All right," I conceded. "Let me try again. Why are you here with me instead of one of the others?"

"That's a much better question. You see how your initial query wasn't sufficiently open-ended? This one gives me an opportunity to really explain."

"Go ahead."

"I choose not to at this time."

I checked to see if Arundel was wearing his creepy "gotcha" smile. He actually appeared chagrined that he needed to withhold information from me. "Will I at least get to meet the others?" While he was feeling merciful, I thought I'd press him a bit.

"We'll see." The grin was back.

"Is your friend who's an angel one of the others?"

"No. She is an independent entity."

The tingling had either dissipated or I was no longer tuned into my body sensations. "Do you recall any of the early childhood trauma that you've suffered?" All MPD cases are created by the need to escape experiencing intense, repeated abuse before a certain age. It used to be four, now they've made it six. Don't ask me how they can change a diagnostic criterion so facilely and expect us all to buy into it.

"I wasn't there, so I don't remember it, but I am familiar with the general details."

"May I speak to someone who was there?"

"No. It was the usual sort of thing. Their parents were members of a Satanic cult. There was a pattern of ritualistic sexual and physical abuse."

This was told to me with completely flat affect. Arundel could've been reading an actuarial table aloud.

"It seems as though you have no feelings about it," I pointed out.

"Why should I?"

"Most people would be horrified or disgusted. I am." In truth, I wasn't—at least not in that moment. I was up in my head—the part of my brain that generated words and failed to notice my ongoing emotions.

Arundel shrugged. "Such is life. I am interested in the current ramifications of the trauma in terms of how we're organized, but other than that…It was a long time ago."

I paused before continuing, reminding myself that for all intents and purposes I was talking to a cautious English professor.

"Have you ever been diagnosed as having dissociative identity disorder?" I asked.

"No. I've known, of course. I'm not like some of the others with their heads in the sand. But you're the first therapist I've seen more than once."

"I'm not surprised," I admitted.

"Why is that?"

"You're rather difficult to work with." Surely he knew that. Who could be such a pain by accident?

"Yes, I see. Actually, I was the one who ended my relationships with the other therapists."

"Why was that?"

Arundel shook his head slowly and began to answer.

"Don't tell me," I interrupted. "It would work out better if you don't reveal that now, right?"

"Yes."

I tried a new tack. "How old are you, Mr. Arundel?"

"Forty-eight."

"Your way of being has worked for you all these years?"

"By and large. As you can imagine, our sex life hasn't been satisfactory, and I, for one, never watch certain types of movies. But basically—yes."

"Any sleep disruption?"

"Nightmares that wake me up, yes. And headaches that worsen at night. But it's a small price to pay."

"Does everyone in there agree with you?"

"Of course not. There is probably nothing in the universe that we all agree on. But I assure you that the side effects really are a small price to pay." He nodded vigorously to emphasize his response.

"What do you mean?" I was genuinely curious, not expressing interest for its therapeutic value.

"The array of personalities works." He sat back and assumed his constipated pose.

I could no longer remember what it was supposed to represent. This time he closed his eyes for a moment, and I could see the muscles in his cheeks tighten. I could hear him breath as well, due to a slight wheezing.

"Then why are you here?" This was a wonderful arrow to shoot at self-satisfied clients in need of deflation. Why indeed, if they're truly perfectly happy with themselves?

"For another reason entirely, which I'm not going to discuss today," he informed me.

I felt like giving him a Bronx cheer or a cuff on the ear. Unfortunately, my scope of practice didn't encompass such satisfying interventions.

"Will you tell me how your way of being works for you?" I asked. I hoped my annoyance hadn't revealed itself.

"Certainly. One of us is a virtual genius with money. Thus, we are rich. I don't care for social gatherings—parties and the like—so others attend them, and I am spared the experience. And so on."

I was reminded of a story my own therapist had told me once; I decided to share it. "Have you heard about the man who learned to walk on water? It took him twenty years and all sorts of self-discipline and practice, but he finally did it. Then a wise old man came along and asked him why he didn't just pay his dollar to the ferryman."

"I don't like stories," Arundel replied.

"But you understand that one?"

"Of course, although you told it wrong. It's a Buddhist parable."

"Is that right?"

"Yes. Your version eliminates the whole guru-disciple relationship and the questions of spiritual ambition, pride, and self-satisfaction. It's been gutted, or let's just say Westernized, eh?"

"Fine, but back up a minute. You said you dislike parties. Couldn't you just not go? Doesn't the parable propose that the simplest solution is usually the best?"

"Sometimes it's necessary to attend. My point is that everyone has strengths and weaknesses, likes and dislikes. Our system matches the personality with these qualities with the appropriate circumstances." Arundel fussed with the hem of his pants, trying to cover his patterned socks, a two-tone herringbone pattern. If he was embarrassed to be wearing them, why put them on in the first place?

It was time to try another approach (again). "If I tortured you, who would experience it?" I asked.

"There is an early personality named Gooey who can experience such things without suffering."

"How is that?"

"Gooey doesn't have feelings."

"Do you?"

"Oh yes. They're under control, of course. There's a world of difference between Gooey and myself."

"Can I talk to him?"

"No. He's preverbal."

I was fascinated but concerned that my fascination might interfere with the business at hand—Arundel's therapy. In other words, was I interrogating my client at this point purely in response to my own curiosity or did it serve a therapeutic purpose? To be on the safe side, I decided to refocus on Arundel in the here and now.

"What are you feeling right now?" I asked him.

"Slight discomfort."

Bingo. I'd tapped into something nonmental for a

change. I surveyed his body language but discovered no confirming evidence. Other than his attention to his hem, he hadn't moved in several minutes. He sat with his right leg crossed over his left, his hands folded in his lap, as usual.

"Tell me about it."

"My foot has fallen asleep. I have a tendency to stay in one position too long."

"Could that be metaphorical for the rest of your life as well?" This fell out of me without thought.

He stared at me for a moment, wincing as if I'd poked him with a sharp stick. "I guess it is. That was astute."

Suddenly Arundel's demeanor dramatically shifted. His features softened and reformed into someone much younger, less defined. The contrast was remarkable.

"Who are you?" I asked.

"Jeff." The voice was unsure of itself. "Who are you? You're awful big."

I'm six foot five, and I weigh about 230 pounds. "I'm ugly too, aren't I? My name is Tom Dashiel, and you're in my office. How old are you?"

"Fourteen."

"Do you know why you're here?"

"No. Did I do something wrong?"

"Not at all. It's a little hard to—"

"That's enough. I'm back," the professor broke in. "Sorry about that. We don't have all the bugs worked out in this context yet. When something unexpected happens, well, you see the result."

"What was unexpected?"

"Actually, that you would generate a useful insight." He had the decency to appear sheepish, shifting his weight to the side and lowering his head momentarily.

"Thanks a lot."

"I didn't select you because of your therapeutic skills," Arundel informed me, glancing back up.

"Why then?"

He smiled his creepiest smile yet and held my eyes for a few seconds. "Not yet," he cautioned. "Be patient."

I squelched my irritation again. With most clients, I'm quite content to pace the work around their readiness. After all, three sessions into a course of therapy is still a preliminary stage. Why should a client fully trust me? It's healthy to feel safe before opening up. In some cases, I slow people down who don't know how to take care of themselves around safety and trust.

But Arundel's behavior smacked of gamesmanship, and I've found that the more I do this work, the more intolerant I grow of game playing. Intellectually, I knew that as a survivor of very serious abuse, my client was doing remarkably well simply to be walking and talking. In a sense, his history gave him dispensation to use any means necessary to protect himself. Nonetheless, I experienced my compassion stretching particularly thin at that moment in our session.

"So I gather you don't normally slip up and change personalities like that?" I tried.

"Absolutely not. As I said, certain circumstances demand certain personalities. I'm in charge of all that, actually."

"Really? That sounds like an important job."

"Oh, it is. Without me, the whole thing would fall apart."

"Do the others recognize that?"

"Some do. Some don't even know about me, let

alone appreciate what I do." The usual emotional expressions that might accompany these statements were missing.

I watched closely to see if Arundel might evidence any micro expressions—tiny tip-offs about his internal state. Nada.

"So there's a real variety of folks in there?"

"Oh yes. Men, women, children—even a dog."

"A dog?"

Arundel nodded. "I'd let you meet her, but she isn't house-trained and she's likely to get excited and urinate on your rug."

I smiled, sure that he was pulling my leg. "That's very hard to believe," I told him.

"I've researched it. It's not uncommon in full-blown MPD."

"You're serious?"

"Yes."

My eyebrows shot up. For some reason, this struck me as being the strangest aspect of the entire Arundel experience. "Well, in that case, can you direct me to some up-to-date literature? I see that I need to do some catching up on this."

"Of course." Arundel produced a list from a back pocket. "I anticipated your request. And do try to avoid the popular material—*The Three Faces of Eve* and all that—it's terribly distorted."

"Sure. You're the expert."

I checked the clock, saw that we needed to stop, and informed Arundel. "Same time next week?"

"Yes. See you then. Perhaps I'll bring the angel."

"Really?"

"We'll see."

Chapter 4

Three recent client graduations cut into my schedule and bank account more than usual the following week, so I had a chance to read quite a bit about MPD. Success in my profession can be measured by a client's move from dependence to independence, which translates to replacing $140 a week with an annual Christmas card— if that. The better I do my job, the sooner and more permanently my clients disappear.

So during my unsolicited light week, I discovered that MPDs really did develop animal personalities, among other things. The material was a testament to the flexibility and imagination of the human psyche. Isn't it astonishing that a three-year-old child can produce alters as a coping strategy—entirely independent personalities that even respond differently to medications?

Hard to believe in another way were some of the histories of abuse detailed in the case studies. Hitler gassed all sorts of people, but they weren't his own children. I honestly found the stories too horrific to describe here. That adult survivors function at all after the incredible pain they've endured…Thank God for MPD. It's saved a lot of them.

****

Arundel escorted an unlikely-looking angel to our next session. She was a barefoot young woman, with long, tangled black hair. Faded blue denim overalls covered most of a faded gray T-shirt. Her loose clothes accentuated her slight build and short stature, suggesting a child playing dress-up. Dark-complected, her delicate features didn't hint at any particular ethnicity, but the effect was quite attractive. She could have been twenty-two or twenty-three.

"This is Zig-Zag," Arundel told me. "Zee," he said to the girl, "this is Tom Dashiel."

Zig-Zag extended her slender hand, and I shook it. Her grip was surprisingly strong, and she flashed dazzling white teeth at me. As she released her hand, I spied a small, artful tattoo of a green flame on the inside of her slender wrist.

"Let me rearrange the chairs," I told them, placing two seats about four feet in front of my own. When everyone was comfortable, I spoke first.

"Mr. Arundel tells me you're an angel," I began. A direct approach seemed worth trying, despite my track record with the young woman's companion.

"I'm not," she replied quickly in an unaccented, educated voice. "What I am is an environmental crusader." This latter statement was uttered pridefully. Her eyes defied anyone to challenge her right to this claim.

"Crusader?"

"Activist. I'm saving your goddamn planet." Her fierce expression suggested I didn't deserve saving, and not only that, I probably threw away cans as well. I was tempted to thank her—after all, who doesn't want their planet saved?—but I settled on a continuation of my direct questioning. Arundel seemed to be enjoying the interaction so far. He was smiling and alternately scanning our faces. I was momentarily distracted by his rounded teeth, wondering once again how they'd been shaped. This time, his combover was impeccable, and he wore a gray suit with a gleaming white shirt.

"Why do you think Mr. Arundel believes you're an angel?" I asked.

"Ask him. He's sitting right here, isn't he?" Her tone remained mildly contentious, but she smiled playfully, ameliorating the effect.

Arundel spoke in his most professorial voice. "There are numerous clues. I've delineated them to Zig-Zag, but she is quite resistant to her destiny."

The young woman snorted and rearranged herself, moving each limb in turn so the maneuver took several seconds. At the end of the sequence, she pulled her legs under her in a modified lotus pose.

Arundel continued. "First of all, my friend here is the illegitimate daughter of Krishnanda."

"The deceased Indian guru?"

"Exactly. He was no ordinary man, and she is his only offspring. Next, we have the fact that her mother's last name is Cassiel, which is an angel name. Then there's the fact that without any training whatsoever, Zee here sees people's auras."

"Really?"

Zig-Zag and Arundel nodded in unison.

"What does mine look like?" I asked.

"Mostly purple with a golden glow around your throat," the young woman reported, nodding.

I had no way to glean the significance of that but decided not to pursue it further. This session wasn't about me. I noticed I'd unconsciously moved my hand up to my throat, as if to feel the ascribed color, which was patently absurd, so I pulled it down.

I suddenly felt as if I were in a surrealistic film. One week it was multiple personality disorder, the next I had guru offspring seeing auras. I yearned for a nice obsessive-compulsive who just washed his hands too much.

"Have you always had this ability?" I asked.

"Sure," Zig-Zag replied. "It's no big thing."

"Next," Arundel continued, "there are the prophetic dreams, the sensitivity to ethereal energy, and the moles."

"The moles?" Now I felt like a straight man in a comedy team.

"The moles on her back," Arundel explained. "They trace a pattern—wings."

"You mean if you played connect-the-dots with them, that would be the picture you'd end up with?" I asked.

"Exactly. And there's more…But this is all I'm at liberty to say at this time."

I looked at Zig-Zag, and she gazed back at me, expressionless—no help there. I caught a whiff of patchouli oil, which I hadn't smelled since my college days. I thought things over for a moment and then spoke to Arundel.

"I don't understand why you're telling me all this. I'm not qualified to adjudicate spiritual matters, and if you don't have a psychological problem with your beliefs, then I don't either."

Arundel paused, licked his lips, and cocked his head. It was a stage actor's version of deep thought, or perhaps a cocker spaniel's attempt to discern if food was in the offing. "It's time to lay some of my cards on the table," he finally told me. "Can you name any angels, Thomas—

from the Bible or folklore?"

"Well, let's see. There's Gabriel and Raphael. Uh…that's all I remember." I had no clue as to what Arundel was up to. Was he trying to seize control of the session by playing teacher again?

"How about Michael, Gaddiel, or Adriel?" he prompted.

"Michael, I know, of course. I'm not sure about the others."

"Put your detective skills to work," Arundel instructed. "What do all those names have in common?"

I pondered for a moment. "Well, the endings are similar phonetically."

The man actually clasped his hands in delight. "And…?" He leaned forward and peered brightly at my face.

"Wait a minute. There's no Dashiel in the Bible," I protested.

Arundel sat back with a self-satisfied smirk on his lined face. "Your last name is an angel name, Thomas, and I wouldn't be surprised if you had a significant birthmark or pattern of moles as well. That's how it works—one thing verifies the other."

I felt like telling him he was crazy, which needless to say was not an appropriate response. It did clue me in, though, to just how far afield we'd strayed from a traditional client-therapist relationship. I needed to wrestle the conversation back into the therapeutic realm.

"Tell me more about your beliefs," I suggested.

Arundel stared at me. Zig-Zag rolled her eyes as if to say "Good luck with that approach, buddy."

"How long have you believed in angels?" I tried.

Even Arundel rolled his eyes at that one.

"Look, exactly what do you want from me?" I finally asked, my frustration leaking out.

"Just be a person," he replied. "Talk to me like a person. This doesn't have anything to do with your being a therapist."

Oh yeah, I thought. I'd really be having this conversation for free.

"All right," I agreed. "The whole thing is ridiculous. I don't share your point of view, and obviously I'm not going to suddenly espouse a new belief system based on somebody's moles or last name. There are real-world explanations for everything you've mentioned, for one thing. The unconscious is a powerful force. It can create stigmata, moles, illusions of auras—none of that surprises me. Anyway, the only birthmark I have is a totally amorphous blob on my ankle."

"May I see it?" Arundel asked.

I thought about that. I wasn't under any compulsion to bare my flesh to clients, but humoring him for a few seconds might convince him of his folly. On the other hand, most delusional systems as complex and entrenched as Arundel's have a catch-22 in place to prevent contradictions. I decided I'd need to encounter his particular catch-22 at some point anyway, so I rolled down my brown argyle sock and displayed my dark red birthmark. It really was just a blob; I defied Arundel to make a case for it representing anything at all.

The girl gasped; Arundel smiled.

"What? It's just a blob." I stared at my ankle to see if the birthmark had changed its configuration when I wasn't looking. Nope.

"My father had one exactly like it," Zig-Zag told me. "It's the shape of his aura, too. And I know because I've seen it." She turned to Arundel, who was still grinning. "This is too weird, George."

"*Stai calma*," he replied in Italian, and then turned to me. "Do you see now why I've come to you?"

"No."

"It's obvious. You're in that body for a reason, Thomas, and it isn't so you can listen to neurotics whine and complain, any more than Zig-Zag's true calling is to blow up power stations. A new era approaches, and my job is to find and awaken the key figures involved in the upcoming transition. People like you—people who are more than people. We all have a great deal of work to do if things are going to unfold in the manner they are designed to. Do you understand?"

"I hear the words, Mr. Arundel. But no, I can't say I truly understand. Do you honestly expect me to believe all this?"

"Right now? Of course not. But you will. If I'm right, then events in your life will begin cooperating with this process of awakening. You'll discover who you are because the universe will orchestrate what needs to happen around you. It's not my job to convince you. I'm a catalyst, not a teacher."

"Look at me, Arundel. Have you ever seen a less likely candidate for angelhood?"

"I sure haven't," Zig-Zag chimed in. "You're a motherfucking monster."

"Thanks, sweetheart," I growled, forgetting myself momentarily. Sarcasm was one of the first ingrained behaviors I'd had to jettison when I became a therapist. "Anyway," I began, trying to save a deteriorating situation, "angels don't say 'motherfucking' either, now do they?"

"How do you know?" Arundel asked. "You're both in human bodies, with human minds and human tongues. I'll grant you that. But so what? Did Jesus swear? Was Buddha overweight? Surely you can see how ridiculous such concerns are?"

It was time to insert some reality into the proceedings. "I'm not going to argue with you," I told Arundel. "You're entitled to your religious beliefs. But I'm concerned that your view of here and now reality is radically different from the prevailing mainstream, and yet you aggressively advocate it to Zig-Zag and myself. Idiosyncratic thinking is one thing—it doesn't necessarily harm anyone. But when you begin promoting a self-aggrandizing viewpoint out in the world—this concerns me. Don't you find that all this interferes with your ability to develop satisfying relationships?"

"Let's not digress into psychobabble," Arundel responded, scowling. "I'll see you next week." He stood. "I cede my remaining time to Zig-Zag. Why don't you two get to know each other better?" As soon as he'd finished speaking, he turned on his heel and strode off.

When the door closed behind him, I focused on Zig-Zag. I was still feeling off-center, but perhaps she could help me understand Arundel better.

She shrugged, and one of her overall straps slid off a slim shoulder onto her upper arm. "Well," she said, "that's George." She smiled wanly as if she understood how little help her comment had been.

I was struck by how alert her dark brown eyes were. And her mouth's default setting seemed to be a sweet half smile—a better one than I'd ever mustered.

"This is typical behavior?"

"Yup. Well, typical if he thinks you're an angel."

Her face had gradually softened during the session, and now she smiled widely, showing her perfect teeth.

"What's your relationship to him?"

"He's my godfather. He was close to my father. George was the one who took me to the zoo or whatever while my father was in samadhi."

"Samadhi?"

"Like an extended trance. He spent a lot of time doing things like that."

"Was your mother Indian as well?"

"No. She was from Berkeley—Cassiel—remember?" Zig-Zag yawned, which I sensed was sleepiness, not boredom. "How in the world do you psychoanalyze someone like George?" she asked.

"Beats me. Got any ideas?" This departure from professionalism was a calculated risk. By matching her vocabulary and tone of voice, I was creating an alliance of sorts. It was possible she actually had some interesting ideas about treatment, too. She'd known George Arundel for a long time.

"Well," she began thoughtfully, "he's not really crazy. Mostly he's just like all the Krishnanda people."

What a horrifying notion, I thought—dozens, maybe thousands of Arundels loose in the world.

"Are you aware of his…other problems?" I asked, treading lightly on the thin ice of confidentiality law.

"You mean the extra personalities thing?"

I nodded, relieved.

"Well, sure. But I think it works out pretty well for him."

"How's that?"

"He's rich, he's successful, he's as happy as anyone I know—what more do you want?" She peered at me intently, as if she expected me to add to her list with something inappropriate or foolish.

"That's plenty. I was just wondering. So what do you make of this birthmark deal?"

"I'm gonna have to think it over," she told me. "And I've gotta get to work."

We both rose, and I handed her my card. I towered over her by a foot and a half.

"Call me if you need to," I told her, unaware of what that simple largesse would lead to.

Zig-Zag tucked the card into the bib pocket of her worn overalls, slipped her strap back onto her shoulder, and offered her hand again. "Nice meeting you."

"Likewise," I answered, shaking hands while maintaining eye contact. Once again, I was moved by her eyes; they were more liquid than most and reflected an unusual intelligence.

After she'd departed, I sat and stared at the two empty chairs while my next client fumed in the waiting room.

Chapter 5

George Arundel not only suffered from MPD, he also harbored a delusional disorder. I'm not usually preoccupied by labeling my clients—clinical diagnoses can be heavy albatrosses to lug around. But in Arundel's case, the relationship between the two disorders was something I needed to examine carefully. I knew from my reading that the mission-from-God business was not likely to be universal throughout Arundel's personalities. Clearly, the professor character—the one I thought of as my client, actually—was driven by the paradigm, but Jeff, the fourteen-year-old boy I'd met, hadn't even known who I was. Was he privy to the overall plan, but not the details? Or was Arundel more thoroughly compartmentalized? This seemed likelier to me, but there was no way to know.

If I could contact a responsible, non-pain-in-the-ass adult within Arundel's array of personalities, I might be able to ally with him. The idea of organizing an internal revolution and staging a coup d'état to overthrow the irksome professor…well, needless to say, this was an attractive notion to me. Insofar as the others were aware of his role and his manner, surely they experienced him as a despot.

Traditionally, a therapist helped an MPD client by facilitating an integration of the parts, not by fomenting further conflict. But first things first, I reasoned, and dissipating the delusions seemed to be a precursor to any integration work.

Even after all my research, I was still confused about the influence of the unconscious in multiple personalities. Ordinarily, Arundel's denial that my role as a therapist was relevant to his behavior would be a telltale clue. While a client might have a conscious reason to see me that doesn't include my idea of doing therapy, I trust his unconscious has guided him to me nonetheless and will participate at some level in the healing. In other words, it might be quite pertinent that the man Arundel had seized on as an angel (me) happens to be trained in working with the problems Arundel happens to exhibit (big nutty ones).

I don't believe in coincidence anymore. I tried valiantly to hang onto the concept during my tenure at graduate school, and I still maintained a few shreds of belief while an intern. But for years, my simple mechanistic view of the universe, especially people, has been rendered obsolete. Sometimes I wonder exactly what has replaced it, since the current perspective is so much more amorphous. I know it has something to do with the way everything is put together. I guess it's still mechanistic—just such an incredibly intricate relationship of parts that I know I'll never understand it as a machine, per se.

To reach this perspective, I needed to let go of a great deal, including my faith in science. I've gradually dragged substantial portions of my interior into congruence with my perceptions of the external world. I once entertained a fantasy of founding a new theoretical orientation—Congruence Therapy. But God knows, there's enough of that sort of thing in the world.

Thus, it was no accident George Arundel had become my client, and I felt a duty to peek at the clockworks of life on his behalf whenever I could. The more I understood the nature of our relationship, for example, the more I could help.

As usual, at about this point in my reasoning, the penguin metaphor wafted into my mind. I hate penguins. For all my talk of changing and concocting theories, that elusive key factor that enables one to establish useful values—to know which rock is which—well, I wasn't much closer to discovering it. A therapist I saw briefly while in my early thirties postulated that it was the very construct of there being something to understand that was my problem. I could accept that idea intellectually, but how did it help? I still had to bumble through my life since I didn't know what I felt I needed to know.

****

The next day, I met with Mrs. Volkov, a large, middle-aged woman who was both very depressed and, periodically, extremely anxious. For months, she had been discussing birds, which for a still unknown reason, scared her silly, and I use the term literally. She was not my favorite client, although I was her favorite therapist. Lord knows why.

As usual, she wore a tattered housedress—this one was pale pink— and her hair was hidden under a black silk scarf. A round, nondescript face peered at me. Her glaringly red lipstick was the only feature that distinguished her from a million other women. She smelled musty, as if she'd pulled her dress from the back of a rarely used closet..

Not as usual, she began relating a dream she'd had the night before. This was new. According to her, she didn't dream.

"Doctor," she began in her high, squeaky voice, "it was a wonderful dream, but I don't know exactly what it means, so you listen close and tell me."

I nodded agreement.

"I was in a foreign country. I don't know which one, but it was very dirty. And hot. I remember thinking that I wish I was in Florida visiting my sister where it's hot too, but it's very clean. She has the nicest place, Doctor. Palm trees and everything. And so clean. So I was sitting on the sidewalk in this dirty foreign country, which I would never do, of course. I mean you don't sit on the sidewalk here, even. There could be dog dirt or germs or God knows what. So I don't know what I was thinking, but there I was right on the sidewalk. And it was so hot, Doctor. I thought I'd die." She fanned herself with a lily-white hand and let out a dramatic breath.

"Then what happened?" My initial interest was flagging in the face of Mrs. Volkov's narrative style.

"The strangest thing. You know I'm not a religious person, Doctor. I mean I try to be a good person and everything, but I don't go to church, and I even change channels when one of those preachers comes on. They are so tacky, those preachers. You know what I mean?"

I nodded.

"So here I am in this dream just sitting there minding my own business when I get this urge to look up. And there she was." She waited for encouragement again.

"Who was that?" I obliged.

"The angel."

"What?" I couldn't think for a moment. My mind was blank.

"There was an angel floating in the air above me.

She was so beautiful. I could hardly breathe," Mrs. Volkov reported. She pantomimed holding her breath while obviously continuing to inhale and exhale through her nose, pointing to her substantial chest in case I failed to notice her demonstration. With her mouth pursed tight, if I didn't know better, I'd have thought she was angry at the angel.

My first thought was that Arundel had bribed her to tell this story, but I knew Mrs. Volkov. She wasn't capable of that sort of pretense. So it must be one of those non-coincidences. Maybe they both had angels on their minds because of some recent TV show or something.

"Tell me about the angel," I prompted.

"She was all in white, kind of like she had on a wedding dress, and she had these big gold wings. Her hair was black, which surprised me because I always see them with blonde hair on TV and in the movies. And she was smiling this beautiful smile, and I felt her love inside me like I'd just had a hot chocolate on a cold day."

Her face was a sweet picture of contentment. It was like seeing a pig fly. I had no idea she was capable of these feelings. I knew her as a stuck, depressed sack of misery. Or at least I thought I did.

"What are you feeling now?" I asked.

"The love. I'm feeling the love, and I never want it to end." She closed her eyes and radiated warmth.

I could actually feel it in my gut as if I'd drunk hot chocolate too. "Stay with it," I coached. "Stay with the love."

By God, she did. The rest of the session was twenty minutes of watching Mrs. Volkov feel love. It was a wondrous sight—one of the most miraculous events in my experience as a therapist. She closed her eyes and gradually relaxed her features into the most peaceful expression I'd ever seen in a session. She could've been the after image in a before-and-after mental health poster.

Mrs. Volkov was a client I'd been inches away from giving up on more than once. Antidepressants hadn't helped, anti-anxiety medication gave her hives, and talk therapy usually made *me* feel depressed. I didn't expect one sublime event to change her life, but what the hell did I know? Clearly, I had drastically underestimated my client. Maybe by next week she'd be hosting her own self-help talk show.

****

One of my most entertaining clients called himself Bug. After years of life-disrupting involvement in popular conspiracy theories, he had recently shifted his attention to his own idiosyncratic obsessions. I had no idea if this change constituted progress, regression, or just lateral movement. But since Bug needed to talk about his theories and no one else would listen, I served as an audience as much as a therapist in our sessions.

Before his head injury in a bicycling accident, Bug had been Peter Alexander, an insurance salesman who couldn't have cared less who had offed JFK. Sometimes organic brain damage transformed an individual beyond possible restoration to their historical self. It could be very frustrating to work with these clients, but as I said, I enjoyed Bug.

I saw him several days after Mrs. Volkov's breakthrough.

"How's it going?" I asked.

He was classically handsome, in his late thirties, with striking light green eyes and a perfectly symmetrical cleft chin. His aviator-style glasses convincingly implied that he was actually a pilot. A sparse blond mustache downgraded him from a ten to a nine to my eyes. Everything else fit together tidily. He wore black jeans, a T-shirt advertising an Idaho ski resort, and leather sandals. In a crowd, Bug would be the last person you'd select as a head-injury survivor. He was unrelentingly mainstream in his looks, demeanor, and behavior until he spoke.

"I'm doing good," he told me. "I think I've discovered the link between all the Perfects."

According to my client, the Perfects were people like Elvis, Hank Williams, and Marilyn Monroe—flesh and blood archetypes who'd died before their time.

"That's great, Bug. Tell me about it."

"Well, you know about some of the ideas I've been kicking around. Were they aliens? Examples of hyper-evolution? A secret government experiment gone awry?"

I nodded.

"I've been waiting for a sign, and now I got one. It's really exciting, Tom. I think I may be able clear up a lot of things for a lot of people." His mouth hung open, his eyes widened, and he brought his hands up alongside his face. I recognized this as Bug's expression of excitement.

"Really?"

"Yup. Like is there a God? What happens when you die? And what's the meaning of life? Stuff like that."

"Well, don't keep me in suspense, Bug. What do you think about those things?" I felt a tingle of excitement myself; he might be talking about a therapeutic breakthrough, à la Mrs. Volkov.

"I gotta tell you about the sign first. It was a couple of nights ago. I couldn't get to sleep because I was thinking about the Masons again."

"I thought we were through with the Masons." If I never heard another word about the Masons, I'd be happy as a clam at high tide.

"Hey, so did I. So I was up real late, and then I finally fell asleep and I had this dream."

Two dreams in one week? I was exceeding my quota. When I'd gotten into this field, I'd been expecting dreams galore, but I rarely heard them.

"I was in Egypt," Bug told me. "I knew because there were pyramids all over the place—big ones, little ones, even one covered in blue down comforters."

"Blue down comforters?"

"That's right. And I was sitting on this park bench except there wasn't any park, just a lot of dirt all around. And it was really hot."

I was struck by the similarity of Bug's dream and Mrs. Volkov's. Both had transpired in hot, dirty foreign countries.

Bug continued, his eyes closed now. "Suddenly, there she was," he reported.

"An angel?" I interrupted. Shivers ran up and down my spine.

"No. Not an angel. A little dog. She looked like a schnauzer, or maybe a Scottie."

I breathed again, inserting a loud "whoosh" into the conversation.

"She could talk, and she said, 'Follow me,' so I did," Bug continued, "and we went to a rug shop where this girl handed me a note and the note said the Perfects were sent to advance mankind's spiritual progress. What do you think about that, Tom?"

I didn't answer, still recovering from the angelic near miss.

"Are you okay, Tom? What's the matter? Are you sad it was a dog instead of an angel? I'm not. She was a beautiful little dog."

"I'm okay. Can I ask you a few things about your dream?"

"Sure. Go ahead."

"What did the girl look like?"

"She wasn't anyone I know, but she was pretty," he answered.

"Do you remember her hair color or what she was wearing—any details at all?"

"Gosh, I don't know why you need to know that, but let me see…" I was reminded of myself during Arundel's interrogation. "Sure—here you go," Bug replied. "She had dark, wavy hair, and she wore old overalls. And I remember the name of her store. It was 'Ziggurat Rug Shoppe.' "

This was beyond synchronicity. What the hell was Zig-Zag doing in Bug's dream? Did Arundel have some sort of psychic power that enabled him to control dreams? Was he messing with my clients? Hypnotizing them, maybe? Was I going crazy?

My gut churned, and my face heated up even more. As Bug told me all about what the dream meant to him, I tuned him out and continued to desperately generate rational explanations. Perhaps Arundel had hired Mrs. Volkov and Bug months before in order to set up an elaborate con game. They could be professional actors. On the other hand, I didn't have any money to be bilked out of.

Maybe it really was a coincidence. After all, our culture is saturated with New Age advertising and Christian-oriented symbolism. It wouldn't be that strange for three people to be thinking about similar things in a given week.

Maybe Arundel was clairvoyant. If he knew what I was going to hear in session, he could backtrack and bring it up first. Zig-Zag could be in on it, since she and Arundel were buddies. I only had their word for everything except the two dreams.

There were holes in these theories, but I liked all of them much better than Arundel's grandiose vision. It dripped pathology. How convenient that in his version he was a messiah-like figure entrusted with transforming the world. It was a classic abdication of personhood. When the going gets tough, the schizophrenics bail out.

"And so," Bug concluded, "there are probably Perfects among us now, helping to raise our consciousness."

"What do you think they're like?" I asked, pretending I'd been listening. I hated to introduce inauthenticity in a session, but at that point, what choice did I have?

"They're perfect, just like the ones we know about. Everything about them is charismatic—the way they look, the way they sound. Everyone is drawn to them. I just hope I meet one someday."

Our hour was up. I was tempted not to charge Bug since I'd been so self-involved for the latter part of the session. But then I'd be divulging that I hadn't listened to him, which could lower his shaky self-esteem. Clearly, some truths are better left unspoken.

Chapter 6

The evening before I was due to see Arundel again began innocently enough. I perused the newspaper while eating a tub of raspberry yogurt at my kitchen table.

The serial murderer had struck again, I saw. Martin DeVilliers had been an assistant produce manager in Capitola, a town five miles southeast of Santa Cruz. Once again, seven stab wounds established the modus operandi of the killer. It was the only factor so far that linked the victims, furnishing the police investigation with very little evidence or motive. An accompanying article detailed the arrival of the national media in the county now that the number of victims had surpassed the current threshold for major attention. Apparently, this was four, although a few years ago it had been three, and speculation was rife that victim inflation would push it to five soon.

Other news was more typical. The mayor wanted to declare Santa Cruz pesticide-free; his opponents claimed this was irrelevant since there was virtually no farmland within the city limits. "The issue isn't about relevance," the mayor retorted. "It's about feeling good about ourselves." Three gay women were petitioning the zoning committee for a variance to build a women's-only carwash. The concept was proving to be a political hot potato, spawning a slew of absurd letters to the editor.

On the last page of the newspaper, there was an

advertisement for a local bookstore's upcoming book signing. Audrey Wilson would be in town shortly to pitch *They Walk Among Us: Angels in the Twenty-First Century*.

My reaction was purely intellectual this time, which suited me. I was already sick of my body's reactions to events. If the ad had been running for a while, it could explain a great deal, serving as the unconscious trigger for all the dreaming. Perhaps Arundel had read the book and absorbed Wilson's ideas into his delusional system. Just seeing the concept in print normalized my experiences somewhat, too. If an author could manage to get a book like that published, then the notion itself wasn't as crazy as I'd thought. Well, maybe just as crazy, but more culturally crazy than personally crazy. I even considered attending the book signing, just to see what it felt like to consort with that subculture. Was there a perceivable difference between Audrey Wilson and Arundel? Perhaps he was just a few steps beyond the norm. After all, only a fine line separated religious fervor from delusion.

I realized I was thinking too much again, trapping myself up in my head. It was one of the dangers of living alone. So I grabbed a sweater and embarked on a walk.

In the evening, Santa Cruz's downtown neighborhoods softened and blended. There was no sunlight to etch in the harsh details of the weathered homes, and the darkness erased the property lines that separated the area into discrete parcels. I strode toward the wharf, conscious of my breathing and heartbeat. Since my knees had retired from truly active duty, walking was one of the only forms of exercise available to me. Simplemindedly, I felt virtuous whenever I marched around town. I guess after all those years of playing basketball, I still framed the idea of not exercising as moral turpitude.

After four or five blocks, one of my clients encountered a difficult social situation—me. Clients never seemed to know how to relate to me outside the office. Was I best dealt with as though I were a friend? A stranger? Invisible?

Bob Granger—an overweight dentist—opted for an analogue of acquaintanceship, first asking me how I was ("Fine"—I was always fine to my clients), then telling me briefly about his day. His sister was moving to town, and he'd been scurrying around scouting housing for her. Bob was twenty-nine, looked like a young Ben Franklin after a severe binge-eating episode, and was subject to premature ejaculation. This was the sort of thing, of course, that a real acquaintance wouldn't know, and I wished I hadn't remembered. But I always do. Bob could have been a giant, spurting penis and I wouldn't have been any more conscious of his problem as we stood under a soaring eucalyptus tree on Center Street. The wind whistled through our leafy canopy. A twig with several leaves landed on Bob's shoulder, and he brushed it off.

"So I think I found a really nice apartment for Angela," he told me.

"Angela, huh? I'll bet she's from Los Angeles too, isn't she?"

"Yes, but she hates it down there—bad air, traffic, and really scary crime in her area, too."

We exchanged platitudes for another minute or two, and then I was in motion again. This angel business was beginning to annoy me. My face heated up, and my arms and hands were fraught with tension. A sharp breath whistled out through my nose. It wasn't okay with me that my free time was being invaded by a client's fantasies. From my perspective, Angela and all the rest comprised a leakage of Arundel pollutants into the sea of my life. It happened to be angels instead of pesticides or sewage, but so what?

I was aware that my anger was not a particularly mature or compassionate response to an unusual set of circumstances. But I also knew that whatever I thought, I was powerless in the face of such a growing, strong feeling. I didn't like George Arundel, and I didn't like whatever was going on that he'd catalyzed. At that moment, I didn't care if the ultimate source of the phenomenon was God, an overactive imagination, or poor toilet training.

As I walked, my anger subsided, and I became aware of waves of self-righteousness and self-pity. This was a typical progression for me. Next, I'd feel disgusted with myself, impatient for the feelings to dissipate, and then hungry. Knowing all this, I turned left toward Pacific Avenue to put myself on course toward my favorite coffeehouse. All those years of my own therapy and professional training allowed me to feel everything I always feel, but now I could get an unhealthy snack five minutes sooner.

As I nibbled on my baklava in the pseudo-warehouse atmosphere of Cafe Beatrice, I listened to the college radio station on the array of high-tech speakers and watched an assortment of students reading, typing on laptops, and covertly scrutinizing each other. UCSC students tended to wear costumes rather than clothes. I enjoyed the spectacle.

One young woman at a nearby table loudly proclaimed her allegiance to a band I'd never heard of as she adjusted her bright purple beret. Her Italian accent was marked and musical to my ears. A bald young Black man wore a brown and orange ikat sarong. My favorite outfit was sported by someone of indeterminate gender. Perhaps he/she would even object to the concept of gender, but since there are no thought police, I didn't worry about that. They—I'm giving it a try here—had selected an irregularly-shaped jade bolo tie, highlighting a powder-blue corduroy sport coat and bright-red pants ensemble.

Before I finished my tart, the KZSC deejay began playing "Earth Angel." I left.

That night I dreamt I was flying over a football game, wearing overalls and spitting on all the bald-headed spectators.

****

George Arundel arrived on time, and the professor greeted me in his stilted, formal manner. They were wearing—I mean, he was wearing—khaki cotton pants and a hideous Hawaiian shirt. This orange and purple monstrosity dominated the room. Pineapples and surfboards seemed to be battling the diminutive hula girls scattered in their midst. I wasn't sure if the shirt represented passive-aggression or was simply a testament to monumentally poor taste.

His combover smelled of whatever hair gel he used to get his sparse strands to stick to his scalp. Why would anyone want their hair to smell like limes?

"I need to ask some questions, and I'm not going to be satisfied with your usual evasions. Is that clear?" I began.

"It's started, hasn't it? How exciting." Arundel clapped his hands together once as if he were beginning to applaud and then remembered he wasn't attending any sort of performance. The sound was loud enough that I worried my suitemate might hear it in her session.

"Have you been tampering with my clients?"

"Of course not." His denial was punctuated by a vigorous head shake.

"Are you aware of everything the other alters do?"

"No. I don't need to be."

"I think you do." I glared at him; his arrogance was aggravating.

"I have much more experience with this type of thing," Arundel responded. "So let me assure you there's no plot against you, you're not crazy, and whatever else you're wondering about probably isn't the case either. This is simply how these things work."

"What things?" I wanted answers, not vague reassurances.

"That which I have previously discussed with you—your angelic legacy. How else could the universe tell you who you are?"

"A letter?" I heard my sarcasm and reigned myself in with some difficulty.

"Would you believe it?"

"No, but I don't believe this either, do I?"

"Not yet. And that's sensible. For every legitimate spiritual event, there are ten thousand fraudulent ones. I could be a confidence artist or simply deluded. For that matter, coincidences and such crop up all the time, even when there is no profound meaning associated with them. You probably aren't accustomed to noting them. Now you're tuned in. At any rate, you must proceed carefully. I agree."

"Somehow, your agreeing with me fails to console me. My God—now you've got me talking like you." I threw my hands in the air, my exasperation shattering any vestiges of professionalism.

Arundel smiled and leaned forward. "Look at it this way, Thomas. Something very interesting has happened. That's all you can accept for now. And if what I'm saying turns out to be true, is that really so bad? An angel? With a mission to help transform the world? There are worse fates."

"That's beside the point."

"Hardly." He paused and rubbed the bridge of his nose where his missing glasses would rest. "Aren't you even open to the possibility that I know what I'm talking about?"

"No," I replied. "I'm not. And I'll tell you why. To consider that I might be an angel would be a form of psychic suicide, given my current outlook. I can't be the me I know and do that. It's like telling one of Mother Theresa's nuns to go hold up a 7-Eleven. You don't know what you're asking."

"Yes, I do. I'm very much aware of what is entailed. You will need to reorganize almost everything about yourself to accept who you truly are. But it can be done."

"That's easy for you to say."

"Hardly. Do you think I was born with the capacity to hold all this gracefully? I've been in your shoes. I know how difficult it is to undergo a spiritual emergence. But ultimately, you're going to have to choose between going crazy and your destiny. That's what it will come down to. It always does. And I feel confident of your adaptability. Remember, I questioned you carefully before embarking on this."

"My favorite color? House pets?"

Arundel nodded amiably.

"I'm supposed to risk my sanity on the basis of that?" My face tightened—all of it—and my hands clenched as I involuntarily raised my voice. I took three deep breaths and tried to calm down. "Wait a minute," I continued. "We're way off topic here. I still need some questions answered." I bent my head and kneaded my brow while I continued to regroup. "Can you control dreams?" I finally asked, looking up.

"No. I don't possess the skills to do that."

"But it can be done? Is that what you're saying?"

"Certainly. Krishnanda did that."

"Could he be involved in this?" I asked.

"I'm sure he is, but he's been dead for nine years, so that's probably hard for you to accept."

I was belatedly aware that I was solely focused on my reactivity to Arundel's words at this point, ignoring facial cues, body language, and everything else available to me. Ignoring this potentially useful insight, I plunged on. "So you're saying he's creating the dreams as a ghost or something?" I asked.

"No. You asked if he is involved. That's the question I answered."

"Well, now I'm asking if he's messing around with my dreams."

"I'm not a confidante of the subtle realm's personnel department, Thomas. Why does it matter who or what is orchestrating your coming-out party? The fact that you're receiving signs—this is what matters."

I resorted to logic, an old friend when my nervous system became aroused. "There are all kinds of signs, and they don't prove facts in any case. At best they corroborate things, and nothing's happened that can't be explained much more easily by ordinary means."

"Then why are we having this conversation? If you're so secure in your understanding, why ask me anything? Is this your idea of a therapeutic intervention?" He leaned back, confident he'd scored points with me.

He was right; this wasn't therapy. I was scratching an itch—a really big one. "I'm sorry," I told him. "This isn't my idea of therapy, either, so I won't be charging you today. And I am shook-up over what's happening. I can't deny it. It's downright weird, and it makes me angry."

"Understandable. There are stages in this process much as there are in grieving—denial, anger, and so forth."

"You make it sound so inevitable. Aren't you open to the possibility that you're wrong?"

"Of course, but nothing's happened to support that hypothesis," Arundel asserted. "This is what I do. If a client came in with a classic array of symptoms for some familiar disorder, wouldn't you feel confident that you understood him? Your training and experience would serve you, just as mine do."

This arguing was getting us nowhere. We were trying to settle an issue of faith, not logic. He had it, I didn't. It was as simple as that.

"How do you know," I asked, "that your alters aren't running all over town producing so-called coincidences to dazzle me with?"

"I know."

"But how?"

"I can't explain," he answered, his smirk demonstrating his smugness.

"Can't or won't?"

"Can't. You haven't developed the appropriate receptor sites for the information, so there would be no place for it to attach." The smirk was still there.

"We're not molecules. Try me," I suggested, exhaling loudly to release my excess energy.

"It's akin to speaking in another language. It wouldn't make sense to you."

"Try me," I repeated more firmly. I was back in control of myself and emphasizing my words consciously now.

"I'm sorry, Thomas." For once, his facial expression appeared to be congruent with his words. He'd raised the inner corners of his eyebrows, loosened his eyelids, and pulled down the corners of his lips. He really was sorry.

I paused and wondered what to do next. Arundel seemed to consider himself my mentor, which obligated him to answer some questions and not answer others. It also kept him at the helm of our conversation, as usual. Perhaps if I mustered something unpredictable or insightful, another more forthcoming personality would emerge. That had happened before.

"What about Zig-Zag?" I asked. "She doesn't believe she's an angel either. Haven't the signs failed with her?"

"The young can be stubborn and foolish, and she is somewhat inured to the extraordinary. But I have no doubt she'll see the light."

"See the light? There's a phrase with more than one meaning."

"Yes."

It wasn't much of an insight, I had to admit. "Part of your mission is to help me, right?"

"Yes."

"Well, you're not helping."

"Yes, I am. You just don't like it. Perhaps a phrase devised by Krishnanda would be appropriate to share here. 'Yield gracefully to what is.' If I were you, I'd write that on my bathroom mirror."

"If you were me, you'd do exactly what I'm doing since you'd be me," I said. "Anyway, we're out of time. Are you interested in continuing therapy?"

"No. Call me when you're ready."

"Ready? Ready for what? To save the world?"

Arundel smiled tolerantly and marched out, his hair gel following him out. I had survived another hour with the king of noncooperation.

Chapter 7

The eerie synchronicities continued, averaging about two a day. Part of me grew accustomed to them; another deeper part was shoved further and further off-center as the tally accrued. It was like being a juror in a trial in which the prosecutor presented a myriad of circumstantial evidence. Eventually, inferential or not, the overall mass of the presentation directed a guilty verdict.

I really didn't want to be an angel. Oh, on some level it would feel good to be special—more than special, really—a legendary creature. But then I wouldn't still be Tom Dashiel, and as miserable as I often was, it was what I knew. My clients commonly faced the same dilemma. They showed up with certain attitudes and behaviors in tow, swearing they were sick to death of all the problems these evoked. Then quite a few of them fought me tooth and nail to hang onto their sense of themselves and not change. A great deal of psychic energy is reserved for maintenance of the status quo.

Another issue was responsibility. I didn't need the burden of some holy mission to transform the world. Maybe that sounds selfish, but I definitely preferred that somebody else save anything bigger than individual people. My job was hard enough as it was.

Of course, all of this was beside the point, anyway. The whole idea was crazy, and this type of thinking represented nothing more than my susceptibility to this particular form of craziness. I was who I was, regardless of Arundel and all the noncoincidences.

If God told me himself…Well, then I'd think about it. Short of that, I was protecting my sanity any way I could.

****

The phone rang at three a.m., and I debated for several rings whether to answer it or not. I handed out two sets of business cards. One only listed my answering service; the other included the landline that was ringing. I gave these latter cards out sparingly, which meant that only people I was willing to talk to in the middle of the night could disturb me. Nonetheless, I usually equivocated before answering.

"Hello," I rasped.

"Hello? Is this Mr. Dashiel?" It was an unfamiliar young woman's voice, fraught with urgency. Her words loudly tumbled out.

"Yes, it is."

"This is Zig-Zag. You know—George Arundel's friend?"

"Sure. What can I do for you?" I was about three-quarters awake at this point.

"It's an emergency. A friend of mine is freaking out, and I don't know what to do." Her words ran together now as she hurried to get them out.

"What do you mean by 'freaking out'?" I asked. I've found that clients employ the idiom to describe a wide variety of behaviors, from simple crying to actually running amok.

"It's like she's paralyzed, only she can talk some. It's really scary. Can you help?"

"Where are you?"

"On Brommer Street near Seventh."

"Okay. I'll be there in fifteen minutes."

"Thanks. I really appreciate this. I'll be standing by the side of the road."

"Right. See you soon."

I don't know why I agreed so readily to rush off in the middle of the night to meet a stranger in crisis. Perhaps it was because the last time a client of mine had become inert, her housemates had called the cops, who handcuffed her and locked her in the back seat of a police car—the standard procedure in Santa Cruz County for hauling someone in for a seventy-two-hour observation period. Unfortunately, her breakdown had been spawned by paternal mistreatment. Her father had been a highway patrolman who had locked her in a closet for days on end, among other things. Obviously, the episode was far from therapeutic, setting us back months in her therapy.

My Volvo was a reluctant participant in the house call. First it balked at starting, then it only grudgingly consented to engage its first gear. Hindsight suggests that it may have demonstrated more common sense than I.

Zig-Zag was, in fact, waiting by the side of the road, clad in denim overalls again, underneath an unzipped navy-blue hooded sweatshirt. When she opened the passenger side door and hopped in, I was confused. Wasn't I supposed to get out instead of her getting in? Also, her face was blackened. What did that mean? The only possibility my three-in-the-morning mind could conceive of was a minstrel show. In Santa Cruz? A minstrel show?

"I'll show you where to park. Take a right in that dirt driveway," she directed, pointing with a slim, elegant finger. The smears of wet dirt on her sleeve gave off a fresh, earthy aroma.

The driveway ran along the perimeter of a vacant lot, next to a small church's parking lot. Overgrown weeds brushed against the car's undercarriage as I negotiated a series of potholes on the road, jarring my butt. A few hundred feet in from Brommer Street, several elderly cars huddled beside a tall cyclone fence. Through an open metal gate, I spied the base of a steel tower.

"Anywhere around here is good," Zig-Zag assured me.

I parked next to an elderly Jeep and switched off the ignition. "Why is your face black?"

"It's dark out," she answered, scrambling out of the car before I could ask anything else.

I trailed her to the fence, my eyes gradually becoming accustomed to the dim light. Three African-Americans loitered by the open gate—or were they more White people with blackened faces? They were. I suddenly realized what was going on.

"This is some illegal protest thing, isn't it?" I asked Zig-Zag as we encountered the others. I gestured beyond them at the metal struts of the tower. "That's a power line, isn't it?"

"We don't protest," Zig-Zag answered. "We wreak havoc."

"Havoc?"

"Sure. Right, guys?"

"Right," a short man in army fatigues answered as we joined the trio.

"Havoc's where it's at," an overweight teenage girl added.

"Cripple the machine!" Zig-Zag exhorted.

"Eat the rich!" another figure called, her tone of voice suggesting, thank God, facetiousness. I stared at this last speaker. She appeared to be a tall, slim woman who was actually Black under her blackface. "Kill their heads off!" she added, grinning.

Her smile was both lively and sweet, despite the mock militancy of her words. From what I could see of her face, it was strong, with high cheekbones, a long wide nose, and an exemplary pair of dog eyes. By this, I mean the soft eyes you see on mature dogs that somehow embody the best qualities of the species.

Suddenly, I was conscious of my ugliness. Real dog's eyes didn't care what I looked like, but this woman's probably did. And so I did, too.

"Listen," I finally replied, "I share your concern for our world, but I'm not willing to get involved in something illegal."

"It's Brenda," the especially Black woman told me. "She's halfway up the tower, and she can't move."

Gesturing, she drew my attention to the superstructure dwarfing the power company's transformer site. About forty feet in the air, two dark figures were clinging to the metal cross-bracing.

"Phil's up there with her," Zig-Zag reported. "But he's not getting anywhere."

"So you want me to do therapy in the dark on a tower with someone I don't know who's too scared to move?"

"Exactly," the Black woman answered.

"And I'll be trespassing?"

"Of course."

"And you'll probably expect me to work for free since your cause is so darn just?"

"Naturally," she responded.

"What's your name?" I asked.

"Desdemona, but my friends call me Dizzy."

"If I save Brenda, I'll probably get to call you Dizzy, right?" I couldn't believe my ears. I was flirting. In the midst of this absurd situation, in front of virtual strangers, I was actually flirting.

"That's right," she answered, smiling again.

"Pardon my curiosity, but aren't you Black anyway?" I asked. "I mean under the shoe polish or whatever."

"So?"

"Never mind." I paused and thought a moment. "What are the other alternatives?" The wind kicked up right then, whistling in my ears. I zipped my nylon jacket and turned up the collar.

"We can't leave her," the man said.

"And we're not about to call 911," Dizzy added.

"Jail isn't an alternative," Zig-Zag agreed. "Brenda's wanted as it is. She'd probably get two or three years."

"Why? Did she blow something up? Two or three years seems rather extreme for criminal trespass."

Everyone looked at everyone else.

"Maybe," the large girl replied.

"Great. Is there a bomb up on the tower?"

"No," the man answered. "We had other plans, but they've been scuttled."

"So will you do it?" Dizzy asked.

Obviously, the sane choice was to drive home immediately and go back to sleep. But I found I didn't want to do that. What I wanted to do was concoct convincing reasons to myself to stay and help. I tried for a while, but I couldn't think of any, so I just said yes, anyway.

"Follow me," Dizzy directed, striding forward toward the tower, flashlight in hand. She moved like a dancer, pushing each leg ahead as she walked, while maintaining a stable center of gravity in her hips.

Watching her enabled me to maneuver from the gate to the base of the tower without the interference of sensible second thoughts. An earthy odor akin to the one Zig-Zag had brought into the car permeated the air. Had they been digging? Why?

A metal ladder with tubular rungs and handholds was welded onto the structure, and Dizzy hesitated only a second before pulling herself up and beginning the climb. I paused longer, common sense compelling me to reconsider. I glanced up to assess the danger of the mission, and the vision of Dizzy's tightly jeaned posterior lured me up onto the first rung. I was being seduced by my own projections onto this woman. I certainly didn't know her—she could be married with two children, for example. But my hormones were overriding reality, and my size thirteen feet continued to seek out ever-higher rungs.

As I climbed, two problems surfaced. One was my tendency to enjoy the dimly lit view of Dizzy above me at the expense of concentrating on the task at hand. After slipping off the ladder, clinging to the tower with only my arms—I was scared into a more immediate focus. Worse yet were truly painful collisions between the ladder and my raging erection.

Living a celibate lifestyle created certain drawbacks, among them an inconvenient ease of arousal. I've been burdened with erections from hugging elderly women, watching female joggers' chests rising and falling, and even glancing at lingerie advertisements. Clearly, my endocrine system was completely incapable of distinguishing between legitimate stimuli and whatever else came my way.

I've heard other men describe their type—tall, slim redheads or whatever. I don't have a type; my arousal is completely unpredictable. Once again, whatever criterion the rest of the world uses is a mystery to me. Did everyone else's genitals come with an owner's manual?

On the tower, en route to the acrophobic girl, at least it was dark, and my juvenile response to Dizzy remained hidden. Also, I was consoled that in this instance my conscious self agreed that the stimulus was indeed exciting. It was an erection on merit.

When we finally neared the stricken climber, I could see that Brenda was a pale, ascetic-looking woman in her late twenties. She wore a black karate gi, fastened by a piece of yellow nylon rope. Her very short, dark hair framed her small oval face in an old-fashioned manner— like a Dutch renaissance painting. Unlike the others, she wore no blackface.

Brenda's distress was obvious. Her ragged breathing overrode the increased wind noise from our being aloft. Her eyes were squeezed shut, and her tense body pressed against a cross-strut adjacent to the ladder. Apparently, she'd been maneuvering laterally to reach something I couldn't see on the other side of the tower. She hadn't gotten far before an urge to meld herself into the metal had asserted itself. Immobile, her overall posture was reminiscent of a desperate kindergartner clinging to her mother's leg on the first day of school.

Just above her, squatting on a small platform, a slim,

handsome man in his forties spoke soothingly in an effort to convince Brenda to join him. There was no evidence she even heard him.

The sort of anxiety attack that Brenda was weathering entailed very real physical symptoms. She was probably dizzy, sweaty, and suffering heart palpitations. This latter feature could be extremely disturbing, convincing the person that they were experiencing a heart attack, or even dying. No intervention conducted in the panic-producing context was likely to be effective, so my first task was to devise a way to get her down on terra firma.

As I formed my initial impressions of the situation on the tower and my erection subsided, Dizzy scrambled up next to the man whom she introduced as Phil.

"And this is Brenda," she told me as she settled into a full lotus position on the shared platform. "Brenda, this is Tom. He's here to help."

The panic-stricken woman blinked her eyes open for half a second, focused on my face, and then hurriedly withdrew back inside herself. I felt as if a human camera had just taken a snapshot of me.

"Do you think you can hold onto me?" I asked.

She struggled to respond, finally forcing the air out in audible gulps. "What…do…you…mean?"

I could barely distinguish the words, but her talking at all was a good sign. Some part of her was present and interested in a solution to her dilemma.

"On my back," I told her gently. "Do you think you can lock your hands around my neck?"

"I…can't…move."

"Oh, I'll do all the moving," I assured her. "All you have to do is transfer your grip from the tower to me. I'll do the rest. I'm sort of like a human tower anyway—you probably won't even notice the difference. Dizzy and Phil can hang onto you while you switch over."

"Who…are…you?"

"I'm a friend of Zig-Zag's."

"How…do I know…I can trust you?"

She was speaking in bunches of words now; our conversation was distracting her from her fear.

"Well, Dizzy likes me," I told her. I couldn't think of anything else to say.

"The man flirts good," Dizzy added.

"Why can't Phil carry me down?"

Not only did Brenda articulate an entire sentence, the words were much more comprehensible now. Her breathing was noticeably calmer, too. I was encouraged.

I glanced at Phil, who shrugged. He probably weighed about 140 pounds, and his arms resembled fettuccine.

"I'm really big and strong," I informed Brenda. "I do this kind of thing all the time."

"Really?" She opened her eyes and scanned my face.

"Sure. Why do you think they called me?" I smiled and projected sincerity, not one of my most convincing emotions, but apparently good enough for Brenda.

"Well…okay." She closed her eyes. "Let me know when it's time. I don't want to watch."

What a remarkable recovery, I thought. "Sure," I agreed.

It was much more easily said than done, but eventually, after several false starts, I found myself clambering down the ladder while my human backpack choked the living daylights out of me.

The two other activists followed us, taking turns telling Brenda terrible jokes, which she ignored. Her terror had repossessed her as soon as we'd begun moving; I could feel her heart beating frantically against my back. I experienced difficulty remaining calm myself. All sorts of things could go wrong, after all. Brenda might successfully throttle me, in which case we'd plummet to our deaths, or at least to a pile of broken limbs. Alternately, she could relinquish her grip suddenly and fall on her own. If Dizzy or Phil slipped, they'd clobber us from above and set in motion yet another airborne disaster.

I listened to the jokes, though, and as humorless as they were, I could center myself around them. They served as an anchor for the part of me that wanted to sail off to fear.

Anyway, none of the tragic events I'd pictured came to pass. Instead, Brenda initially refused to abandon her perch on my back once we reached the ground, which was a pain in the ass—literally, since she'd dug her boot heels into my butt. And a squad of sheriff's deputies were waiting for us, handcuffs in hand.

"Oops," Dizzy commented.

Chapter 8

The deputies were utterly uninterested in who was
an environmental crusader and who was a therapist.
Furthermore, my size intimidated them, so they cuffed
me much more forcefully than the others. I had to lie face
down in the dirt while one of them twisted my arms
behind me and another planted his knee in the small of
my back. It was very hard to fully cooperate with this
procedure, since no one announced where any of my
body parts were supposed to be next. It also hurt—on
more than one level. My wounded dignity and self-
respect competed with physical pain for my attention.

I did notice the policemen were gentle with Brenda,
whose anxiety level was still marked. Also, it was
apparent that Zig-Zag, Dizzy, Phil, and the others were
completely familiar with the getting-arrested drill. In
fact, Dizzy addressed one of the deputies by name, and
another policeman told Phil that he wished "you guys
would give us all a break and cut this crap out." It was as
if they were sports rivals or opposing lawyers meeting in
a bar after a trial. I was the only one deeply affected by
the arrest as far as I could tell. Of course, preoccupied
with my self-indulgent pathos, I could've missed
something.

They split us up and farmed us out to the backseats
of several police cars. I shared my black vinyl pew with
the short man in camo gear who'd stayed on the ground.

He told me his name was Emory and that he was sorry I'd been dragged into this mess. He spoke with a slight lisp and a hint of an accent. Irish?

"No sorrier than I am," I told him. "This could play hell with my professional reputation."

"You know," he responded, "it's not that bad. These kinds of crimes aren't self-serving—they're based on moral principles—and people are pretty understanding about that. I'm a professional, and it hasn't hurt my business at all."

"You've been arrested before?"

"Three times. Nothing serious."

"What do you do for a living?" I asked.

"Chiropractic."

Now that he mentioned it, I noticed his chiropractor demeanor—long, unblinking eye contact. It was spooky—the sort of false intimacy that a successful gigolo developed. Did they teach a course on it at chiropractor college—The Look 101? I guess you had to do something beyond the norm to convince people to let you play with their bones.

"Do you think sitting on the front edge of a bench seat with your hands cuffed behind you, your legs wedged against the seat in front, and your head pressed against the ceiling is a healthy posture?" I asked.

"I'll give you my card later," Emory replied. "Stop by my office for a free adjustment. It's the least I can do."

"You don't seem very upset for a guy who's just been arrested."

"Like I said, it's really not that bad. If you think of it in a sociological way, jail is a pretty interesting place, in fact."

In other words, I thought, if you dissociate thoroughly enough to escape the realm of feelings, then you can skate through the experience and pay the psychic price later.

"Personally, I'm scared," I told him, turning my head away to gaze ahead.

"Of what?"

"The kind of people I'm likely to be meeting soon."

"Are you kidding? I hope you don't take this the wrong way, but they're all going to be terrified of you."

"Hey, maybe you're right."

"Of course I am. No offense."

It was a fifteen-minute ride to the county jail. No one spoke for the remainder of the trip, although the police radio squawked periodically, triggering my startle reflex. I lurched forward each time, the handcuffs digging into my wrists, reminding me not to react to the next burst of noise. Who knows? Maybe after a few thousand of these stimulus-response training episodes, I'd calm down. We arrived at the county jail before I had a chance to find out.

The complex sat across the San Lorenzo River from downtown Santa Cruz, and except for the high iron fence and the dearth of windows, it could've been a mid-priced motel. The outside walls were some sort of brown masonry—not cinder block or brick—and the one-story, flat-roofed design sprawled across a well-kept landscape.

Once inside, the differences between the jail and a tourist accommodation became much more evident. Despite the size of the booking area, its ambiance was distinctly claustrophobic, as though traces of apprehension lingered from previous guests. It also smelled like a cross between a hospital and a bar, with the aromatic aftermath of poorly cleaned-up vomit, and remnants of a powerful disinfectant permeating the entire space. The tang of the latter in my nostrils was nauseating.

We were booked as a group, and once again no one was interested in my status as a good Samaritan. I was promised, though, that I could tell my story at a hearing later in the morning. By now, it was about four a.m.

Next, we were sorted by gender, unmanacled, fingerprinted, photographed, searched, and our possessions were confiscated. The county personnel were polite but very impersonal; they were hiding themselves in their roles. Finally, Phil, Emory, and myself were led to a large holding cell in which five smelly drunks were lying on orange plastic benches. As well as cheap alcohol and rank body odor, a puzzling combination of mildew and wet dog assaulted our noses. Clearly, incarceration provided a cornucopia of unpleasant odors. If I ever wrote a sociological textbook, I'd make sure to include that.

As Emory had predicted, none of our fellow arrestees wanted any part of me. Rousing themselves, they stumbled to the far corner of the room to resume sleeping off their various states of drunkenness.

My own fatigue overwhelmed me shortly after reclining on the uncomfortable, too-short bench nearest the cell door. I dreamt I was lying on an orange plastic bench in a holding cell. In the dream, I drifted in and out of sleep, dreaming (in the dream) that I was a gorilla looking for food who fell off a cliff and hit his head, and then hallucinated he was a goldfish trapped in a small muddy puddle.

It was probably the strangest dream I've ever had. I couldn't tell who I really was, which scenario, if any, was real, and what any of it meant. I was hopelessly confused, or at least my subconscious was.

Much too soon, we were awakened by a loud, cheerful voice.

"Rise and shine, campers. Up and at 'em!" a guard called.

"Shut up!" one of the drunks shouted back.

"Now, now. Let's not be a grumpy Gus," the guard admonished.

I sat up to get a look at this character. He was almost as big as me, and although he couldn't have been over thirty-five, his buzzed hair was pure white. His teeth, on the other hand, revealed in a broad smile, were quite yellow.

"Why not?" the drunk rasped. I expected this guy to look down and out, but aside from wrinkled clothes and a major scowl, he could've been a car salesman.

"Nobody likes grumpiness. It just doesn't say, 'Hey, I want to be your friend.' " His voice was musical, as if he were performing in a light opera.

"Fuck you."

"And we all need friends."

"Fuck your mother."

"Much as I'm enjoying our repartee, I need to make a general announcement. Listen up, gentlemen. You've got ten minutes to primp for your hearings. If you're back in here afterward, we'll feed you. Any questions?"

"Fuck you."

"You'll need to reorganize your thought into the form of a question."

"Fuck you?"

"That's better. Have a nice day," he added as he turned and departed.

"What's this primp shit?" one of the other drunks asked. He was extremely skinny, with a bedraggled ponytail.

"Beats me," his buddy answered. "Just some wise-ass shit, I guess."

He had a point. There was no mirror or sink in the room—just a lidless toilet. I stumbled over to it and peed. So much for primping.

We were herded down a wide, well-lit hallway by two new guards, who were armed with batons and fierce scowls. I missed the facetious guy already.

The hearings themselves were boring, list-reading affairs. When my turn came, I simply explained the circumstances, admitted I'd broken the law, and asked for mercy. I was told that if I paid a $200 fine, I was free to go. I could call someone to bring the money, or wait until another unspecified official decided I could be released on my own recognizance. My cohorts were all charged with more serious crimes, and their bail was set at $5000 each. Brenda shook when she heard this outcome, but the others took it in stride. Dizzy turned out her pockets in a mock search for hundred-dollar bills, accusing Zig-Zag of taking them while she'd slept. Phil made a speech likening their cause to anti-war demonstrations in the 1960s until the elderly judge told him he was even more annoying than Vietnam-era defendants had been.

I decided to wait and see if they'd let me go without my needing to prepay the fine. Back in the holding cell with the same motley crew again, before I could find out, the merry guard informed me that my fine had been paid by a "kind gentleman" and I was free to "depart this vale of tears some call home."

Chapter 9

In the lobby, George Arundel and Zig-Zag were waiting by the exit door. She didn't look worse for wear. She'd tucked her hoodie under her arm, and a strap of her denim overalls had once again slipped off her shoulder, creating a vulnerability of sorts that I found endearing. Arundel was the one who looked as though he had spent time in jail. What was left of his black hair tilted en masse to one side as though it weren't composed of separate strands. Wrinkles upon wrinkles spidered across his blue dress shirt and black slacks in no particular pattern, and the dark pouches under his eyes that I'd spied before were back with a vengeance. As I drew closer, strong body odor emanated from him. Could his night have been worse than ours? Hardly, I decided.

"Brunch is on me," Arundel declared. His voice was raspy, as though he'd recently been shouting.

While it wasn't kosher to hobnob with a client, it would've been rude to turn my back on a benefactor, so off we strolled to a nearby pancake house. No one spoke on the way, which was fine by me. I would've appreciated total silence, in fact, but a street sweeper whirred and scraped to the side of us, an enormous motorcycle rumbled by, and a crazed dog barked continuously for the last block. I blamed them for my burgeoning headache.

June's Breakfast Place was a relic of whatever era

mistakenly believed that Americana decor was the epitome of dining ambiance. The booths still wore patterned ruffled skirts, and wooden wagon wheels with lantern-like globes served as light fixtures. Every detail in the restaurant manifested the theme, including the salt and pepper shakers (wooden piglets), the menu (nicknames for every dish), and the wall decor (patchwork quilts I actually liked). Whenever I ate at June's, I felt the presence of glowering grandparents ready to swoop down and catch me using poor table manners.

"Thanks for bailing me out," Zig-Zag told Arundel after we'd installed ourselves in a maroon corner booth. I would've waited for a greeter to guide us to it, but Arundel seemed familiar with how things worked at the restaurant, so we followed him there. The duo sat across the yellowed Formica tabletop from me.

"Yes," I agreed. "Thank you, George."

He nodded his acknowledgement to me and turned to face his goddaughter. "This isn't the first time," he reminded her.

"Maybe it'll be the last," she replied.

"You're ready to give up this foolishness?"

"Nope. I'm willing to not get caught again, though." She grinned, flouting his serious tone.

"There's no guarantee of that. The only sure way to stay out of prison is by opening up to your angelic nature."

She rolled her eyes. "Here we go again." As Arundel continued to speak, she marched a salt-shaker piglet around the circumference of her red paper placemat, clanking its base against the Formica.

June's dining room smelled of pancakes, syrup, and

sausages, catalyzing my hunger. I felt like grabbing a plate from a nearby table. When would someone come and take our order? A few seconds later, as if she read my mind, a cute, diminutive Asian server sidled up with a tablet in her hands. Her pleasing voice was surprisingly low-pitched, like a note on a clarinet—warm and rounded. I looked at her more closely. She wore an old-fashioned gingham apron over jeans and a scoop-necked, yellow T-shirt. It was as if she were a hybrid of cultures, styles, and eras.

After we'd ordered, Arundel addressed Zig-zag. "I'm surprised you haven't begun receiving information about your mission," Arundel told her. "When that happens, even you won't be able to resist."

"Wanna bet?"

"What do you mean?" he asked.

"I've been having visions for days now."

"Really?" I asked. I wondered if this would happen to me too.

"Yup. I'm supposed to go to a certain bookstore and look at a particular book. Page fifty-three, second paragraph." She leaned back and crossed her arms. Her eyes defied him to compel her to do a damn thing about it.

"What did it say?" I asked. "Was that in the vision?"

"I'm not going. Who cares what it says?"

"I do," I asserted. "Aren't you even a little curious?"

"Well, a little. Sure. Who wouldn't be?"

"You must go," Arundel told her.

"No way." She backed away farther, pressing herself into the booth's cracked vinyl upholstery.

"Suppose I go?" I suggested. "You can tell me the details from your vision, and I'll check it out."

Arundel chimed in. "That's a reasonable compromise, Zee. Let Tom do it."

"All right. But I don't necessarily want to hear about it. And, George? You have to stay off my back about all this. Is that a deal?"

"Agreed. Just one more thing…"

She glared fiercely at him. "I'm not up for your games today, George. I spent the night in jail, and I'm tired. Okay?" Her volume had risen with each word. The "okay" got the attention of the only other table of diners in the room. I glanced at this fivesome of older men who could've just come from an AA meeting. Their interest quickly faded, and one of them began gesticulating at a companion.

"I understand," Arundel replied. "Perhaps I'll take my leave and let you two get on with things."

"What about your food?" Zig-Zag asked.

He waved his hand in the air and grunted.

"I'll eat his pancakes," I told them. "I'm starving."

I once again expressed my appreciation for Arundel's financial help at the county lock-up as we stood and shook hands. His was clammy. I resisted the urge to immediately pull mine away.

"It's the least I could do," Arundel told me. "And I have yet to thank you for your efforts in our therapy sessions."

He seemed to be serious. "I can only recall one moment that could be termed therapy. If I didn't know you better, I'd think you were joking." I smiled to soften my words.

"Sometimes, even a single insight can be transformative," Arundel replied.

I raised my eyebrows.

"Of course," he continued, "that wasn't the case here."

"I thought not."

He smiled one of his creepier smiles before he strode away.

"George is George," Zig-Zag sing-songed.

"He certainly is. Listen, are you sure you won't go to the bookstore with me?"

"Oh, maybe I will. As long as George doesn't know about it."

"I won't tell."

Our food arrived, and the thirtyish server smiled at me when I asked her to leave Arundel's dish on my side of the table. "Big men need lots of food," she told me. "And there's more where that came from if you need it."

"Thank you."

"I like a big eater," she continued, grinning now. She reached down to straighten my fork, her face alongside mine. I caught a whiff of coconut. I also felt the heat of her smooth, white skin next to mine about the same time I noticed my arousal. When I turned my head toward her, I involuntarily glanced down her loose shirt at her modest, unfettered breasts.

"I'm Jun," she told me as she caught me and then straightened up.

"You own the restaurant?" I knew that wasn't the case, but my face was flushing and felt too ashamed to gather my thoughts.

"No, that's just a coincidence. I'm Jun without the E. You can call me Junie if you have a hard time distinguishing me from a seventy-three-year-old German woman. Or maybe the view from where you're sitting took care of that." Her grin told me she hadn't revealed herself by accident, nor did she mind where my eyes had strayed.

"I think I can manage. I'm Tom, and this is my friend Zig-Zag." I gestured at my companion in an attempt to deflect Jun's attention.

Zig-Zag was already digging into an omelet and laughing about as much as she could with a mouthful of food.

"I think I'd better start eating before things get cold," I added.

"Sure, Tom. You do that."

She sashayed away, confident that I'd watch her go. She was right. My erection was in charge again.

I put my head down, brought a forkful of blueberry pancake up to my lips, and tried to ignore Zig-Zag. I needed to regroup.

She leaned forward to get my attention, and once again, I smelled patchouli oil. "Yeah, your silverware really needed rearranging, Tom. You should ask her out. She is so into you. And her boobs weren't big, but I liked her nipples, didn't you?"

I kept eating.

"Oh, come on. Don't be like that. I had to say something, didn't I? She flashed me, too. Do you think she's a sex addict or something? I'll bet this doesn't happen to you much, no offense."

"Sometimes my bestial repulsiveness could be said to exert a horrid fascination."

"That sounds like something out of a book."

"It is. My own words escape me. What am I supposed to say?"

"I'd go with 'yippee!' Another option would be 'excuse me, I need to go get Jun's phone number.' "

"None of those feel quite right. I think I'll just eat."

"Go right ahead."

When we'd finished—I had no trouble devouring two portions—Jun returned.

"I'm sorry if I made you uncomfortable," she told me. "I know I can come on kinda strong." She held my gaze unflinchingly and placed the check on the end of the table, eschewing the opportunity to hover close to me again.

"I'll say," Zig-Zag replied.

"Who are you again?"

"Just a friendly bystander. Don't mind me."

"It's okay," I told Jun. "I just didn't know how to handle things. With my face, I'm not used to a woman's interest."

"What about your face?"

"The burn scars."

"Who cares? It's what's here that counts." I expected that when she reached forward, Jun would touch my heart. Instead, she laid a gentle hand on my crotch. "Big men have big treats for their women."

Zig-Zag laughed again, this time drawing Jun's attention.

"Hey," our server said with heat, "I've got something going here. Back off!" Her hands were on her hips now, and she widened her stance as if she were preparing to do physical battle.

Zig-Zag held up her hands in mock surrender. "I'll see you outside, Tom." Then she scooted across the bench seat and scurried off, leaving me in the surreal scenario that breakfast had turned into.

I turned to Jun. "I appreciate your interest. But why are you doing this? You could get fired. I could be a dangerous guy. And doesn't this sort of behavior go against your value system?"

"I'll level with you, Tom. George stopped in earlier and told me how special you are. I was supposed to say something about it, but I don't remember exactly what he said. I had a big table of surfers right then. He said I shouldn't tell you he told me. I remember that."

"But you did."

"I did. You don't lie to an angel."

There it was—Arundel had definitely tampered with my life. "Why do you believe him?" I asked.

"It's a long story. I met another angel once. Listen, I've gotta get to my other tables. Here's my phone number." She handed me a slip of paper.

"Okay, thanks."

"Call me or don't, but I guarantee you some amazing fireworks if you do."

Zig-Zag was sitting on the curb when I reentered the sane world. The noisy sane world, as it happens. A logging truck idled a half a block away.

"Well, that was weird," she said as she arose, a cloud of dust drifting up around her.

An ambulance roared past, its siren wailing. Was the universe conspiring to keep me flooded with sounds and smells? I watched it and waited to respond. "It certainly was. It turns out George put her up to it."

"Oh, I doubt that. He's a prude. You even say the word sex, and he shuts you down."

"He told her I was an angel, and apparently, that substantially upped my status in the dating world."

"Jun didn't want a date, Tom. She wanted to jump your bones."

"She guaranteed fireworks," I told her. "I guess she

meant something tantric."

"Anyway, I'm never coming back here," Zig-Zag said. "Besides slutty Jun, it's like 1950 in there. Weird. And the blueberries in my pancakes were frozen. Frozen! They grow them ten miles from here. Ridiculous."

"Be that as it may, shall we skedaddle over to the bookstore in your vision?"

"Okay. Let's go. It's that antique one downtown. You know, the one near the library?"

"Sure. We can walk over to the impound lot, get my car, and drive there. How's that sound?"

"Let's go."

Our route wound through one of the few semi-industrial areas in town, which was sprinkled with homeless people and stray dogs. I guess owners of warehouses, building materials, and machine shops were less likely to complain about their neighborhood's demographic.

On a street corner by a wholesale bakery, a young white man with blond dreadlocks asked us for a handout while three adjacent friends chatted about which variety of meth was the most bang for the buck. One of them held a small, round device that played reggae music. The beggar's yellow-and-black dashiki completed the I-wish-I-were-Black ensemble. Zig-Zag handed him a dollar.

On the next block, a particularly skinny red dog who'd been hiding behind the legs of a stocky man barked at us until we'd passed. His curly tail wagged the whole time; he liked barking.

A pickup truck with a bed full of seated women in gray uniforms made a left turn so sharply in front of us that we had to lean back to avoid being hit. The sign on the side of the truck—Courteous Housecleaners.

Finally, we passed a positive scenario. Squeezed between a tire store and a small manufacturer—United Drip Lines—a tidy white cottage sported a sky-blue picket fence. In the paved front yard, an Asian man was teaching his young daughter how to ride a bicycle. Just as we passed, she triumphantly managed to stay aloft on her own. Her father cheered, and we joined in. The smile on the girl's face was sublime to behold. What adult can match the sheer joy that shines forth from a child?

On the way, Zig-Zag filled me in on her unusual life. She'd been born on an ashram in India, and her mother had suffered some sort of permanent nerve damage during labor. I told her I'd never heard of that happening, and she responded with a one-word explanation—"India"—and then shrugged.

According to my companion, everything was different there—the air, the sky, the colors, the people. I expressed skepticism, and she tried to describe what she meant.

"It's like the colors are brighter—no, more intense. They're not really brighter. And everything is more three-dimensional, and it's like the air is charged—full of potential for the next thing to happen. Do you know what I mean?"

"No. Could it be because you were younger when you were there?"

"Oh no. I was older then. I've only gotten young since I came to the States."

"Now I'm really confused," I admitted.

"You get a different perspective growing up around someone like Krishnanda. Hell, George was one of the most normal people there, according to Western standards, if that gives you any idea. My father could perform miracles. I mean, when I was a baby and I was cutting new teeth or something, he'd do a miracle or two to distract me from crying. I still remember the time he levitated to get my kite out of a tree. He didn't let other people see that kind of thing, but to me it was just part of the deal. So I know anything's possible. It's not a theory to me. It's something I know."

Crassly, I fantasized what a great book a case study of Zig-Zag would be. I struggled to stay in contact. "So are you saying that because you know there are more possibilities than other people think there are, you can notice things about India that sound odd to someone like me?"

"More or less. Our brains filter out most of what we perceive, right?"

"Yes."

"So suppose someone's filter was less effective— more porous, more open-minded. Then you could recognize the subjectivity of all experience."

"I didn't realize you were interested in metaphysics," I told her. "I feel like I'm in first grade." I was taking a one-down position to encourage her to keep sharing.

"That's okay. Americans don't know anything about what really matters. And I had to be interested in metaphysics in order to survive—or at least in order to make sense out of what I saw and heard as a kid. So do you see what I'm saying? Suppose you grew up thinking it was okay to sense differences in the air. I don't mean smog or temperature or anything like that. Then you'd see what there is to see. It's simple really. Even regular American tourists know something's up when they get out of their airplanes. They use words like vibrant or an assault on the senses, but it's the same thing. Matter vibrates. Well, there isn't any matter, really. Energy vibrates so it looks like matter. This is in physics books, too. And in India, all the vibrations are more intense."

It was an odd experience being lectured in metaphysics by a young woman whose life focus was clearly elsewhere. I was very curious to hear more about her life.

"So the rules are different in India?" I tried.

"Let's say the parameters. There aren't any rules."

"Okay. So it's possible for something to happen in India that can't happen here?"

"Not can't, just doesn't or hasn't happened yet."

"I think I understand. With all this in mind, I'd love to hear more about your childhood."

"Sure. Some of the Krishnanda people wanted me to be my father's successor, and they started working on that when I was only six. They made this special little robe, and I used to bless people by touching them on the head with this peacock feather. It was really fun for a while, but then I got bored with it and I wouldn't do it anymore."

"Was George one of the people encouraging you?"

"No. He and Krishnanda thought it was hilarious."

"Really?" I found this surprising. My eyebrows shot up.

"Sure. My father found most of what his followers did totally amusing. He laughed at them all the time."

"That doesn't sound very compassionate."

"Well, they were pretty silly. Anyway, after that I hung out more with the Indian kids, and I got some exotic form of encephalitis. My temperature got up to 107

Fahrenheit, which usually kills you, but my father did something so I didn't die. I did have hallucinations for a week, though."

"What was that like?"

"Scary. I was only eight or nine, and they were really intense." She paused and looked up. "You know, I just remembered something. In one of the fever dreams, I was walking down the street with this big man with scars on his face like yours."

"You're kidding."

"No. And at the end, we both flew away." She glanced at the dismay on my face. "Look, I don't like this any more than you do."

"Yeah?" I stopped and stared at her intently. I'm sure my face reflected my urge to compare our displeasures.

"I've got plans. I'll bet angels don't even have sex. I've got a lot of living to do. After fifteen years in an ashram, what do you think? I want to sign up to give my life away?"

"Is that what this is?"

"Of course. Don't you even know that?" Zig-Zig scowled as she stared back into my eyes.

I stepped back involuntarily. "I guess I do." I felt a sinking sensation in my chest as I admitted this out loud.

"And there's no way to tell what's really going on, either. That makes it worse."

"What do you mean?"

We started walking again. "Well, it could be some weird guru doing all this, or it could be my father from beyond the grave, or maybe one of us is accidentally doing it, or I don't know what else. There's no way to tell." Zig-Zag's scowl gave way to something milder—

irritation? She shook her head, her eyes narrowed, and her lips compressed.

"Do any of those appeal to you more than the others?" I asked. Yet another vehicle drowned me out. This time it was a forklift backing up. I repeated myself when the obnoxious beeping ended.

"Well, yes and no. If it's bogus, then I'm right to resist. But if it's really the universe itself, then we'll have to do it sooner or later, and I don't want to."

"I see what you mean, but have you considered how unlikely it is that this is for real? There are thousands of people in institutions all over the country that spout apocryphal nonsense. Historically, there have always been plenty of grandiose religious delusions. It's dirt common. Maybe even Krishnanda himself was unbalanced. I mean, if I could do miracles, I'd probably get a little confused about who I was."

"You don't believe he did miracles, do you?" She turned and stared me in the eyes again as if to determine the honesty of my answer.

"I'm trying to, but no, I guess not."

"That's okay. I don't mind. I just hope there's nothing too great in this book we're going to look at."

"Amen, sister."

****

After ransoming my Volvo and driving back downtown to the bookstore, we were greeted by a well-groomed border collie just inside the glass front door, who acted as if we were old friends. She seemed especially pleased to see my companion.

As far as I could tell, there was no one else in the place. We both tried calling out to no effect. After this excited boy-it's-good-to-see-you-again routine, the little black-and-white dog padded a few steps up a narrow, crowded aisle between ceiling-high shelves of dusty books before stopping and turning her shaggy head to glance back at us.

"I think she wants us to follow her," I told Zig-Zag.

"I can see that, but I think I'd prefer some human help. Hello?" she called one more time. "Anybody here?"

There was no reply. The dog watched us assiduously, her eyes gleaming. When we still didn't move, she yipped, took another step, and coquettishly cocked her head again.

"I'm coming," I told her. "I can't disappoint an old friend."

Zig-Zag sidled forward with me, and together we negotiated a maze of poorly lit aisles by following our canine guide. It was an eerie experience following this strange dog in an empty antique bookstore on a spiritual mission based on someone else's vision. If at any time in my life prior to this, I'd been informed this episode was going to be part of my future, I'd have laughed.

We found ourselves in a back corner of the store in the fiction section, according to the faded blue notecard affixed to nearby shelves. The dog barked again to get our attention and then reared up to put her paws on a small black volume near the bottom of the stacks.

"That's the one, huh?" I asked, reaching down to pat her head.

She evaded my hand and barked again. It was an alto bark, not too deep and not too yippy.

"Get that book," Zig-Zag said. "I want to see what it is."

As if she understood, the little dog returned her front

paws to the green linoleum floor, her nails clicking loudly. Then she watched me lean forward and snare the slim volume.

The book was bound in soft black leather and yielded easily to my grasp. There was no title or any other writing on the cover, so I opened the book, flipped past several blank pages, and found the name of the work. *An Account of Bat-Ool, the First Prophet in the Time Before History*. It was written by Captain M. Larris in 1886.

I read all this aloud to Zig-Zag, who began swearing softly.

"What?"

"It's the one from my vision. God damn it." She pronounced the blasphemy carefully, enunciating each letter.

"Really?"

"Of course. That probably wasn't even a dog."

I looked around for our furry salesclerk. She'd disappeared.

"I didn't see her go, either," Zig-Zag told me. "Let's get this thing over with. Page fifty-three, the second paragraph."

"Right."

The printing was crude, and not all the pages were numbered, but I found the passage, enduring a strong musty smell.

"And so Bat-Ool let it be known that although life was hard for the people of the big river, there would come a time when everything would change and the plants would grow taller and stronger and the diseases would be gone from the land. When the people asked their prophet how this great change would be affected

[sic], he told the people in a fine strong voice that men and women with wings would fly down from the heavens and defeat the spirits who made the life of the people hard. 'When will this happen?' the people of the big river asked, and once again their striking prophet spoke. 'You will know when the time of change is nigh,' he told the people, 'as everything will be doubly reversed from that which you know, and death and killing will be as eating and sleeping, and there will number among the people too many to live in peace.' "

"Well," I said after we'd both read it, "at least it was in the fiction section."

"What do you think 'doubly reversed' means?" Zig-Zag asked.

"The opposite of how things are, maybe—in some exaggerated way?"

She nodded. "Let's get out of here."

"Wait. I want to buy this book and read the rest."

"Go ask the dog how much it is." Zig-Zag's eyes narrowed, and she glared down the row of bookshelves. Obviously, she was still quite angry that the book had matched her vision. "There's no one else here."

"Hello?" I called out as we wandered back to the front of the store. I tried a few more times, but there was no sign of the dog now, let alone her owner.

I left the book on the store's high, wooden counter with a note saying I'd be back the next day to buy it.

"I've got to get to my office and see some people," I told Zig-Zag outside the store. "Can I give you a ride somewhere?"

"No, thanks."

"Let's talk on the phone about this soon."

"Good idea."

For some reason, I wasn't very shaken-up. Maybe I just couldn't assimilate any more weirdness. I don't know.

Chapter 10

The next day, I stopped by the bookstore on my way to see my first client. A wall of slack-key Hawaiian music assailed my ears as I crossed the threshold. A slim young man with a shaved head was perched on a high stool behind the front counter. He wore a forest-green velvet sports coat with wide lapels over a white silk shirt, which created a Dickensian effect. He might have been the eldest son of some early English industrialist, or perhaps a young dandy whose entire fortune had been spent on a class-climbing wardrobe.

The expression on his face hinted at low-grade boredom, which was consistent with the I'm-only-working-here-as-a-favor-to-a-rich-relative   impression I'd formed. He reached below the counter and turned down the music. His smile, when it finally arrived, was reasonably sincere.

"Good morning," he chirped.

"Hi. I'm here to buy that book I left on the counter," I told him.

"What book is that?"

"It's by a guy named Larris, and it's a novel about a prehistoric prophet."

"Hmm. Let's see."

Without moving from his stool, he began typing on a desktop computer. After a while he glanced up at me from across the wooden counter.

"Was it supposed to be the *Account of Bat-Ool*?"

"Yes. That's it."

"I'm sorry, but I've never had one of those. I can't afford it, frankly. There are only eight of them, according to my information service," he told me, tapping the computer screen with a slender index finger. "The last one auctioned was in 2014, and it sold for $44,000."

"Wait a minute. I was just in here yesterday, and I held it in my hand. It had a black leather cover. Why don't you look and see if it's under the counter somewhere?"

"I don't keep books under the counter, and the store was closed yesterday."

"No, it wasn't."

"I assure you it was, since I was attending my cousin's memorial service." He was losing his patience, and his tone of voice reflected that.

"Could I speak to the owner?"

"You're looking at him."

I held my hands up. "I'm sorry. I just assumed it would be someone older. You know—antique books— the whole eccentric-old-man thing?"

"I understand."

"Do you have a dog?" I asked.

The man looked alarmed.

"I'm not crazy," I told him. "In fact, I'm a psychotherapist. It's just that yesterday the door was open, and there was a small black-and-white dog in here. It was about noon, I guess."

"I have no explanation. I don't have a dog. Who waited on you?"

"Well, the dog sort of did." I noticed his expression again. "Look, I know how this sounds. I just want to buy a particular book, that's all. I can show you where it was in the stacks."

"My assistant isn't here, and I can't leave my stool."

"Just for a minute? Surely no one's going to rush in and steal anything in just a minute. This is very important to me."

"I'm sorry. I really can't leave my stool."

"Can't we even discuss this?"

"You don't understand. I'm dying. I literally can't leave my stool. I can't stand or walk anymore."

"Oh God. I'm sorry. I've put my foot in my mouth again." I lowered my head and glanced to the side, unable to meet his steady gaze. The poor guy.

"It doesn't matter—it's the least of my troubles. That's one thing you can say about dying. It gives you perspective on the little stuff."

"I know what you mean. It's kind of like that after a big quake. Getting cut off in traffic or something just doesn't seem too high up on the Richter scale after that." I offered this to repair my blunder, although it was scarcely up to the task.

"Yeah. So I can't help you, and anyway, as I said, there's no way you saw that book here. It's rare, it's expensive, and there aren't even any on the West Coast, let alone in Santa Cruz."

"Okay. Fine. Let's just say I'm confused. Can I go look in the stacks anyway?"

"Sure. Help yourself."

Needless to say, the book wasn't back on its shelf. There wasn't even a gap where it had been. I was glad Zig-Zag had shared the experience so I didn't have to diagnose myself.

Later that day, after work, I once again tried to sort

through my thoughts. Either I was enmeshed in some sort of group delusion, a very elaborate hoax was in progress, or the world was not what I'd always assumed it to be. The notion that I was experiencing psychosis was the easiest to dismiss. I was trained, after all, to differentiate this condition from other possibilities, and trying to cram all my experiences into that box just wasn't feasible. The hoax theory was still viable, but the incident in the bookstore spoke of the enormous resources needed to generate my experiences thus far. Either someone had access to a $44,000 book or the means to create a convincing simulacrum. Further, they would need to gain access to a locked store, train a dog to perform a complex series of tasks, and hire all sorts of talented actors to play various roles the last few weeks. As events continued to unfold, the scope of the potential hoax became harder to accommodate. But was the third alternative any easier to swallow?

Zig-Zag had outlined some of the possible scenarios in this realm. Her dead father could be the mastermind? Give me a break. Some other person with mystical powers was doing it? Who? And why? We had no clues, unless George was more than he seemed to be. This idea intrigued me. A hitherto buried alter could be psychic or whatever he needed to be to generate everything. There didn't seem to be any limit to how many or what types of alters an MPD could have. That wasn't mentioned in any of the literature, at any rate.

I found myself grasping onto this idea with vise-like intensity. Sure, I told myself, it makes the most sense. I'd need to discard the smallest bundle of hard-learned life experiences to accept this extraordinary-alter concept, and all the responsibility for events would be limited to the current cast of characters. In science, they say that the simplest solution is both the most elegant and the most likely. Why not accept this quasi-supernatural, non-paranoid solution?

My entire body relaxed when I figured this out. As a working hypothesis, it enabled me to move on and take care of business, and God knows my clients needed my full attention.

****

A few days later, my new four o'clock client, D.L. Farr, turned out to be Dizzy, or more properly, as I discovered later, Desdemona Lucille Farr.

"D.L.?" I asked as she sashayed into my office in green yoga shorts and a tight black T-shirt. Her legs demanded my attention. Their muscularity confirmed my dancer theory. She smelled great, but I couldn't differentiate the exact scent. Maybe it was just her.

"I didn't know if you worked with acquaintances," she explained as she slid into the client's chair.

"I don't."

She didn't seem disappointed, but unlike most people I knew, I was no whiz at reading her. With her brown eyes and wide mouth held perfectly still, I imagined she was concocting arguments to further her agenda. When her features relaxed and her tongue wet her lips prior to speaking, I guessed that she'd successfully mustered something she believed would be convincing.

"Oh. Well, in this case it's a matter of life and death, so you'll probably want to waive your usual policy."

"Really? Life and death?" I wasn't impressed. That was a facile phrase to throw around.

"Well, I'm not sure. Either it really is or I'm

paranoid, and I'd rather be paranoid, so I'm here so you can tell me I'm paranoid, which would mean that nobody's trying to kill me."

I leaned back in my chair. "Tell me about it." I was hooked.

"Some guy is stalking me, only I'm the only one who seems to notice, and that counts the police who say there's no one, it's all in my head. God, I hope they're right. And then yesterday as I was walking home from work—I'm a limousine driver—I got this totally creepy feeling, so I started running, and I think the serial murderer was chasing me, but since I made it home and he didn't kill me, I've got no proof, and the police said I should 'seek counseling,' so here I am. I'm really scared, Tom. Suppose I'm right. Suppose he's after me. Maybe the victims of the serial killer weren't random. Maybe he picked them all out ahead of time, and I'm next."

She huddled on the chair, her knees pulled up to her chin. Even in her misery, I was arrested by the holistic grace of her body and visage. It all fit together and formed a striking tableau.

"Have you ever had these feelings before?" I asked.

"Yes. And nothing happened."

"So you think it's nothing this time?"

"No. I think somebody's trying to kill me, but I hope it's nothing."

"Let's get clear about why you're here," I suggested. "You want me to decide if this threat is real or not. Is that it?"

"Yes."

"How do you imagine I can do that?"

"I don't know. Can't you recognize paranoia when you see it? Didn't they teach you that at school?" Her tone was sharp but not offensive.

"I must've been sick that day. And I'm afraid I don't have any business seeing someone I've been arrested with. It's not ethical to have a dual relationship, and there are good reasons for that."

"So what are you saying? You can't help me?" Her smooth voice went up in pitch at the end of both questions more than called for. It was a novel form of emphasis.

I thought about it for a while, and she let me. In hindsight, my decision-making was skewed by my attraction to Dizzy, much as my tower climbing had been. So I made a leap to an even more inappropriate behavior than she was asking. "I'm not going to take your money, and I'm not going to be your therapist," I told her, "but I'm still a human being, and as such I can do whatever the hell I want outside the office, can't I? As a human being, I care about what happens to you, and I'll help in any way I can. Do you know what I did for a living before this?"

"No, but let me guess. Pro football?"

I shook my head.

"Fireman?"

"No, but that's a good guess. It would explain the burn scars."

"I give up. Just don't tell me you were a serial murderer, okay?"

"I was a private investigator."

"You're kidding."

"Nope. And I still have a gun and a permit to carry it."

"So what are you saying? You're gonna shoot everybody suspicious-looking?" Ironically, she was looking quite suspicious herself. Her eyes flitted to the side, and she shifted restlessly. In a crime TV show, she'd have just revealed to a savvy interrogator that she was the perp.

"Dizzy, you're looking at your new bodyguard."

"Really?" Her eyes widened, and she raised slender, dark eyebrows.

"If you want me." I held her gaze, feeling vulnerable. For some reason, I was already emotionally invested in my plan.

"You'll be wasting your time if this is all in my head," she warned.

"No, I won't." I smiled winningly.

She smiled back. "There's that flirty guy I used to climb towers with."

"It's a big gun too," I told her.

"Oh boy."

"The murderer's only got a knife."

"Yippee."

"Of course I'll have to accompany you all the time."

"Of course."

"Into the ladies room, on dates…."

"In your dreams, shrink."

"Well, I do have other obligations too, like all these pesky therapy clients."

"Who pay you, right?"

"You'll be a hobby, Dizzy. A lovely temporary hobby. They're going to catch this guy soon. He's not that careful."

"I hope you're right. I can't live like this. If you couldn't help me, I was going to go stay with my aunt up in Oregon."

"Let's keep that in mind as plan B." I leaned back

and let out a deep breath, suddenly aware that I had been holding myself rigid. My lower back yowled at me in protest.

"Sure, but tell me more about plan A," Dizzy requested. "Are you serious about protecting me? Do you really have the time?"

"I'll make the time. I'm perfectly serious. Even if it's unlikely you're in danger—and I'm not saying it is— we'll probably have fun hanging out and getting to know one another. And if you're right—if there is someone stalking you—we'll be saving your life, and maybe taking a killer out of circulation. I don't see how we lose either way."

"What if he kills us?"

"Well, that would qualify as a sub-optimal outcome, wouldn't it?"

"Sub-optimal? Damn straight!" She smiled, and her eyes widened again, this time for something other than surprise. I wasn't sure what. "You think you can prevent that?"

"Yes. Just being there is probably enough. All the victims have been alone. And I know how to use a gun, and I'm big and strong as well. Would you attack us?"

"Hell no, but I'm not crazy," she pointed out.

"I don't think this guy is either—not in the way you mean it. His actions aren't senseless or arbitrary, anyway—just hard to understand. In his way of being, what he's doing is internally consistent, even if it doesn't share the same roots in reality that ours does."

"Maybe they could catch him if somebody like you told them all this." Her face relaxed as she contemplated this possibility.

"They have forensic psychologists who are much

better at profiling than I am," I told her. "The FBI has a whole branch that works with local authorities on serial killings. But even then they need a lucky break. The usual methodology—looking at motive and so on—doesn't help much. I helped profile somebody on a case like this a long time ago before the FBI was available in the county."

"Well, anyway, I'd sure appreciate your help. Thanks. I feel like I ought to pay you for today, too. You could've had a real client instead of me."

"Don't worry about it. You could've had a real therapist too, right? So we're even."

We worked out a schedule when Dizzy needed bodyguarding and when I was available, and the two overlapped well for the most part. When we'd finished arranging to meet at her apartment later that day, Dizzy blessed me with a wonderful hug before leaving. I had that hot-chocolate-in-the-tummy feeling again, and I liked it a lot.

****

After finishing my workday, I stopped off at my place to pick up my pistol, holster, and the voluminous cardigan sweater I customarily wore when I was carrying. As usual, close examination suggested that a large gun-shaped tumor was sprouting beneath my armpit. But I wasn't someone who invited detailed scrutiny—my stature and scarred face tended to dominate the viewer's attention.

Dizzy lived in a neighborhood called Beach Hill, which lay between downtown and the Boardwalk. At one time, it had been the high ground the wealthy had staked out, and it was easy to understand why. A sea breeze, a spectacular 360-degree view of the Monterey Bay and the Santa Cruz mountains, and a feeling of isolation from the troubled world that lay at its feet all made Beach Hill desirable still.

Now the area consisted of elderly Edwardian and Victorian homes mostly broken up into apartments, and relatively upscale condominium complexes. Dizzy's apartment was on the ground floor of a purple fairy-tale monstrosity on a side street that was usually clogged by tourists in tourist season. Santa Cruz's maze of streets confused visitors in patterned ways, disgorging them onto certain streets while leaving others pristine for local use.

Dizzy's doorbell announced me with a loud insect-like buzz that was one of the more obnoxious sounds I'd heard lately.

"Just a minute," she called. "I haven't got the hang of these new locks yet." A series of clicks and metallic scrapes ensued.

After finally swinging the door open. Dizzy retreated to the middle of the room. There was an overwhelming smell of oil paint and the large studio apartment was very brightly lit. Every square inch of the walls was covered by canvases and every canvas was a portrait of one subject—a Black female angel.

"Do you like her?" she asked.

I was too stunned to answer at first. I'd thought I was inured to synchronicities by now, but I guess I'd developed unconscious expectations in some arenas and not in others. For whatever reason, I was shocked to discover that Dizzy was looped into the angel phenomena.

"It's from a vision," she told me. "The only one I've ever had."

"She's magnificent," I responded, moving forward to stare at the largest of the paintings.

The angel was a creature of great age, with lines of knowing and wisdom etched onto her jet-black face. Her body, though, retained a litheness, a supple grace that was explicit in Dizzy's depiction. As a painter, her technique was, for the most part, equal to the task of realistic portrayal. Even the black feathery wings invited the viewer to reach out and palpably feel what Dizzy had seen. The Black angel was naked but completely asexual. The background was a Greek temple, and the grain of the white marble was clearly delineated, as well as a bit of graffiti that resembled the outline of a dolphin. Each canvas was slightly different, yet each contained all these essential details.

"Why so many?" I finally asked.

"I'm trying to get it right. I'm close, but I haven't gotten it yet."

"How many are there?"

"I don't know. Twenty or thirty so far."

With a wave, Dizzy invited me farther into the sparsely decorated room, and I ambled in and sat at her simple wooden dining table, continuing to study the paintings. Belatedly, I realized that modern jazz was softly playing from a compact stereo on her tidy, beige kitchen counter. It wasn't like me to miss something like that, especially since I hated that genre.

"What does it mean?" I asked.

"I told you. I'm trying to get it right." Her irritation was right at the surface, easy for me to trigger.

"No, I mean the vision itself."

"Oh. I don't know. Zee says it doesn't mean anything, but that's like saying disregard the biggest thing that's ever happened to you, and I'm not about to do that."

"Did the angel say anything?"

Dizzy was still standing just inside the doorway, but now she strode to the other side of the table and lowered herself into the only other chair. "No. But I knew what she was thinking. She was thinking that the world was sad and also beautiful—like they were the same thing— and then I knew that she totally loved me, more than I've ever felt from anyone. It was wonderful. I started sobbing, and it didn't stop for hours. I think every ounce of fluid and mucus came out."

"Yuck."

"You're missing the point." She pointed at me as she uttered the word "point."

"I know, but it's easier to respond to the mucus part."

"Yeah, I get it. I haven't told too many people."

I considered whether or not to share my angel experiences. It would be nice to reciprocate and repay her trust, but on the other hand, my information might be unsettling or even traumatic. The fact that she'd created so many paintings based on her vision indicated her propensity to overreact.

"I appreciate your telling me," I decided to reply. "I feel honored."

"Well, hell, if I'm going to trust you with my life…"

"Good point. Want to see my gun?"

"No."

"Want to see anything else?"

She smiled. "Not right now. It's time to get going to my women's group."

"Is that what I'm taking you to?" I'm sure my

surprise was evident.

"Yup. And I thought it would be fun if you came in and guarded me there."

"You're kidding, right?"

She shook her head.

"Isn't it run on a confidential basis?"

"Nope. It's not a therapy group, and there's no leader. Mostly we moan and bitch about men."

"Gee, that sounds like oodles of fun."

"Great. Let's go."

"Don't you recognize sarcasm when you hear it?"

"No," she answered, grabbing my hand from across the table and pulling me toward the door.

Chapter 11

So I attended my first women's group. There were nine of us—well, eight of them and one of me. We sat in a circle in a cramped living room, whose only remarkable feature was a giant abstract painting on the wall facing me. Vertical streaks of red, orange, and purple were superimposed onto a black background. Whatever the painter's intent, I found it disorienting.

I'd buttoned my cardigan to thoroughly hide my gun. In Santa Cruz, let alone in a women's group, the very sight of one induced panic. Dizzy sat next to me and introduced me as her bodyguard.

"Are you really her bodyguard?" an older woman with a New York City accent asked. You could've used her frizzy hair to scrub a sink.

I nodded. It didn't seem right to inject a male voice into the proceedings.

"I'm not comfortable with him here," a Latina woman complained. Her accent was strong, and I had to struggle to understand her. I studied her face, which clearly displayed indigenous roots—high, sharp cheekbones, slightly canted eyes, and straight black hair. Perhaps her initial tongue hadn't been Spanish.

"Why not?" Dizzy responded.

"He scares me. I can't open up with him here. It's not safe."

"It's not safe for me if he leaves. I think somebody's

trying to kill me," Dizzy told her.

"Oh my God!" another woman exclaimed. Upon closer examination, she turned out to be the sister of a former client. According to my client, this woman, whom I had observed once through my office window, was constantly campaigning to convince their mother to cut my client out of her will. I wished Santa Cruz was bigger as I surveyed the other group members.

There was no obvious common denominator in the assortment of women. The rest ranged from early twenties to at least seventy, from Black to lily white, from expensively dressed to sporting slapdash, stained outfits. It was as if someone had done their best to assemble a completely disparate group, plucking members from what would seem to be mutually exclusive subcultures.

"Does he talk?" a skinny woman asked in an abrasive smoker's voice.

"Sometimes," Dizzy answered for me. She'd been slightly smiling throughout the conversation, and now it broadened.

"How are we supposed to talk trash about men with that brute in here?" she complained.

"He is an intimidating fellow," an elderly matron agreed.

I smiled disarmingly.

"That's the idea," Dizzy told them. "Bodyguards are supposed to be scary."

"That's true, and he does have a disarming smile," the matron admitted.

I smiled more.

"It makes me want to smack him," the frizzy-haired ex-New Yorker shared.

"I wouldn't advise it," Dizzy warned. "He's trained in eleven different martial arts, including how to maim and kill with just one finger."

Although this was news to me, I brandished my right index finger and wiggled it menacingly while I scowled at my foe.

"I didn't mean I'd really do it," the woman explained hastily. "I was talking about my feelings."

"Smacking isn't a feeling, Ruth," a tall woman in a blue business suit commented.

"I didn't say it was. I said I felt like smacking him— that was the feeling. You never listen to me, Brenda. We've been over this before."

"You don't speak clearly. That's the problem."

"Fuck you, too."

There was an awkward pause while everyone decided to ignore them.

I decided to smile again.

"He thrives on our conflict," the conniving sister proclaimed, pointing at me with a stubby index finger of her own, one that looked much more capable of mayhem than mine.

"Maybe he's just friendly," someone said.

"I think he's retarded or something," someone else added.

I exchanged a glance and a smile with Dizzy. We were both having fun with this.

"Anyway," Dizzy interjected, "I know we're all anxious about the serial killer, but I am truly terrified. I've seen him stalking me."

"Jesus!"

"Holy shit!"

"No wonder you're spooked!"

Dizzy glared at this last speaker.

"No offense," the woman added. "I meant it in the sense of ghosts. You know I'm not a racist, Dizzy."

Dizzy nodded her acknowledgment.

"Have you been to the police?" someone asked.

"Yes, and I couldn't believe it. It was just like in the media where they treat traumatized women like they're hysterical over some fantasy. I mean they never even asked for a description of the guy, not that I got a good look at him. There was just this sense they weren't going to take me seriously, no matter what I did. That was the worst."

"Haven't you done this before—gone to the police?" New York asked.

"So?"

"So it's like the boy who cried wolf."

"Say what?"

"You don't know that story?"

"No."

"Really?"

"I'm Black. That's probably some White story. Why don't you tell me so I won't be culturally deprived anymore." She shot the woman a withering glare and sighed heavily.

"Okay."

So we heard a long, boring rendition of the tale, replete with detailed descriptions of everyone's clothes and even the weather.

"Fuck that," was Dizzy's response.

"I support you," someone else told her.

"Me too."

"You poor thing."

Eventually the group moved on to other topics,

including domestic violence, menopause, and rude Uber drivers. Procedurally, the women continued to engage in a free-for-all, occasionally confronting each other scatologically. Everyone forgot about me, it seemed, until the end of the two-hour session, when the older matron reported that she'd gotten more out of the group with a male witness present. Several others agreed, although they didn't understand the phenomenon. The group decided to discuss the possibility of a permanent male witness at their next meeting.

It wasn't going to be me. Observation of the group made it clear that these weren't people I was eager to consort with. As usual, my projections onto an attractive woman had proved to be incongruent with her actual personality, too. As the hour progressed, in this case, Dizzy had demonstrated that she was younger and more superficial, strident, and impatient than I had assumed. I'd convinced myself of something I'd wanted to believe, and now the discrepancy between this desire-driven pseudo-reality and the way things actually were was making me feel like an idiot—an old, ugly idiot who should know better.

I was quiet in the car as Dizzy drove us back to her apartment. I fumbled with one hand to unbutton my sweater in an effort to look less like a mutant Mr. Rogers. I guess I still cared how I looked in Dizzy's eyes.

"It's a zoo of a group, isn't it?" she offered.

"It certainly is," I answered dully.

"Are you bummed? What's going on?"

Just then, someone honked at us, and my startle reflex kicked in, feeding me energy.

"It was hard being there after a while," I told her. "I realized some things about myself that I don't like."

118

"Like what?"

"Oh, it's nothing new. How I con myself and play games with reality."

"Well, hell, we all do that, right?" She made a left-hand turn, her blinker clacking frantically. One of her bulbs was out.

"I suppose so."

"Sure. I had this whole fantasy about you, for instance. I mean I hardly know you, but I convinced myself that you're really wise and powerful, not to mention funny and sexy. And maybe you are—I don't know yet. So I came to you for help when I normally would never get near a male therapist. Is this the kind of thing you mean?"

"Actually, that's exactly what I mean. I wasn't able to hang onto my fantasies about you tonight. You're you and there's nothing wrong with that, but compared to my projections…Well, it's a process of disillusionment, and ultimately I'm most disillusioned with myself for not having graduated out of this crap yet."

"I know what you mean, but maybe we should celebrate moving further into reality. That's what happened. You got more authentic, right? That's a good thing."

"It's the contrast. When I suddenly see how things really are, I feel like a moron for how I've been up until then."

"I understand, but isn't that a common deal? Everybody does it. You may be a therapist, but you're still an everybody, too."

"You know, you're right."

"Sure. Lighten up."

"Of course your saying all this is fodder for a new

fantasy."

"Naturally. I don't mind. Mine's changed too. I love that vulnerable thing of yours, but it kind of ruins the all-knowing thing. You know?"

"Yes. It's hard to hang onto something like that even when in this case, of course, I'm actually God-like in so many ways."

"Yeah, right."

"Don't forget about my finger of death. Show some respect, mortal."

She flashed her finger of obscenity, which I now understood had more to do with her sense of humor than her depth as a person.

There was no one lurking in Dizzy's building or immediate neighborhood, so I hugged her goodnight and drove off. Our hug was perfunctory, which surprised me. Why were neither of us putting energy into it?

As I pulled up to the stop sign on the corner, a glint of something caught my eye off to the right. I shifted to reverse and backed up to investigate. Just then, another car turned down the street in the opposite direction, its headlights sweeping across the front lawn near me.

A figure trying to hide behind a slim tree took off running, a large knife in his or her hand. I slammed my brakes and jumped out of the car. As the figure darted down a dark driveway, I lumbered in pursuit, hauling my gun from its holster. Whoever it was certainly wasn't an athlete, but my worn-out knees were already killing me after a few steps. I concentrated on my footing as the hard asphalt yielded to a recently watered backyard, but before I'd gained any ground, I encountered a sprinkler head, wrenched my left knee, and went down hard. For just a second, I considered firing my gun as a warning shot, realized that would be inappropriate, and then watched helplessly as the figure blended into the darkness of the garden next door.

I could barely limp back to my car. I'd be serving time in my Rube Goldberg knee brace for quite a while. When I called the police and got hold of a sergeant I knew reasonably well, he dispatched cars to scour the area. My credibility, unlike Dizzy's, was still intact. Within minutes, two detectives joined me back at Black Angelville and took copious notes as I sat at the table again and detailed my experience.

Across from me, Dizzy couldn't stop shaking, although her version of this was almost too exaggerated to be believable. Perhaps she was working hard to get the police to take the incident seriously. Periodically, she moaned softly, which also seemed inauthentic. Of course, as a therapist, I knew that everyone responded idiosyncratically to stress.

Both detectives looked to be in their mid-fifties and shared several attributes that seemed unusual for cops. For one thing, they sported close-cropped blond beards. Also, their voices were high-pitched, and they wore thick-lensed glasses. They weren't brothers—they had different last names—but these likenesses initially overrode the obvious variations in their features and size. When I studied the taller of the two, for example, it was clear that his nose was twice the size of the smaller man's. And his skin was much rougher—he was even pocked on his forehead from bouts of acne. At any rate, they were polite and methodical, which was what I'd come to expect from Santa Cruz cops. When I surrendered my gun for their examination, the shorter one smelled the muzzle and handed it back without a word.

They questioned Dizzy extensively as well, since she represented a live victim who could help determine what, if anything, the targets had in common. Strangely, neither guy asked her about the canvasses surrounding us. It wasn't until I was hobbling to my car with them that the shorter detective asked me if she was crazy.

"Why do you say that?"

"The paintings seem to be evidence of an obsession, wouldn't you say? And one of the people killed was a therapist—like you. Maybe that's the connection."

"She's not crazy, or maybe I should say no more than anyone else around here. And I doubt if you're going to get anywhere with the therapy angle. But let me know. What else are you going to do?"

"We're assigning a car to watch her," the other policeman told me.

A third cop I hadn't noticed called to us. He was over by the tree down the block.

"I've found something," he shouted.

"Don't touch it!" the detective yelled. "We'll be right there."

I started to walk with them, but the tall one reached across my chest to restrict me. "We'll handle it from here. Thanks for your cooperation."

"Sure." I asked him to give me a call the next day to let me know the status of the case.

"Yeah, yeah," he intoned in his high-pitched voice as he hurried away.

****

In the morning, when, to my surprise, the detective called, I discovered the suspect had left a mostly intact footprint of an extra-wide size-ten running shoe. The extra-wide part was a promising clue, the detective told me.

"Probably he ordered them through the mail or bought them at a specialty shop," he added.

"That makes sense," I replied.

"Also, he eats bagels."

"Maybe that's how his feet got so wide."

"I beg your pardon?"

"Never mind. Did you find crumbs on the ground?" I asked.

"Better. A half-eaten cinnamon-raisin bagel with at least three toothmarks."

"That's great. You've finally got something to work with."

"Exactly. And please keep all this under your hat, okay?"

"Of course. That's what I do—I'm a therapist."

"Well, Sergeant Mamer says you used to be a private investigator, and I can trust you. In fact, he said you might even have some ideas that could help us."

"Not right now, but I'll stay in touch."

"Fine. Take care."

"Bye."

Next, I called Dizzy.

"You're my hero," she told me.

"Aw shucks, ma'am."

"Now don't be modest. You saved my life. How's your knee?"

"It's been better." That morning, it was about a seven on the pain scale—four or five numbers higher than my baseline. It wasn't bad enough to limit my movements, but whatever I did would hurt.

"You poor thing," Dizzy said and then clucked.

I'd never heard a cluck outside of a film or a TV show. It was an odd sound for a human to make.

She continued. "I feel I owe you big-time, and I want to pay you back."

"Do you usually pay off with perverse sexual favors?"

"You wish. I had dinner in mind. At the restaurant of your choice?"

"That sounds good, too. Esposito's?"

"Tomorrow night? Around seven? I'll meet you there?"

"Sure. Do you need to talk about last night?"

"At dinner, you mean?"

"No, now."

"Oh. I guess so. I still feel pretty shook-up. The main thing is the whole 'you could be dead any second no matter how much you forget or pretend the world's some other way' thing. That's what gets me. It's like the universe showed me this big black hole that might suddenly appear under my next step when I thought I could count on solid ground."

"That's a normal reaction."

"So?"

"I mean it's an appropriate response."

"What are you—God? I don't care if you think it's normal or not. Is this what you do with your clients? Judge their responses and announce how close to normal they are? Jesus."

Every time I began to feel comfortable with Dizzy, she did or said something that confused me as to who she was. This latest example was typical. I had no idea how to reply to her.

"So what do you have to say for yourself?" she

finally asked.

"I'm sorry, I guess."

"You guess?"

"Yes. I guess. I'm not sure."

"Well, in that case I guess I accept your apology. Anyway, I don't think we should talk about this anymore. We're obviously on different wavelengths, and things are tough enough right now."

"You're right. I'll see you tomorrow."

"What about between now and then? Aren't you going to keep protecting me?"

"The police assigned someone to you. Didn't they tell you?"

"Yeah, they did. But I'll bet he's not as big and scary as you."

"And I'll bet he runs faster, has better access to reinforcements, doesn't have to see clients, and has more training in surveillance and disarming people."

"Sometimes you're annoyingly logical, Tom."

"It's my job. I'm a guy."

"You certainly are. Take care."

She hung up, and I was left alone with my unappreciated masculinity.

Chapter 12

There is always a threshold beyond which a psyche can't hold challenging experiences without disrupting the integrity of the container itself—me. I was dangerously close to discovering where my threshold was, I realized. The encounter with the killer represented one more bizarre hot potato I was constrained to juggle instead of filing away neatly. It wasn't one too many, but what if the next one was?

I needed help, but I was dubious that my own therapist could sort through the mess I was toting around in my head. Roberta was a gifted practitioner, but I required a specialist—an expert in the occult. Someone with an explicitly spiritual background who could provide a reality check for me.

I knew a colleague of mine was a follower of Matthew Ferguson, who billed himself as "the guru with a regular name." This local, middle-aged man was reputed to be more playful, accessible, and sensible than most folks in his business. In fact, my colleague saw him weekly to sort out the "weirdness" in his life. This wasn't a term I usually identified with, but I was desperate and I knew my acquaintance could set up a meeting on short notice. In fact, I saw Ferguson the same day I made contact with him.

Ferguson had written several books, including *Dying into Sanity*, which had sold well. I hadn't read it, but I knew it was a quasi-psychological exploration of nondenominational spirituality—basically, the kind of book Santa Cruzans read instead of seeing therapists. When it didn't save them and their desperation mounted, then they came in, and together we unlearned whatever they'd read.

Surprisingly, Ferguson preferred to meet in my office and wouldn't accept a fee for his time. It hadn't been necessary to reveal the nature of my concerns to arrange things, so I had no hint of the man's attitude toward angels.

He was about six feet tall and big-boned. His initial demeanor was friendly and open. Based on looks, I would never have picked him out of a guru line-up or chosen to bare my soul to him. Other than rather alert light blue eyes, there was an ordinariness to Ferguson's features. His nose and mouth were pleasant enough, yet not particularly evocative of strength or wisdom. The patterns of wrinkles on his face implied some squinting into the sun, some frowning, some smiling—nothing unusual. I was disappointed. I hadn't realized it ahead of time, but I wanted him to look impressive, even majestic. Anything less represented a sub-par set of credentials.

Once we'd exchanged greetings—he possessed a low, mellifluous voice—I sat him in my chair and became a client.

"What can I do for you?" he asked.

"I'm confused. I don't want to be."

"Sometimes confusion is worthwhile."

"Maybe. But just listen first. Some very strange things have been happening."

Without referring to anyone by name or hinting that clients were involved, I related my bizarre story to my consultant, who listened carefully, his eyes fixed on mine. I tried to emphasize what had happened outside my office—the supposed corroboration of Arundel's news. These were the parts that disturbed me the most and were also the least confidential.

"Well," he began. "That's fascinating, and the first thing I'd say is that you need to be open to all the possibilities. That's the value of true confusion. It opens you up. If you really don't know something, there's room for whatever it is to show you its meaning. You aren't restrained from the truth by your usual filters of logic or experience."

"I'm not sure what you mean in terms of my situation."

"There is a continuum of possibilities implied in your narrative. At one end, it's all craziness—none of it's real. At the other end, it's completely true—you are an angel. Then there's everything in between. I'm saying that your best bet is to begin by opening up to the entire continuum." Ferguson's relaxed pose in my chair made me wonder if I looked tense when I worked.

"Tell me why again?" I felt like an idiot. For some reason, I couldn't understand Ferguson's perspective at all. I felt myself narrow my eyes, and I frowned.

"The best version of confusion entails perceiving all the possibilities as possible," he replied.

"So I might be an angel?"

"Of course. I might be a spider."

"I doubt it."

"Of course you do." His responses seemed effortless—without forethought.

"What do you mean? Because I'm sane or because I'm close-minded?"

"They're the same. Take your pick."

"I like sane better."

He nodded agreeably. "How do you like my help so far? Pretty nifty stuff, huh?"

I stared at him, unsure how to respond. Finally, I asked if he understood our process in the room—a typical therapist's perspective.

"Certainly."

"Tell me."

"You are resistant to some of the alternatives inherent in your situation. As I suggest you stay open to them, you either don't understand or express doubts. This is only natural. I'm accustomed to this type of interaction."

"What do you mean by natural?"

"If you become an angel, or even substantially different in some other way, Thomas Dashiel dies. To the ego, enlightenment represents the ultimate threat."

"Who said anything about enlightenment?" I asked.

"Gee, I think it was me, but I might be wrong."

He grinned, and I realized that was his visible credential. I felt warmed by the depth of positive emotion his mouth conveyed.

"Look, let's back up a little," I suggested. "Why is it best to consider all the possibilities?"

"I'm not telling."

"What?" I couldn't believe I'd heard him properly.

"I'm not telling."

"You sound like a fifteen-year-old."

"Thank you."

I paused and leaned forward. "Will you tell me why you won't tell me?"

"Sure. It doesn't matter, and I don't feel like it.

There's nothing fun about trying to convince people about things. I prefer to offer my point of view. If it resonates, great. If it doesn't, well that's fine, too."

"Okay, that's your prerogative. But what about all these synchronicities?"

"Yes. What about them?"

"Did they really happen?"

"You said you're sane, so I presume they did."

"Do they mean anything?" I asked.

"Of course."

"What?"

"Beats me."

"Thanks a lot. Could they be an affirmation of something?"

"Yup."

"Disproof of something else?"

"Yup."

"An indication of what color underwear people in Mali will buy next year?"

"Now you're getting the hang of this. It certainly could," he agreed.

"Terrific."

Ferguson smiled. "All your questions seem to lead to more questions instead of answers, don't they?"

"I guess so."

"Perhaps this is an indication our meeting today is not going to prove fruitful."

"Why do you say that?"

"If you ask a question but aren't moved by my answer, why bother asking?"

"Because I'm very uncomfortable not knowing," I told him, my frustration leaking out in my tone.

"Listen to me closely. This is the crux of the matter.

You are even more uncomfortable knowing what there is to know. That's clear."

"Are you saying the truth is some monstrous thing?" Alarmed, my chest tightened.

"I think my comment was focused more on you than on any particular truth."

"So I'm incapable of dealing with reality? Is that what you're saying?"

"More questions. They're piling up and burying us."

"Do you know George Arundel?" I asked.

"No. Why do you ask?"

"Never mind." I gathered myself again. "This is very frustrating. There doesn't seem to be anything I can do to settle things."

"Oh, but there is. Live your life. The future will show up, and you'll find out what it is."

"Isn't that rather a simplistic notion?"

"Sure. Got a problem with that?"

"I guess I do. I guess I have a problem with all of this."

Ferguson suddenly began singing in a mellow baritone voice.

Like a moth to a flame, I'm drawn by your will.

Consumed by your fire, but my love can't be killed.

Like a moth to a flame, I know that it's right

that I should transform on this fiery night.

I was deeply moved, much to my surprise. My frustration disappeared, and tears filled my eyes. Then there was heat in my chest as though someone had rubbed Bengay directly on my heart. I hunched over, bringing the heat to my lap. I didn't understand what was happening. I began sobbing as Ferguson continued to sing. The experience was so intense I have no idea how long it continued. My mind was completely shut off, and my experience was rooted in my flaming heart.

When I recovered, or at least became coherent again, Ferguson was gone. Had this been some sort of help? What had he done? Was I still me?

Chapter 13

There didn't seem to be any ill-effects from my music appreciation experience, other than the contrast it provided with everything else. Whatever had happened had been so intense and so sublime that now life in general felt pallid—a charcoal sketch by a fifth-grader. I assumed this impression would fade and my world would return to its usual ninth-grade watercolor status, if not something better. In the meantime, I did my best to ignore the phenomenon.

I was still, of course, accumulating even more concerns than I was capable of ignoring. From a mental health perspective, I knew that stuffing emotions didn't defuse their energy; it just postponed their release. In fact, when the feelings made themselves known down the line, they would probably explode out of their compressed state with far more power than they'd started off with. Nonetheless, I kept signing up for this disastrous process; I guess the alternatives were even less appetizing.

Gradually over the next few days, I noticed something that was at least as positive as the stuffing was negative. The easiest way to describe it is to say that my heart had been jumpstarted, and now I was (temporarily?) aware of it as an active participant in my day-to-day life. I don't mean heart in the sense of rescuing kittens or crying at movies portraying terminal illnesses. Lower case heart was distinct from upper case Heart in a way that I now felt viscerally. The latter wasn't part of the emotional realm. It wasn't connected to events or thoughts, either. An unconditional quality of the love I felt transcended what I'd known before, and my ability to describe it accurately. In short, I knew it mostly by what it was not. Perhaps, to say that some force had stripped away the layers of crud that had stood between me and my essential self—my heart—would be less misleading, although my heart also participated in its own emancipation. Anyway, something was different and I liked it.

****

Dinner at Esposito's ("where you never want to say basta to the pasta") was always a treat. For one thing, the furnishings and decor reminded me of where fat-cat Mafiosi hang out in old films. The booths were constructed of dark wood and black leather buttoned upholstery, sitting on a black-and-white checkerboard tile floor. If the place was classier, I'd have called it a chessboard floor, but it was hard to picture anyone playing anything more complex than checkers in Esposito's.

I felt like I was in New Jersey when I walked in to meet Dizzy. My grandmother had lived in New Brunswick, and memories of summers there still nourished me. I smelled tomato sauce, bread, and pepper. The music in the restaurant was evocative, too. A well-recorded smooth crooner sang a fifties-style song in Italian.

I spied Dizzy in a corner, a tall drink sitting on the white tablecloth in front of her. Her cobalt-blue Chinese-style tunic top almost matched the drink. She may have

134

applied subtle makeup. I was terrible at determining that. At any rate, her brown eyes looked bigger than I remembered, and her lips redder.

Dizzy could sense I'd undergone some sort of transformation. She shared her impressions as soon as I sat down across from her.

"You're warmer and lighter," she told me, nodding. "And your eyes are different—softer."

"Softer?" I was quite curious how an outside party might experience post-song Tom.

"Yup. It's nice. What happened?"

"I had an intense experience where I was in my heart so thoroughly I didn't know which end was up. My mind was shut off, and all I knew was love."

"How wonderful! What's her name?"

"Huh?"

"Weren't you with someone?"

"It was a man."

"You're gay?"

"No. What are you talking about?"

"When that's happened to me, it's always been with a partner. After sex, actually. I just assumed…."

"He was a guru—he sang a song."

"Really? Wow. So you're spiritual, huh? I had no idea." She leaned forward on her elbows, markedly shortening the distance between us. I liked it.

"I wouldn't describe myself as spiritual, per se. It's hard to explain." I felt hesitant to share based on Dizzy's history of unpredictable responses.

"Try."

"I'm mixed up in something I don't understand." Hearing myself hedging, I decided to go for it. "In fact, it has to do with angels."

"I knew it!" She actually hopped up a bit. And snorted. "I knew there was something more than just chemistry between us. What did your angel look like?"

"Ugly. Really ugly." I was thinking of myself, of course.

"How strange."

"Listen, have you ever thought particular people might be angels?" I asked.

"No. Have you?"

"Lately, yeah. I don't want to, but some experiences seem to be pointing that way."

"Like what?"

I told her about the dog and the book, leaving out Zig-Zag, who, after all, knew Dizzy better than I did. She would've already mentioned it if she'd wanted her to know. I was surprised how easily the story unfolded.

"So what do you make of it?" she asked when I'd finished.

A very short young man approached and proffered menus. "I'm Jason. The special tonight is calamari with ginger sauce and salmon parmigiana."

"Really?" I said. "What happened to traditional pasta, risotto, gnocchi—all my favorites?"

"Don't worry. We still have our old menu. The boss decided to jazz up the specials to attract a younger crowd." He shrugged in an effort to distance himself from the decision.

I looked around the half-filled room. Everyone besides Dizzy was over forty. "I get it." I turned to my companion. "Do you know what you want? I do."

"No, I need to look at the menu."

"Sure."

"I'll be back," Jason told us, meandering to a nearby

table full of loud golfers arguing over some obscure rule.

"So I was asking you," Dizzy said, "before the bizarre specials scared us both, what you think about what you were telling me. I still want to know."

"There's more to this life thing than meets the eye?"

"Can you be more vague, please?" She smiled.

"I don't think so."

"Me neither. Do you think the thing with the dog and the book really happened?"

"Oh, yes. That's not the issue. What I wonder is how I need to shift my reality paradigm to accommodate experiences like these."

Dizzy frowned and shook her head vigorously. "Reality paradigm? Accommodate experiences? Who the hell talks like that? If you can't say it simply, it's crap. That's what my grandmother told me, and she's right."

"Your grandmother uses the word crap?"

"Not anymore. She's dead."

"Sorry."

"For who? She's fine. There's nothing wrong with being dead."

"Fine. I'm beginning to wish we weren't having this conversation. Why do you have to give me such a hard time?"

"You're a man. You're full of shit, and you don't even know it. No more than other men, I'll grant you that, but it's enough."

"So what are doing here with me? You're the one who sought me out in my office, weren't you? You're the one at this restaurant with me. I didn't twist your arm."

"Like you could care less, huh? Who are you

kidding? Some men undress women with their eyes, but every time you look at me, you practically knock me up with fucking triplets."

"You seemed to enjoy our flirting," I protested, my gut tightening.

Dizzy continued as though I hadn't spoken. If anything, her fierce frown was more intense now. "Anyway, I tried to be a lesbian. It didn't work out for me. So you're my first foray back into the straight world. It's hard for me. This is a hard time right now. I mean I'm being stalked, I got arrested again, and it's back to goddamned cock. Sorry I'm not currently meeting your standards," she finished sarcastically.

I held my hands up in surrender. "Whoa. Calm down. I'm not attacking you. I just wanted to know why it feels like *I'm* under attack. Now I know. Fair enough."

"Circling the wagons, huh? It's too late."

"I feel like I've got a target on my chest. Why should I get dumped on because of your generalized anger and frustration at men?" My own anger was gradually revving up. I let out a sigh that partially defused it.

"Because you're a man. You're not exempt. You're not some special exception. You're part of the problem." Her glare hurt.

"I don't recycle plastic either, and I ran over a snake once," I told her, alluding to her environmental interests. I'd had enough. "Between being male and imperfect, I guess I'm disqualified from deserving considerate treatment from people with problems. I guess I ought to be a punching bag."

She stared at me a moment, her eyebrow shooting up in surprise at my counterattack. Then angry Dizzy returned. "Damn straight," she snarled. She loudly shoved her chair back, almost toppling it, and stalked out before we'd even ordered.

So much for opening up to beautiful women and sharing intimate anecdotes. I responded to our squabble by retreating back up into my head; I was completely out of touch with my heart again.

Then I ate lasagna and salad, most of a basket of bread, and tiramisu. I got in touch with my stomach. It was better than nothing.

****

George Arundel made an appointment through my answering service, and I wondered why. Had he become impatient with me? Had he finally recognized his need for real therapy? Did he merely miss playing his game of let's-see-how-frustrated-I-can-make-Tom?

He looked the same as he strode into my office—a middle-aged man with slightly oversized features and odd, rounded teeth—although his bald pate under his skimpy combover was pinker than I remembered. He wore a new khaki ensemble straight out of a yuppie catalog, except for shiny black plastic sandals with brown socks.

"Greetings, Tom," he began, sinking into the client's chair with an air of satisfaction as if he'd been on his feet for days.

"Hello, George. How have you been?"

"Busy. Much too busy. In fact, that's enough small talk. Tell me about your ethics around confidentiality."

"Okay. Everything in a session is completely confidential, except for certain situations which I am mandated by law to report."

"What are those?"

"If you tell me about child, dependent adult, or

senior abuse or neglect. If you are intent on harming yourself. If you speak of a credible plan to seriously harm a specific person. And then there are special cases such as court-ordered counseling, clients involved in litigation who tell the court they're in therapy, and if a client signs a release of information form."

"So is there anything I've said to you that you can talk about?" He watched me intently.

"No. I'm obliged not to. If I did, I could lose my license and even go to prison."

"Suppose I told you I was the second gunman in the Kennedy assassination?"

"I would keep that a secret."

"Really?"

"Absolutely. I take confidentiality very seriously."

"Suppose somebody offered you a million dollars to break your rules?"

"It wouldn't matter." Clearly, Arundel wanted to tell me something but wouldn't go ahead until he felt satisfied it was safe.

His eyes narrowed. "Suppose you knew I was going to kill someone?"

"I could only report it if you said who it was and I was convinced it was a serious threat. So do you have something you want to tell me?"

"Perhaps. Are you saying that you'd stick to the rules even if it might cost a life?"

"Well, I've never been in that situation, but if clients don't feel they can trust their therapists, we wouldn't be able to help much. So yes, I'd certainly try to never break the rules."

It's been my experience that the revelations that follow this sort of probing are usually anticlimactic. One man's shameful confession is another man's "is that all?"

"Trying isn't the same as doing something," Arundel pointed out.

I was tired of this, and his pronouncement irritated me further. I shook my head slowly, sending a mixed message as I agreed to his request. "All right. I promise I won't divulge anything you tell me unless the law mandates that I must. Is that satisfactory?"

"Yes. I believe you."

He still appeared hesitant, but in a moment, I realized what was actually transpiring. He was changing personalities, and he had slipped into neutral for a moment while the gearshift disengaged and then reengaged.

"Let me introduce myself," the alter began in a flat, low-pitched voice that I seemed to hear as much in my gut as my ears.

Immediately, it struck me that this time a client's hidden secret might be much more than anticlimactic. This voice was chillingly unemotional; in fact, a-emotional would be more accurate. It was the way a sentient robot would sound—an entity without a heart or a soul.

"My name is Credula. I am not human."

"No?"

"No. Can't you tell?"

Involuntarily, I nodded.

"Good. George assures me that I can be straightforward with you, that this meeting is necessary to convince you of certain things."

I nodded again. I couldn't summon speech. Credula was clearly an inhuman, no, nonhuman personality. All the factors that lent warmth, character, and even personal ego were filtered out by that awful voice. It was well beyond the way a psychopath would sound if you stripped away the artificial charm and scraped down to the bone.

I realized that in all my experiences of evil, pathology, or whatever you want to call it, I had only experienced various versions of dilute good. There was a world of difference between what I'd known before and Credula. He embodied no hint of goodness; in fact, evil and good seemed to be completely irrelevant concepts as I listened to my new client. I don't know how I knew all this, but I did.

"Thomas?"

"Uh…yes?"

"Do you remember the names of the victims who've been stabbed?"

Oh God. I couldn't make my mind translate the words into sense. There was brief relief in this self-induced brain damage, but then Credula spoke again.

"Thomas?"

"What?"

"The names of the dead."

"Heilman. I knew Denise Heilman."

"Heilman, Horn, Klovin, and DeVilliers. So far," it told me.

Oh my God. That "so far" penetrated deep into me. I was too stunned to register anything else, but I knew something intense and awful was looming.

"They're devil names, Thomas. Devil names."

"Devil names?"

"Yes. It was necessary that they die."

"Necessary?"

Suddenly, meaning flooded me. This was the serial

murderer. Raw fear spiked my adrenaline and revved up my metabolism, sending me into fight or flight mode. I would've chosen flight if this physical response hadn't been trumped by the psychological paralysis I felt in the face of this entity's voice.

Credula had been hiding inside Arundel, and now he was sitting in front of me, confessing and explaining the insanity that motivated him. And I was supposed to keep his secret? I realized I could be the next victim if I played my cards wrong.

My heart pounded harder, and my breath sped up until I gasped. My hands trembled. My focus narrowed and intensified despite these distractions. Credula's face was etched against the backdrop of my bookcase. It was both familiar and unfamiliar. And terrifying.

"How do you know it was necessary?" I asked. I was barely able to muster these words. They emerged as a croak. The rest of me continued to roil as chaotic energy surged through me.

"You're an angel. There are devils too—well, demons, technically." Credula had held himself— itself—perfectly still throughout his series of proclamations. Now he paused and then leaned toward me, triggering my startle reflex.

I involuntarily leaned back as far as I could.

He continued. "It's almost time for the ultimate battle. The more we identify and neutralize the opposition, the better chance mankind has to survive and flourish."

"I knew Denise. She was a lovely person."

"A cunning impersonation of a lovely person. I saw the demon leave the body. I know what I know."

"Why are you telling me this?"

"We need your cooperation. It has been determined that you are an archangel. Congratulations." The dead voice conveyed no emotion.

A reply popped into my head. "Does that mean I outrank you?"

He nodded solemnly. "You will. Your role is pivotal."

I tried to think. Surely anything this crazy must incorporate some degree of inconsistent logic. I wanted a debate—a chance to refute Credula. Better yet, I wanted to push a button and make him disappear.

My guts churned now, and my face heated up to the point where I thought I couldn't stand it. I began shaking all over, and I gripped the arm of my chair as tightly as I could, digging grooves into the palms of my hands.

"Why does telling me this make me more cooperative?" I asked. "That doesn't follow."

"We are changed by what we know, Thomas."

"I'm not changed—except for the additions of horror and disgust." My mind was back online, freed from my fear—for now.

"You will be."

"So you know the future?" This tactic showed clients their magical thinking; a lot of irrational thought lay behind problem attitudes.

"Yes," Credula asserted.

So much for that. "How does it work?" I tried. "Do you read tea leaves? Does God tell you?" He didn't reply. I tried something else. "Why is all this happening here in Santa Cruz? Four devils, two angels that I know of—this isn't exactly a metropolis, is it?"

"The energy here is pure and strong. This is where it starts."

Performing the role of stooge for a string of Credula's oracular pronouncements wasn't helping. As I physically calmed down, even as my mind continued to scream at me to run, I remembered I was a therapist.

"Tell me more," I said.

"No."

"What are you feeling?"

No reply. Even I knew that had been a stupid question. Obviously he—it—wasn't feeling anything, and never would.

"So you're going to kill again?"

"I wish I could. Unfortunately, I am merely banishing demons from this plane, but yes, there may be more to deal with."

"What do you really want from me? Right now, I mean."

"Nothing. Do you recall the various phenomena that followed George's announcement that you were an angel?"

"Yes."

"You will experience the new proof you seek in much the same manner."

"I'm not seeking anything."

"That isn't important. The work has been accomplished on the energetic level. It will manifest shortly on the physical."

"What do you mean 'on the energetic level'?"

"Our work here is more than words. Our energies have merged and danced, and that which was in me will now guide that which was in you."

"How did you do that?"

"You misunderstand. It is an impersonal process, different only in magnitude from what happens when any two people sit and talk."

"So in this sense, you're like a person."

"No. It is the very absence of a body and a personality that allows such intense energy to reside in me."

"What's that sitting in my chair, then? It looks like a body to me."

"It is George's. His lungs move the air, his tongue forms my words. We are a symbiosis, made possible by George's rare ability to step aside and allow others to dwell within him."

"It's a disorder, not a glorious achievement, for Christ's sake." I was surprised I could become angry in such a dire circumstance. Credula didn't trouble himself to respond. "And speaking of Christ, where does he fit in? You seem to be working from a Christian paradigm, yet no one's mentioned Christ or even God so far."

"Christ? God? What do you mean?" George was back.

"George?"

"Yes?"

"What do you know about Credula?"

He smiled his creepy smile and remained silent.

I remembered something he'd told me in one of our first sessions. "You said you were the number two man in an organization, right?"

He nodded. "You have a good memory."

"Is Credula number one?"

"Perhaps."

"Is the entire organization contained within you?"

"That's enough. I need to be somewhere else."

"This is craziness, George. Lethal craziness."

He stood and extended a hand. "Good luck."

We shook hands, and in a moment I was alone with my thoughts.

What a mess. My client was a homicidal maniac—no, make that a homicidal psychotic—and I was supposed to be shackled by the law and my ethics. But how could I stand by as the body count mounted? Was my honor more important than human lives? If I was really working with Arundel—engaging in effective therapy of some kind—that might be different. In that case, I might be able to stop him by helping him to understand the wrongness of his actions—or Credula's actions, actually. But as it was, only a breach of confidence could protect the innocent.

I decided I'd make an anonymous phone call to the police. Unfortunately, if they didn't nab him, he'd probably know I ratted on him, and I wasn't sure that my archangel status would protect me.

I'd never heard of an actual criminal with multiple personality disorder, although I'd seen one on a lawyer show on television once. Certainly, killers like Son of Sam had obeyed voices, as paranoid schizophrenics tend to do, but kowtowing to an alter was somewhat different. The legal ramifications were unknown to me. Would they lock Arundel up in prison, execute him, or send him to an institution? My best guess was life in prison, but I realized these concerns weren't a significant factor in my choice to call the police.

There was a knock on my door at this point. Startled, I remembered I'd scheduled another client immediately following Arundel. Vincent Perone had recently shaved off a sixteen-year-old beard and was having trouble adjusting to his exposed face. I experienced an adjustment of my own as I unsuccessfully tried to focus on the remainder of my clients that afternoon.

Chapter 14

A friend once suggested that if I was experiencing problems with a given client around a confidentiality issue, I ought to discuss it in a session with my own therapist. After all, she was obliged to keep it confidential too, and I would be discussing myself, not the client per se. Although I'd already decided what to do, I wanted to feel better about my choice.

Roberta Chan wasn't Chinese, or even Asian. She was a slender sixty-six-year-old who had married Bob Chan, who was also a therapist. This therapist-to-therapist liaison was common in Santa Cruz. I reasoned that only another trained professional could withstand prolonged exposure to someone as screwed-up as a therapist, but a male colleague of mine, when drunk, always proclaimed that only highly qualified individuals deserved the bliss of being with a wise partner. After a few more drinks, he'd shout that once you've had a therapist, you can never go back.

Roberta's office was in Aptos, an unincorporated town eight miles down the coast from Santa Cruz. She was situated above a small, upscale restaurant, whose cook was a former client of mine. I always felt surreptitious when I parked in the rear lot and climbed the back stairs, as though my ex-client would catch me needing therapy myself. It was irrational, especially since our paths had actually crossed once and all that had transpired was a friendly wave.

The interior of her office reflected her interest in folk art, especially pre-Columbian stone work from Latin America. Museum-quality sculptures crowded her shelves. Sometimes I wondered if this served less as a decorating scheme and more as a warehouse for the pieces that wouldn't fit in her house.

Her furniture was Danish modern, with blond woods and smooth black fabrics. Surprisingly, the two styles complemented each other, perhaps contrasting so drastically that the basic qualities of each were highlighted.

Roberta was an outstanding therapist, elevating her livelihood into an art form. She worked with a great deal of intuition, derived from a vast wealth of experience, having begun as a twenty-three-year-old back when licensing requirements were virtually nil.

"Hi, Tom," she greeted. Her gray hair was piled elegantly in a loose bun on top of her head, exposing her long, thin ballerina's neck.

"Hello, Roberta. Thanks for fitting me in."

As usual, traffic noise penetrated her office's thin walls. A truck's back-up beeper almost drowned out my greeting.

"No problem. Have a seat."

When I settled on her couch, a familiar scent wafted my way. Roberta always wore a complex floral perfume—just enough to be discernible.

I closed my eyes for a moment to connect with myself. It was a ritual that aided me in transitioning from therapist to client. Usually, after thirty seconds of this, all thoughts of technique, diagnosis, and self-consciousness disappeared.

"I'm confused," I finally began. "I'm seeing someone with full-blown multiple personalities who's involved in wacky spiritual stuff and some very serious crimes. My legal obligations and morals are clashing."

"You mean you don't know how you want to respond?"

"Not really. I think I know. I promised and I'm bound by law to respect his confidentiality. But morally, I feel there's a higher priority to prevent further...uh, damage to the world. Am I being clear?"

"I think so. Because of the particulars, you think you should break confidentiality in this case. Is that it?"

"Yes. And the particulars are very compelling."

"How do you feel right now?"

"Scared. Nervous. Weak."

"Where are they?" She meant where was I feeling them in my body.

"The fear is a tightness in my chest, under my sternum. I'm nervous in my gut. It's tingling and feels strange. And I feel weak all over, especially in my arms."

"Your arms?"

"Yes. It's like if you told me to lift something, I don't think I could do it—even something light."

"Is what you have to lift light?"

"God, no. It's incredibly heavy." I didn't even know exactly what we were talking about, but I knew it was heavy.

"So you can't lift it?"

"No, I can't." I felt tears welling up. "But I want to."

Roberta was silent.

"I feel I need to," I added.

"But you can't."

"No."

"Is it too big?"

"No, just too heavy. I could never budge it."

"And this is sad?"

"Yes. It hurts."

"Where?"

"In my head."

"Suppose you hired someone to lift it for you?" she asked.

"It wouldn't work. I have to do it myself."

"But you can't."

"Don't you think I know that?"

"You don't know anything," she declared.

"Yes, I do!"

"No, you don't. You don't know anything, and you can't do anything."

"Yes, I can. I know what to do."

"You don't."

"I do. I can tell the police!"

"I thought that was too heavy."

"What? Too heavy?"

"Yes."

"No, it's not too heavy. I can do it."

"Are you sure?"

"Yes."

I flipped into my therapist self, although I'd never done that before in a session with Roberta. I saw she had been using my awareness of my body sensations to allow my unconscious to express itself, then she'd helped me intensify my feelings around that, and finally she'd successfully employed a paradoxical intervention to help me defeat my own weakness. It was a seamless sequence she'd probably never conceptualized in these terms, if at all.

"Where are you now?" she asked, noticing the shift.

"Up in my head. I'm dissecting your work."

"That sounds painful."

"Painful? No, I don't think so. For who?"

"For you. I've always thought that in dissection, the greater violence isn't to the corpse or the animal, it's to the dissector."

"I'm not sure I understand."

"That's all right."

"But I want to understand."

"Yes. You do."

"But you won't tell me?"

"No. What do you feel?"

"Frustrated. Annoyed."

"Are you still up in your head?"

I smiled. "No, you little sneak."

Roberta smiled back. "Are you going to tell the police?"

"Yes. I need to."

"Why?"

"Uh…I don't know. I just need to."

"Good. Good work. We're done."

"There's still a lot of time, actually."

"We're done."

She rose and opened the door for me.

"Okay, we're done," I conceded.

She nodded crisply.

I left.

Problem solved.

Maybe.

****

I made an anonymous call to the authorities from a pay phone at the bus station. Maybe I was being paranoid, but I planned to complete it in less than a minute to thwart them from tracing the call. On television, cops don't capture kidnappers if the phone conversation is sufficiently brief.

"Santa Cruz Police Department," the woman's voice answered.

"Listen closely. I know who the serial killer is. His name is George Arundel. That's A-R-U-N-D-E-L. Be careful. He's crazy."

"What is your name, sir?"

"Never mind."

"How do you know this?"

"He told me," I replied, and hung up.

****

I felt a great deal of relief following the disclosure. I had expected to pay a high psychic price for my behavior, perhaps feeling treacherous or unclean. But I didn't. I just felt lighter. I also experienced an urge to spend a few days in a nice motel somewhere far away, perhaps under an assumed name. However, my sense of responsibility to my clients restrained me.

I wondered how the police would proceed. Assuming they could locate him, they couldn't very well search George's house based on one anonymous call. They would check to see if he had a criminal record and maybe follow him. Perhaps they'd just knock on his door and interview him. And how would Arundel respond to that? Would he switch to a disarmingly innocent personality? Even a trained detective would be deflected by that. Would he cease the killing when he knew he was under suspicion? That didn't sound like Credula.

Since I had no pending appointments with Arundel, my best source of feedback was Zig-Zag, although contacting her was just as unethical as tipping off the police. The second step on the road to therapist hell, however, proved to be much easier than the first.

I called her the following morning during a break between Mr. I-want-custody Jacobs and Ms. I-can't-face-turning-fifty Carlyle.

"Hello," a woman's voice answered.

"I'd like to speak to Zig-Zag. I'm afraid I don't know her real name."

"That is my real name, Tom. My mom named me Zig-Zag Love Cassiel. 'Zig-zag love' was some idea of hers about lightning and love and God. I've never understood it."

"Have you ever thought of changing your name?"

"When I was a kid, I went by Jennifer for a while, and then I tried Zelda, but they didn't stick."

"I actually like Zig-Zag, but I know it's hard to have an unusual name."

"You're not kidding. So what can I do for you?"

"I was just wondering how you and George are doing. Is he still bugging you about being an angel? Have they set a trial date for the arrests at the tower?"

"George is relentless. Dizzy's lawyer asked for a continuance because she's going to be out of the country for a while."

"Dizzy?"

"No, her lawyer. We can't go anywhere. We're out on bail—remember?"

"That's right. Speaking of unusual names, how is our friend Desdemona?"

"She doesn't use that name—just Dizzy or her middle name. She's pretty upset right now to tell you the truth. She might have to serve some time."

"God, I hope not. What about you?"

"No chance. This is only the second time I've gotten caught. I haven't been doing this as long as some of the others."

"How about George?"

"Hell, I doubt he's ever even gotten a speeding ticket."

"I mean, how's he doing?"

"Oh. Well, I haven't seen him for a few days. He's probably fine, though. He isn't a real up and down kind of guy."

"No, I guess not."

"How about you?" she asked. "What happened when you went back to the bookstore?"

"The book wasn't there anymore, and the owner said he never had it. On top of that, the store was supposed to be closed the day we were there."

"It figures. I'll bet the dog was my dad."

"Really?"

"Oh, I don't know. Maybe. What do you think?"

"I don't know what to think anymore," I told her. "I guess I still attribute most everything to George somehow. I'm very disturbed by the whole thing. That much I know."

"It must feel kinda creepy to you, huh?"

"Yes, it does. I can't integrate most of this into the rest of me. Do you know what I mean?"

"Yup. How about the mess I got you into with the police? How're you doing with that?"

"Not too bad, really. I paid my fine—or George did—and I'm free and clear. I'm glad they didn't mention me in that newspaper article. That could've been a real problem for me."

"Why? Don't you think crazy people care about the planet?"

"Of course they do, but they also care about a safe space with someone they trust. Some people don't trust lawbreakers. All things being equal, would you want to work with a big scary guy who's also just been arrested?"

"Gotcha. You've got a point there. I wondered about you being so big before. I'll bet it scares off some people."

"I thought I was a 'motherfucking monster.' What's this 'big' thing?"

"Aw, come on. You still remember that? That was just a weird situation. I thought I was going to help George with some problem he was having, and the next thing I know you're bringing up all that angel shit. I was kind of pissed off."

"Speaking of which, are you still having phenomena happen around the angel business?"

"Oh sure. Just yesterday I had a good one. But that kinda stuff happens all the time, right?"

"Not to me."

"You get used to it."

"I hope not. I hope it just stops."

"Well, anyway, thanks for calling."

"Oh, sure. Take care."

It was a thoroughly dissatisfying conversation in which I'd learned nothing about Arundel.

Over the next several days, though, I received three phone calls that were much richer sources of information.

The next day, Matthew Ferguson told my answering service he'd be available that evening if I wished to call him. I'd tried phoning him after our meeting, but he'd failed to return my calls. After dinner, I sprawled in my oversized armchair and punched in the new number I'd been given.

"Hello?"

I recognized his voice immediately. "This is Tom Dashiel."

"Hi, Tom. Thanks for calling. I felt an urge to check in with you."

"I appreciate that. Whatever happened when you sang to me was a profound experience I don't really understand."

"Good. Trying to understand it would be a mistake," he told me.

"Why is that?"

"You would need to reduce it—to throw out the un-understandable parts. Some experiences aren't meant to be filtered through the mind."

"I do have that tendency."

"Don't we all. I also wanted to ask you about your invasion of angels. Has it continued?"

"Yes. If anything, it's worse. And I've found out it's mixed in with some alarming criminal activity."

"How peculiar."

"I've taken steps to resolve the problem, though."

"Good for you. So you no longer need my help?"

"I wouldn't say that. I still feel lost—in unfamiliar territory without a map or a guidebook."

"That's exactly it. You're operating in a realm where there are no maps. The trick is to get used to it so your anxiety doesn't interfere with noticing the rather subtle directional cues that are always there in the moment. Perhaps they're in the periphery, or maybe you know them by seeing parts of their shadows."

"Parts of their shadows? Isn't that a little too tenuous to use as a guideline?"

"What else have you got? Anything better?"

"No, not so far."

"We established last time that my telling you things doesn't work. Books don't work. Your own sensory input has become suspect—am I right?"

"Yes."

"So forget about the obvious and pay attention to the subtle. That's the help I can offer. It doesn't challenge your general orientation or bludgeon you with my alien point of view. After all, this is your life, and you're the one who's supposed to live it. It's like getting a friend to take a test at school for you. You really do cheat yourself—it's more than a cliche. At school, the effects are usually minimal, but in your life you can't afford to sidestep your lessons. They're what life's all about, really."

"I understand your reasoning, but I'm a therapist. I believe that people need help sometimes."

"Absolutely," Ferguson agreed. "But you don't."

"How do you know that?" He didn't answer. "Why should I believe you?" Again there was silence on the line. "Are you going to say anything?"

"Yes. Be open. Pay attention. That's it. I'm done."

"Well, okay. Thanks."

"You're welcome. I'd say good luck, but I don't subscribe to the concept. Good-bye, Tom."

"Bye."

I hung up and headed back to the refrigerator for more dessert.

Chapter 15

Dizzy called the next morning. I had just finished trimming the gratuitous hair that had recently begun infesting my ears. I could definitely hear more clearly as she launched into an elaborate apology.

"I was a real bitch the other day at dinner, and it doesn't feel good at all now. I really appreciate what you've done for me—saving my life, among other things. And I'm grateful. I really am. I always hate it when other women use this excuse, but the truth is, it was PMS. My hormones were raging, and I couldn't handle it and you paid the price. So I'm sorry, and I hope you can forgive me."

"Well, it's not like I hate you, but to tell you the truth, I'm quite affected by that kind of behavior. The bottom line is that it's hard for me to trust someone once they've attacked me without provocation. So on one level I feel forgiving, but I can't make the incident just disappear. If you said, 'Let's go camping this weekend,' for example, I'd say, 'No, thanks.' Based on my experiences with you, it would represent too big a risk. I might be trapped for two days in a tent with…Well, I can't think of the right word, but it might not be a laugh a minute. On the other hand, if you said, 'Why don't we go for a walk and see where we stand?' I'd say, 'Sure.' "

"Why don't we go for a walk and see where we stand?"

"Sure."

"You're a man of your word, Mr. Dashiel. Did you have somewhere in mind?"

"Me? You're the one who brought it up. I was only speaking hypothetically."

"Well, hypothetically, then, where might you want to walk?"

"I have to admit that if an attractive woman suggested Fall Creek Park, I'd probably be agreeable to the idea. Hypothetically."

"Are you free next Saturday?" she asked.

"I am. Ten o'clock? I'll pick you up?"

"Great. I hope my cop protector likes the woods. So far the poor guy has had to frisk the pizza delivery boy and a squad of Mormons. Then last night, I got him to drive me to the grocery store. I don't think he's been around Black people much."

"Why do you say that?"

"He's really nervous around me."

"Maybe he's just shy."

"Maybe."

"Anyway, they may catch the killer by Saturday," I told her.

"You think so? Have you heard something?"

"They've got some new clues. I think they'll wrap it up soon."

"Great. That's a relief. So I'll see you here at ten in the morning on Saturday?"

"Yes. Enjoy your day."

"You too."

****

The third phone call was from Credula. Its voice was even less human-sounding on the phone.

"Thomas," the voice declared impassively.

"Yes."

"Do you know who this is?"

"Yes."

"Don't use my name."

"Why not?"

"The police have taken an interest in a mutual friend of ours. Don't say his name, either."

"I understand." The hair on the back of my neck was standing up, and my whole body was rigid with tension.

"We need to meet," Credula said.

"No."

"We need to meet," it repeated.

"No."

"You must be activated. The archangel within you is needed now."

"No."

"If you aren't activated properly, the forces of darkness will be able to use you for their own purposes."

"No."

"This world depends on you."

I decided not to answer. The nos weren't getting the job done.

"You must not shirk your responsibilities. A world of darkness cannot be tolerated."

I hung up.

****

That night I dreamt that Dizzy was a Black angel, and George and Ferguson were White angels, and I was a small gray dog trying to run away from all of them, but they could fly, so I couldn't get away no matter what I did. As a dog, I could only think simple thoughts, and I was very conscious of smells. Dizzy smelled like a paint store, and the others smelled like bread. I woke up panting.

I decided to see my therapist again, and luckily Roberta had a cancellation for the next evening. She looked tired; it was the first time I'd seen her that way.

"Hello, Tom," she greeted.

"Hi. Thanks for seeing me again on such short notice."

"I need the money. What's up?"

"Craziness. Two friends and myself are all having visions, synchronicities, and just plain unexplained events about angels. A client says I really am an angel—no, an archangel—and he's trying relentlessly to get me to buy into in his delusions. Someone's trying to kill a friend, but it doesn't seem to be the serial murderer—who I also know. I can't concentrate on my other clients. And I'm not sure about anything anymore. What's real? What's crazy? What's spiritual? I don't know. I just don't know."

"That's quite a bundle. What do you want to work on first?"

"I don't know. Can't you be in charge?"

She shook her head slowly. "No. You know it doesn't work that way."

"I guess the synchronicities, then. They're all over the place. I'm seeing connections between things that can't possibly be connected, and other people verify they're really happening, too. This has all the signs of early psychosis, but I'm not alone, and I can provide real-world evidence to support it all."

"So you've ruled out a psychotic break?"

"No. That's the problem. I haven't been able to absolutely rule out anything. I know how compelling an inner delusional world can be. And I know I have a tendency toward dissociation—or at least retreating up into my head when I'm stressed. So I can't just assume that my perceptions of my so-called evidence is real."

"So you think you're crazy?"

"No, I don't. I think it's the least likely alternative, actually. But obviously it's the scariest."

"Is it? With murderers in your life?"

"Yeah, it is. I'm not saying the rest isn't hard too, but if I'm thinking straight, I think I can deal."

"I'll level with you, Tom. I'm concerned. Have you thought of getting a diagnosis from someone more accustomed to working with this kind of thing?"

"A psychiatrist? No. And if you can't handle this, what kind of message is that—that I'm too screwed-up for a regular therapist? That isn't what I need to hear." My alarm was genuine. Why in the world would Roberta think my problems were beyond her skill set?

"I'm dying, Tom."

"What!"

"I'm dying. I found out last Friday. I don't know if I'll have the time and energy to see this through."

"Jesus. Oh Jesus. What is it?"

"Bone cancer. I don't mind dying, but I'm scared to death of the pain. It'll be bad near the end." She looked away, tears forming in her eyes.

"Roberta, what can I say?" My mind was a complete blank.

"Say you'll make an appointment with Jim Orsac. He's good, Tom. He can sort this out for you." Her head swiveled back, and she wiped away her tears. "Now let's get back to what's happening with you in the moment."

"So where do I start? Don't bother answering; I

already know—with my feelings. Let's see…I'm upset."

"Stomach gas? Indigestion?"

"You're so mean to me. All right…" I paused and contacted my root feeling. "I'm angry. You can't be there for me, and I count on you—I've been counting on you for six years off and on, and now you're abandoning me. I'm sorry, but that's how I feel. I'm mad."

We worked on this for the rest of the session and concluded with a gentle hug.

Later that evening, I cried myself to sleep. Roberta was precious to me; I would miss her terribly. Why was everyone dying all of a sudden?

****

I took the risk of calling the detective working on the serial killings to see what I could find out about George. I'd met the guy outside Dizzy's place after her attacker escaped.

"Any luck with the serial killer?" I asked.

"Maybe. We've got a suspect under surveillance, and it may not be a coincidence that we've had no more murders for a while."

"You think it's him?"

"I don't know. He's an odd one, but he hasn't got a record. We'll see."

"How'd you get onto him? The footprints near Dizzy's place?"

"No. In fact, his feet are wrong for it. We got an anonymous tip we're still trying to track."

"What do you mean?"

"We've got the voice on tape. If we can find the guy, we'll know more."

I coughed and excused myself. How could I have forgotten to disguise my voice? Was that enough for them to find me? No, I knew it wasn't. But while they were monitoring George, would he contact me again, tying me into the case? With the recording, they could eventually prove I had been the caller. This was a career-ending possibility, but there was nothing I could do about it for now, so I ate ice cream.

I was beginning to understand more of my clients' behaviors as I found myself doing them. Got a problem? Eat. Facing a series of confounding experiences? Go into denial. I had always been familiar with depression, stuffing feelings, self-pity, and lots of other popular favorites. Lately, though, I'd begun filling in the blanks on my maladaptation resume. Would it make me a better person? A better therapist? Crazy? Dead? God knew.

****

Jim Orsac returned my call the next evening. I had met him once or twice years before, but he didn't remember me.

There are several schools of thought on how to conduct oneself during the first contact with a prospective client. Personally, since I wasn't interested in screening anyone out, I left the whole business to my phone service. At the opposite end of the spectrum, some therapists held extensive interrogations, even charging for their time.

Orsac fit somewhere in the middle. He wasn't concerned with the details of my problem, yet he obviously wanted to get a feel for who I was before he agreed to see me. Our conversation lasted about ten minutes, ranging from who'd referred me to what was my earliest memory as a child (falling off a stack of lumber and landing on my chin).

We made an appointment for a week from Thursday,

which was his first available slot, proving that Orsac had built a better practice than I had.

****

On the way to Dizzy's apartment on Saturday morning, I realized I had little idea why I was getting together to take a walk with her, especially with a still-sore knee. True, she was beautiful, but if she invited me to sleep with her, I was fairly sure I'd turn her down. I didn't need the grief that accompanied the short-term pleasure. The angel paintings did hint at some sort of mystical connection, but once again, what difference did that make in the real world? I finally decided that our interaction was unpredictable, and therefore intriguing. There was a certain tension to being with Dizzy. Would she be civil? Contentious? Appreciative? Funny? I had no idea what to expect. I'd experienced all of these traits at one time or another.

Anyway, for better or for worse, I found myself on Dizzy's doorstep with a small, vague smile on my face. I was surprised that my convoluted inner process manifested itself in such a simple expression.

Dizzy looked great to my eyes, as usual, and the sight of her in worn jeans and a purple turtleneck sweater banished my musing. Her mahogany skin tone gleamed as though she'd just stepped out of the shower. Her wide smile dominated her features.

"Hi, big guy. Friends again?"

She reached out for a hug, and I stepped forward into her arms. I wasn't prepared for the intense wave of lust that enveloped us both. It was all I could do to remain standing, and my erection threatened to pierce the intervening layers of clothing. I was also dizzy, nauseated, and sweaty—all in about ten seconds. In short, another novel experience had arrived to help trash my way of being. I broke away before I discovered what came next.

"Whew!" she exclaimed. "That was incredible. What happened?"

"I don't know. I've never felt anything like that. Well, maybe like that, but not that. Oh, hell. You know what I mean."

"I sure do. Talk about chemistry. They could mix our energies together and make a new kind of bomb."

"Is that what it's about—energy mixing together?" I asked. That sounded a lot like what Credula had asserted, which scared me.

"Sure. Because of our karma or whatever, we each have a certain energy configuration, and I guess when you get ours close to one another, all hell breaks loose."

I found myself able to dismiss this simplistic New Age version of lust. "Well," I replied. "We'd better get going."

"Okay. I'm ready. Let's roll."

So we did. Her cop followed us dutifully in what must have been his own car—a blue Honda SUV.

On our route to the park, we traversed an assortment of small-scale ecosystems, including a pine forest, dry scrubby meadows, and stands of redwoods. Every few miles, it was as though we were visiting another region.

In lieu of conversation, I was content to watch the various settings as they presented themselves. As I guided the Volvo on the winding road, Dizzy also remained silent. Eventually we reached the town of Felton and the entrance to Fall Creek Park.

The parking lot at the trailhead was composed of a strange sort of dirt. Most of the time it could best be described as a thick layer of dust, but in the rainy season it morphed into deep, gooey mud that sucked at car tires, shoes, or whatever else was handy, threatening to pull everything down into some messy underworld.

Today was a dust day, so we waited for the dirty clouds to settle before exiting the car. It was warm at the trailhead, but I knew that once we descended to the valley below, I'd need a sweater, so I carried one. At one time, I'd experimented with the sweater-draped-over-my-shoulders look, which in my case hinted of some terrible experiment that had gone awry over in Italy. I'd also tried the sweater-tied-around-the-waist method, but I always seemed to forget it was there until I sat on something filthy.

The first part of the trail was downhill, which was actually harder on my knee than uphill. With each step, I had to catch all my weight, which made something in the joint pull and send pain up into my quadriceps muscles. Even with the aid of my cumbersome brace, I had to work hard to keep up with Dizzy, who hiked as though she could maintain her brisk pace indefinitely.

"I need to go slower," I finally called ahead to her.

"Oh, I'm sorry. I forgot about your hurt knee. How's it doing?" She waited for me to catch up, maintaining eye contact.

"I'll be fine if we go slow and maybe only as far as the lime kilns."

"Sure. We can rest there and talk a while. I brought water in my backpack."

At the bottom of the hill, Fall Creek itself ran through a narrow valley bracketed by steep, forested slopes. The sunlight filtered down through the multitude of conifers. Everything was partially in the light and partially in the shadows. This lent a common context to the disparate elements of the setting, tying them together to my eye. I was conscious of a unity that was ordinarily out of my awareness. As the creek itself raced through all this, its waters were always alongside us, yet always arriving and departing, too. There were no boundaries between the creek's past, present, and future. Its length was seamless—all of a piece, all now. It took compelling scenery to compete with Dizzy, but we'd found it on our hike.

Chapter 16

After a half hour of walking, interspersed with pauses to observe banana slugs and birds, we reached our destination. By then, I was more than ready to shed my knee brace and reclaim my leg.

The lime kilns at the end of the trail were old brick structures that had cooked limestone to extract lime, which was widely used as an ingredient in mortar at the turn of the century. The three kilns were in a line, sharing side walls and sporting small arched doorways. From the front, then, they resembled row houses in some fairyland peopled by gnomes. A path led to the top of the brick walls, which no longer supported roofs, and there were numerous perches up there. Once up on the walls, I've always had the feeling I was visiting ancient ruins.

"It's great up here," Dizzy proclaimed once we'd settled in side by side atop the wall.

"I love this spot," I agreed. "You know my favorite thing here?"

"What?"

"It's when a leaf falls and you watch it all the way down. I love the way it defines the space—makes you aware of the in between places in the woods."

"That's nice. I like that. It's kind of Zen, isn't it?"

"I don't know. Is it?"

"Sure. Everything's kind of Zen. If you're ever at a party and you don't know what to say, just say 'It's kind of Zen, isn't it?' and see what happens."

"Maybe I'll try it sometime."

"Another good one is 'Isn't this boring?' I think everything is at least partly Zen and partly boring. Anyway, even if it isn't either one, people tend to respond to that kind of thing."

I didn't have much interest in this subject, but I managed a grunt while I watched a squirrel stare back at me. Dizzy offered me water, and I drank.

"So what do you really think about angels, Tom?" Dizzy asked.

Her face was turned in profile, but as I studied it, she swiveled her head and caught my gaze full on. She was suddenly very present, perhaps more than she wanted to be. Involuntarily, my awareness blossomed into the moment, and I experienced an intensity of sensory input and emotion that was almost too much to handle. My chest tightened for a moment before something deep in me adapted, and I found myself breathing freely and deeply. An extraordinary calm asserted itself, and despite the continued barrage of sensory information, my peace of mind was unassailable now. I felt as if I were Buddha.

"What's going on?" Dizzy asked. "What's happening?"

"No words," I replied. "New thing." I could hear that I was answering her in Tarzan language, but I didn't care.

"Well, I'm here if you need me," she asserted, grabbing one of my meaty hands and pulling it over to entangle it with hers in the space between us.

I peered out of my body at the intricate puzzle of the world before me. One thing was clear immediately.

Everything out there fit together perfectly, and we were a part of it, too. I didn't know how it worked or how I knew, but somehow I was aware that it was all working just the right way, including Arundel, the murders, and everything else. There was no sense of wrongness, problems, or worries. Nothing needed fixing or even demanded my attention.

And it was all so incredibly beautiful. Each square inch was a universe. Each plant, each rock, each cloud was an amazing creation which both stood on its own and fit sublimely into the whole. I felt that if I just sat and looked long enough, I would become what I saw. It's hard to explain now, but it was as if the delineations between things—where I left off and the rest of the world began, for example—were revealed as arbitrary constructs that could be transcended simply by understanding the oneness in which we all played our parts.

At the time, of course, I wasn't thinking about my state or what words could best describe it. I just was. That's really the most faithful description of that wonderful twenty minutes. I was.

My return to ordinary consciousness was abrupt. One moment I was one with the world; the next I was Tom with a sore knee sitting on a hard rock. Fortunately, the experience remained with me as a strong memory, softening the otherwise harsh contrast presented by my return to normalcy.

"I'm back," I announced.

"Wherever you were, it looked fun," Dizzy told me. "Your hand got really hot too."

"Hmm."

"Can you tell me about it?"

"No, I'm not ready to talk about it."

"Did you see an angel?" she asked.

I shook my head and shifted myself on the rock wall; my butt was killing me.

My ordinary consciousness began nibbling at my experience. As usual, it started with a plethora of questions. Was what happened related to my heart experience when Ferguson sang? Was it just a coincidence that it happened with Dizzy? How was it connected to Arundel and all that? Did it validate the philosophy of naturalists such as Emerson?

As I played with these questions, I was once again off in my own world, and this time Dizzy was less patient.

"Hey!" she called as she poked me in the ribs. "Snap out of it, would you? We're supposed to be getting to know each other."

"Sorry."

I returned my attention to Dizzy and our setting and was struck by how odd it felt to be sitting next to her on the kilns. For one thing, I hadn't spent this much time with anyone Black since my basketball days. There just weren't many African Americans in Santa Cruz.

Also, of course, sitting in the woods with a single woman was a rare event for a hermit such as myself. Dizzy's breathtaking beauty added to the surreal tenor of the context. I decided to share my general impression of my spiritual experience as a way to re-establish contact.

"You've been hanging around with Zig-Zag too much," she told me when I finished. "That girl is the spaciest thing around. I wouldn't be surprised if she had something to do with the angel vision I had."

"She's told you who her dad was, right?"

"No, she never talks about her family or her childhood. Who was her dad?"

"Krishnanda."

"I've never heard of him. Was he Indian?"

"Yes. A guru. She says she grew up with miracles happening all around her."

"That explains a lot. I wonder why she'd tell you, but not me. I'm kind of hurt."

"I'm a therapist. She's not my client, but people tend to tell me things. I guess they know they can trust me."

"You mean they trust you not to tell other people? If that's the case, you just blew it, didn't you?"

"I guess you're right. Oh well." I paused to examine a beetle that crawled across my thigh. Its shell gleamed with a blue-black reflective sheen. "That reminds me. I called the newspapers and the TV stations about your vision. I hope you don't mind."

"Hey, don't even joke about that. I feel crazy enough as it is. A friend of mine keeps telling me it's better to just forget about it since it could be the beginning of a breakdown. What do you think about that? Could I be losing my grip?"

"It's possible. Lately, I've wondered about myself too. But I wouldn't worry about it if I were you. It's not visions or religious beliefs that get people into trouble. It's how they react to them—do they think they're God or get too anxious to function? That's the key thing, and your life doesn't seem as though it's been too disrupted."

"Yeah. You're right. It's not like I'm really freaking out. I'm just painting, and that's how I always spend my free time anyway."

"You're really talented. Have you had any shows?"

This question triggered a long recitation of her

history as an artist. I half listened and half watched the forest around us.

As a result, I spotted Arundel as he surreptitiously worked his way toward us, using redwood trees for cover. He wore camouflage rain gear, which must've been designed for a completely different kind of forest. Something about the particular combination of green and brown clashed horribly with the flora of the hillside below us. There was no sign of either of the cops— Dizzy's or Arundel's.

For a moment, I froze, unable to think, and then my adrenaline kicked in again. We were in trouble. I wasn't armed, and a serial killer was stalking us. Presumably, he was after Dizzy, but it was possible I was the target, based on my being either a reluctant archangel or a stool pigeon. At any rate, Credula wasn't likely to leave witnesses hanging around, so what did it matter?

I spoke to Dizzy in a whisper. "There's a guy following us who might be the one who's after you. We need to get out of here."

She whispered back urgently, "Where's my cop? Can't he deal with this guy?"

"I think he's out of the picture. And there's no cell service here. Follow me."

I stood and walked quickly along the wall toward the back of the kilns, leaving my brace propped against a rock. Arundel was in a position to cut off our access to both trails that led to the parking lot, but as Dizzy hurried to follow me, I discovered a narrow path winding back into the hills. We darted onto it now that we were out of sight.

At first I was confident that our head start and our good luck finding the trail would save us. Then my knee gave out. A few minutes later, limping painfully as I maneuvered along the now rocky path, I discovered that we weren't exactly navigating through the hills either. We were in an old, overgrown limestone quarry; it was probably the only dead-end topographical feature in the entire park, and I'd found it on the first try.

"Shit," Dizzy commented as she realized why I'd stopped.

"We can go back or try to climb out," I said. "I don't suppose you're an experienced rock-climber, by any chance."

"Actually, I am, although I've never done any free-climbing. But you can't climb anything with that knee."

I gave it a try anyway but only ascended a few painful footholds before slipping and falling back onto the rocky ground. I landed on my shoulders, and then my head snapped back and hit something hard.

At that point, I experienced an odd sensation, as if someone had flipped down an on-off switch that controlled me and then thrown it back up before I'd fully shut down. Later, I'd remember this as a key event in the sequence that followed.

"You're right," I answered, continuing to feel distinctly odd. "You scoot up there and get some help. I'll play hide and seek and stall this guy."

"Maybe we could get by him if we double back off the trail."

"I don't think so." We turned and surveyed the scene behind us. "Look at how narrow the opening to the quarry is. If it weren't for all these damn trees, we'd have noticed the layout before."

"I guess you're right."

I slapped her on the back. "Get going. Hurry."

"All right." She gave me a kiss on the neck—as high as she could reach—and lithely scurried ahead.

I stumbled off the trail to find a hiding place. If I could confound my five-year-old nephew in a three-bedroom house, surely I could hold out for a while on the forested floor of this abandoned quarry. And if Arundel missed me on his way up the trail, I could try to limp back before he noticed his mistake.

Once again, I was struck by how surreal everything felt. I wrote this off as a stress-induced response.

Arundel simply tracked me, following the obvious carnage a huge limping man created in an otherwise pristine environment. Within five minutes, he stood a few feet from where I'd sequestered myself behind a gnarled redwood stump.

"The woman is gone," I called.

"I realize that," Credula intoned.

I shivered. That dead voice was worse than I remembered.

It continued. "I've told you we have no interest in her. I am here to speak to you."

I unfolded myself and rose; Credula moved laterally to stand facing me, perhaps six feet away. He assumed a posture of parade rest, as if he were a marine about to receive a medal.

"What do we need to talk about?" I asked. "There's no point in beating a dead horse."

"Unfortunately, we are dealing with matters beyond mere death."

Up until this point, attempting to elude Credula had still been a game. With the aid of adrenaline, I'd responded to circumstances, trying to survive. Now this ungodly entity faced me, and I knew there could never be any winning against such a thing. Its eyes were beyond dead; clearly, they had never lived. Would I soon wish I hadn't, either? A shiver started at the top of my skull and flashed down my spine.

"It is time," Credula continued. "You must declare yourself."

"As an angel, you mean?"

"Yes. If you don't transform now, your energy will be co-opted by the dark forces."

"The dark forces? Isn't that a little corny?" I don't know how I mustered the nerve to say this.

He stared into my eyes, ignoring my comment. I suddenly felt even more vulnerable. Basically, this was an ultimatum—you're either with us or you're against us. And I knew how Credula dealt with those he perceived to be against him.

"Okay, you're right," I said. "It is time. I hereby declare I'm an angel. What happens now?"

"You die," he stated flatly. "The words are not enough. You must mean them."

He reached into his jacket pocket, and I lurched away, trying to run. After two steps, a throwing knife whistled into the muscle mass behind my left shoulder. I went down hard, breaking my nose on a tree root. I could feel the bone splinter.

In a fog of blood and tears, I scrambled and pivoted as Credula approached me cautiously, a large kitchen knife now held low in his right hand. There was no time to think. Reaching backward, I yanked the weapon out of my upper back. As Credula realized what I was doing, he lunged forward.

I threw instinctively, and he took the knife in the throat, just below the Adam's apple.

His lunge became a fall, but the large blade remained on an intercept course with my chest. My follow through had rendered me completely vulnerable—I was a wide-open target. I wriggled and twisted sideways a millisecond before Credula stabbed me in the upper thigh. The knife shaft stuck—God, it hurt—and he fell away, gurgling from the wound in his windpipe. At that point I passed out.

Chapter 17

I awoke the following afternoon in intensive care, my knife wounds throbbing sharply with each heartbeat. The pain was both localized and diffuse. At the center of each of the two major traumas, a searing pain pulsed jagged waves through the surrounding tissue, which, in turn, ached as though someone had been pounding them with a sledgehammer. The thigh wound was the worst.

My nose was packed with cotton and bandaged; my face hurt terribly, too. Even breathing (through my mouth) was a problem. I felt as thoroughly bruised as I felt cut, and the combination was overwhelming.

Gradually my eyes focused, and I glimpsed the back of someone across the equipment-filled room.

"Hey," I called weakly. "Hey, I need a pain pill."

A male nurse clad in green scrubs whirled and hurried over. "Welcome back, hero," he greeted. His smile annoyed me.

"I need a pill," I repeated.

"I can do better than that. Now just hold still while I send you something intravenously. That's it. There you go. Now…"

I was gone again, a flood of warmth banishing me back into blackness.

My next foray into consciousness was, unfortunately, more successful. When it became obvious to the young woman on duty that a dose of major painkiller wasn't going to shut me up, she summoned my doctor.

The car accident and subsequent fire that had scarred my face taught me a lot about hospitals. I now subscribed to the squeaky-wheel school of negotiating painkiller schedules. I needed information, as well. How badly was I hurt?

Dr. Rodriguez was the most reasonable surgeon I'd ever met. If therapists are crazy, then surgeons are arrogant, but Rodriguez displayed little of his profession's core trait.

"Certainly," was his response to my request to self-medicate. His assessment of my physical condition was lengthier but just as cooperative.

"You almost lost too much blood," he told me in a soft, slightly accented voice. "It was close. The smaller knife missed your heart by less than an inch. But actually, it was the thigh wound that gave us the most trouble."

I was having trouble concentrating, but I asked him to tell me more.

"We had to repair one of your adductor muscles, which had been almost completely severed, as well as reroute a damaged tendon, which is not an easy job. But I'm happy to say you're out of trouble."

"You mean I'm going to survive?"

"Exactly. And I think it's unlikely that you'll walk with a limp or be permanently disabled in any other way. But we're keeping you here in IC for at least another day, and you're looking at least six months of rehab."

"Oh boy."

"I know your medical history, of course. From here on, this should be a breeze compared to your post-accident recovery. I'm not sure how you managed that one."

"Me neither."

"So get some rest. I'll leave instructions with the nursing staff concerning your medication."

"Wait a minute. What about Arundel? Is he dead?"

"I don't know anything about that."

"How can I find out?" I asked.

"The police want to talk to you, of course. But I think tomorrow will be soon enough."

"I can talk now."

"No. Rest. Doctor's orders."

For once, I followed orders; I simply couldn't keep my eyes open.

The police chief himself visited me the next day and filled me in on things. He was an unlikely-looking middle-aged character, with curly red hair and black plastic glasses. His nose was squashed flat and his cheeks were concave, but his lips jutted forward as if they were trying to escape his incongruent face. The overall effect was very busy, almost distracting. He told me to call him Fred.

"George Arundel is dead," Fred told me. "Ms. Farr and the park ranger—I can't recall his name offhand—rushed back after calling in, but he was deceased when they got there, and you were in the process of bleeding to death, I gather."

"So I hear." Cruising on painkillers, I was detached from all that.

"The knife in your leg was definitely the murder weapon in the first four serial killings," he continued.

"What do you mean?"

"The knife blade and the wounds match, and we

found microscopic fibers that correspond to some of the clothing the victims wore."

"No, no. What do you mean 'the first four killings'?"

"I'm afraid it hasn't stopped. Since you've been in here, we've had another murder—complete with seven stab wounds. Someone's using a much larger weapon now."

"How could that be?" This news diminished my recent ordeal and even made me wonder if I'd made a heinous error.

"Arundel was guilty," Fred assured me. "There's no question about that. There's a host of other evidence. It looks like we've either got a copycat killer or the deceased was working with someone else. We know he belonged to a cult—it's possible that another member has been ordered to continue the rampage."

Rampage struck me as a wildly inappropriate term for Credula's behavior, but I understood how it must appear to a police chief.

"I don't think he was working with anyone," I offered. "At least not outside himself."

"I don't understand."

"He was a multiple—one of his alters did the killing."

"Really? We didn't know that, which reminds me. When we're done talking, I want to send in a couple of detectives to question you. Do you feel up to it?"

"Sure." I suddenly thought of something important. "Who's dead?"

"I beg your pardon?"

"Who's the new victim?"

"Oh. A waiter named Robert Schatan."

"Shit. It's not a copycat. Somebody is carrying on Arundel's mission."

"Arundel's mission?" the chief echoed.

"He murdered people with 'devil names.' Heilman, Klovin, Schatan—I can't remember the other two."

"Devilliers and Horn. I can't believe we missed this. So it's probably some associate of Arundel's—someone in the same cult."

"I don't know about that, but Arundel believed he'd been called upon to help a New Age begin by activating people with angel names and killing people with devil names."

"Activating?"

"I'm not sure what that means, either. He said I was an angel, for example, but he never convinced me. He was still trying right before he came at me."

"Why would he try to kill someone he thought was an angel?"

"I wasn't cooperating. He said I would be used by 'the forces of darkness' if I didn't go ahead and become an angel."

"So he was insane?" the chief asked.

"That's not a term I'm comfortable with. Let's say he was deeply disturbed."

"Fine, fine. Disturbed, then. Let me get my men in here. We need to get on this right away."

"Sure."

It was a long, tedious afternoon, which I probably shouldn't have weathered in the condition I was in, but the idea that another maniac was on the loose kept me from taking care of myself. The doctor on duty, on the other hand, was firmly focused on my welfare when he arrived at four fifteen. He not only tossed the trio of policemen out of the intensive care unit, he gave them holy hell as well, cursing in English and Farsi.

I felt semihuman the next morning and even better once they moved me out of intensive care into a private room in intermediate care. Not only was the brightly lit room filled with flowers and fruit baskets, now I was entitled to solid meals and television. Until I could read, and I was still too doped-up to manage that, the remote control would be my best friend.

A chubby Filipina nurse scooted in around two to tell me that virtually everyone on the planet was downstairs waiting to visit me. Her name tag told me her name was Susan.

"Well, Susan, what should we do?"

"I took the liberty of having them sign in so you could decide who you wanted to see."

"That's great. Thank you."

It was an interesting list. Several television stations were represented, as well as the newswires. On the personal side, Dizzy, Ferguson, and several clients who I barely wanted to see when they paid me were cooling their heels. I told Susan to send Dizzy up, and then have Ferguson visit a half hour later. I further instructed her to thank my clients and tell them I'd be in touch, and to suggest to the media that they piss up a rope.

Susan giggled; I liked her.

Dizzy was a proverbial sight for sore eyes. She'd dressed up in a brown silk shirt and black slacks, which she tucked up under herself as she sat in an uncomfortable-looking metal chair next to my bed.

"More scars, huh?" was her first remark.

"You just can't have enough," I told her.

"It's that whole Frankenstein thing. You should get

some electrodes glued on your neck."

"Thanks. You really know how to cheer a guy up."

"Actually, I do. But I don't know you that well yet, and I don't think your door locks."

"That's more like it."

"So how're you feeling? Are you in pain?"

"What do you think? Of course I'm in pain," I replied, irritated. "My nose is killing me right now, and my leg isn't great either."

"I'm sorry. They said you almost died."

"I would've if you hadn't gotten back so quickly. Should I thank you or curse the day you were born? That's the question."

"Don't you think it's better to be alive?"

"I'm not sure right now. I guess so," I admitted. "But if I were dead, I wouldn't have to wonder about things like this."

"That's true. Say, can I eat your fruit?"

"Sure. Go ahead."

Dizzy began foraging through the various baskets that littered my room.

"Here's one from your Aunt Dora," she informed me as she snared a small, perfectly-formed tangerine.

"Terrific."

"So why'd you think Arundel might be the guy?" she asked as she stood at the foot of the bed and peeled the fruit.

"He was a client of mine. He told me."

"Why didn't you turn him in then? You could've got us both killed."

"I made an anonymous call."

"Oh, give me a break. That is so half-assed. You let some stick-up-your-ass therapy rule make you chickenshit?"

"You've got a point there," I responded. "I should've done more, I guess. I was covering my ass, to continue the ass theme we've got going here."

"It's too big to cover," Dizzy told me.

"You're so sweet. Let me tell you about my ass. It's a counterweight—think about it."

"That's disgusting." She spoke with her mouth full. I had to struggle to understand her. "Thank you."

"You don't seem so hurt to me," she said.

"I've got raccoon eyes, a nose as big as the Ritz, multiple stab wounds, and I'm out of it on heavy-duty drugs. That's not good enough?"

"You only have two cuts. That's not multiple."

"Sure it is. More than one is multiple."

"No, more than two."

I just stared at her. I couldn't believe Dizzy was arguing about something so petty.

She finished her tangerine, foraged again, and began to peel a banana once she resumed sitting. "Anyway," she continued, "I still don't understand why Arundel was trying to kill me."

"I don't think he was."

"Wasn't he the one behind the tree that night?"

"Probably not. Say listen, I forgot about those cops following you and Arundel. He didn't kill them, did he?"

"No. He conked them on the head or something. They're all right."

Just then Matthew Ferguson strode through the doorway, spied Dizzy, and halted. He wore green cowboy boots that clomped on the hard floor.

"I'm sorry. I didn't know you had company," he apologized.

"No, no. Come on in," I replied. "Dizzy, this is the guru with a regular name—Matthew Ferguson."

"Hi," she greeted, standing to shake his hand. "I've heard of you."

"Hi right back at you," Ferguson responded. "I've heard of you too. My TV tells me that you're a rock-climbing savior who might even play herself in an upcoming blockbuster TV movie. Is that right?"

She glanced at me sheepishly as she sat down. "Well, I might. I've been playing myself for years now, so I've got the most experience."

Ferguson stood beside the bed, watching both of us as she spoke. He wore a pleated yellow Mexican shirt and white cotton pants. He reminded me of a taller, more Anglo Tijuana pimp.

"How's the patient?" he asked me.

"I could be worse."

"That goes without saying. I could poke you in the eye, for example."

Dizzy glared at him. "You better be joking."

He smiled beatifically. "I'm a guru. We never say anything serious—just all this life and death crap."

She wasn't sure how to react, but I was beginning to appreciate the man. He consistently defied my expectations of how a spiritual leader should act, which I found refreshing.

"I hurt a lot," I complained.

"Physically?" Ferguson asked.

"Yes, of course."

"That's terrific. Physical pain is so much easier to bear than the other varieties."

"I guess you're right."

"I don't agree," Dizzy protested. "I think it can be

the worst thing that's ever happened to someone."

"What is suffering?" Ferguson replied. "No—don't answer. I will. Suffering is usually resistance to pain or discomfort—what we feel when we refuse to experience a sensation exactly as it is. Pain is just pain."

"Look," Dizzy began in an aggressive tone of voice, "why don't you keep your philosophy to yourself? Nobody asked you."

"I asked me. Don't you remember?" he replied cheerily.

"That doesn't count."

"Why not?"

"It's obvious."

"Not to me," he told her.

"Hey," I interrupted. "Visit me. This is boring."

"Okay," Ferguson agreed. "So, Tom. How does it feel to have killed someone?"

Dizzy jumped in again. "What kind of a question is that?"

"I think 'incisive' would be an accurate description," he replied.

"I think 'horseshit' fits better," she told him. "Tom's a mess. He doesn't need guilt thrown at him on top of all the rest."

I decided to answer. "I don't feel guilty. It really was him or me. In fact, I don't feel much of anything about it. I guess it'll hit me later."

"You just rest," Dizzy suggested, glaring at Ferguson.

"Isn't this hostility interesting?" he confided to me. "I think I know what it's about, too."

"What?" I asked.

Dizzy continued her withering stare; if anything, it

was even more fractious now.

"I think that a deeper part of her knows she and I are enemies," he answered.

"Enemies?" I echoed.

"Yes. Perhaps it's time to bring things out into the open. Dizzy?"

"What? What do you want now?"

"What name have you used most of your life—when you were growing up, in school and the like?"

She cocked her head, puzzled. "My middle name—Lucy."

"And what's your last name?"

"Farr. Why do you want to know?"

"Lucy Farr," he mused. As he continued to speak, he lifted his yellow shirt and pulled an enormous bowie knife out of a leather scabbard that was strapped to his ribcage. "Say it fast and it sounds just like Lucifer, doesn't it?" He pointed the knife at me, and Credula's voice issued from Ferguson's mouth. "Tom knows what this means. He has chosen to side with you and your kind."

I was too shocked and terrified to react. Dizzy stood up, but Credula waggled the huge blade in her direction and she froze in place.

"Oh yes," the entity continued. "I still live. Did you think I did all my work through George? That killing him would kill me?"

I nodded dumbly. The back of my mouth was awash in bile; the front was bone dry. I tried to move. I couldn't. My bad leg was a dead weight, anchoring me to the bed.

"I am not alive," Credula continued. "I cannot die. I occupy an office—a role—not a physical space." He kept the weapon trained on Dizzy. "Are you ready to die, demon?"

At this point, something gave way inside me. I can't explain it and it didn't match anything I'd ever read about, but it was definitely some kind of altered state. For one thing, everything began moving in slow motion—as though Credula and Dizzy were underwater. Also, instead of normal sounds, I only heard a high-pitched tone—sort of like a tuning fork, but less pure. I wasn't focused on all this; it was just the way I witnessed what came next.

Credula slowly inched forward, holding the outsized blade low and in front of him. Dizzy reached down to her ankle and produced a throwing knife not unlike Arundel's. I was transfixed—a statue watching a film unfold on a screen. I saw Dizzy's mouth move in slow motion, yet I heard nothing but the constant tone. I tried to move, and now I couldn't even swallow or blink. I tried to think, and nothing happened.

Credula lunged forward, and Dizzy danced away. With time slowed down, there was an awful grace to their movements—a defiance of physics that was both gloriously transcendent and horrifically primal.

Once more, he stabbed forward, and once more the Black woman eluded him. This time, as she moved, she raised her much smaller knife and cocked it for throwing alongside her head.

Credula immediately charged her. Would she have time to throw? Did she even know how to?

There was nothing but time. The scene slowed down even more—was it me?—was it them?—and Dizzy's arm crept forward. Just before Credula reached her, the bowie knife extended, she released her blade and dove sideways. The knife was airborne for an eternity. As I watched, I gradually became aware of a feeling that wasn't an emotion so much as a visceral intuition. It was a sense of momentousness and profundity that I realized had been residing in me somewhere but was only now making itself known to the whole of me. Whether that knife struck its target or not Mattered with a capital M. That I knew.

So I waited. And watched. And waited.

Finally, the knife reached its destination, embedding itself in Credula's belly.

Time suddenly resumed its normal pace, and what I observed next happened almost too fast to truly register.

Credula dropped to his knees, and his bowie knife fell with a loud clatter onto the white linoleum floor. Dizzy scrambled and scooped it up, holding the heavy blade in two hands as she knelt in front of the stricken man. With a fast, powerful thrust, she sank the ten inches of steel deep into his gut beside the smaller knife. Then she ripped upward, and blood and gore cascaded out of the gaping wound.

I couldn't believe my eyes. What was going on?

Ferguson crumpled backward onto the floor, and Dizzy maintained her grip on the knife, which slid out of his lifeless torso dripping blood and God knows what. Then she calmly rose, turned, and began to approach me, the knife held high.

"Your turn," she announced.

I tried to shout, but no sound came. I tried to move again, but I was still.

Suddenly I saw Dizzy for who she really was. Horned, fanged, grossly misshapen, the demon she was reached forward with the blade.

I rose off the bed into the air. My heart was suddenly

a pure white light, and it carried me up and over the demon. As Dizzy whirled and snarled, energy flooded through me and the high-pitched tone returned—only ten times louder this time.

I knew now that Arundel had been right about everything, and also that the lightness of my true being was an inexorable force that no entity could withstand. I had lived only to fight this fight. Tom Dashiel was no more. An archangel had claimed his birthright.

"Go," I commanded. "Return to the void from whence thou camest." My lilting voice was the same pitch as the ubiquitous tone I'd been hearing.

"Fuck you," the demon growled, kicking Ferguson's body to one side and dragging itself forward.

The creature was a hideous amalgamation of raw tissue and spare parts, oozing pus from multitudinous sores, and blood from every natural orifice.

Since it was my nature, I loved the demon. I was Love. Love was both my process and my content. I knew that Love, Beauty, and Truth were all reflections of the same phenomenon—the perfect core reality that comprised everything—even the demon. Its very ugliness was perfect. Just as I was Love, it was itself— exactly the way it should be—hideous. The problem was that the demon was trespassing in a realm in which it had no legitimate business.

Quicker than I could react, the creature flung the huge weapon at me, which passed through the white light I had become and sank into the wall behind me. I reached back and willed it into my hand. As the demon cowered and backed away, I apologized to Dizzy. Then I began stabbing what had once been her body.

When the police arrived, I was still stabbing. Over and over, I stabbed. Over and over and over.

Chapter 18

Why did it happen the way it did? Let's just say that everything happened so that this perfect moment right now could be just the way it is. Do you understand? It doesn't matter why penguins give each other rocks. It doesn't matter who died or that I am where I am now. The realm of cause and effect and logic is only meaningful in terms of how it serves the deeper purposes of the cosmos. And these purposes I cannot reveal. Not yet.

The police and the judicial system, of course, operate within certain parameters and therefore can only recognize limited versions of the truth. Not only couldn't they comprehend the basic principles that guided me in my actions, they couldn't even assemble the physical evidence accurately.

So I was arrested and tried for both killings at the hospital, as though a man one day out of intensive care could've managed all that. It was ludicrous, really. Some of the so-called evidence insulted the intelligence of everyone concerned. I guess man's need to generate a sense of closure is more urgent than his quest for the what-isness of a given situation.

I've been in Napa State Hospital for about three months now, and my wounds have long since healed. I think of this place as a high-security warehouse to store people who have been deemed too dangerous to be allowed anywhere else. True, there are criminally insane inmates here, but I've also met three other angels and a man who can make himself invisible. Obviously, if you're beyond physical law, you threaten the power structure. And I for one know firsthand just what happens to serious threats to the cozy prevailing paradigm. We're locked away where our existence needn't be acknowledged, and we're kept doped up on old-fashioned antipsychotics to render us more manageable. Zombies need fewer keepers, which makes the whole farce cheaper too.

Fortunately, I've developed several successful strategies to avoid ingesting my so-called medications. By and large, they monitor us by observing our behavior, so if I imitate the characteristic Thorazine listlessness of the others, they assume I swallowed. No one in an asylum could control himself, after all. Sometimes the ignorant assumptions of the powers that be can be subverted to work for you.

Yesterday afternoon, they decided to let me receive my first visitor. With no advance notice, I was informed by a fat orderly that a young lady was waiting for me in another wing of the hospital. My escort waddled behind me, occasionally transmitting directions by tapping me on the shoulder as we navigated our way through a maze of long hallways. I shuffled convincingly and vacuously, watching my feet as if they were an award-winning film—perhaps a documentary on why anti-psychotics aren't the optimal performance-enhancing drugs for Olympic athletes.

Eventually, we reached a lovely glassed-in courtyard, which was monitored by two nasty-looking, baton-wielding guards. Looking past them, I spotted my visitor sitting in the sun on a lacquered wooden bench beside two potted ferns.

Zig-Zag wore her usual overalls and also sported a red baseball cap, which gleamed in the bright sunlight as if it were brand new. She was so small I wanted to cry, but then I was struck by her beauty, so I smiled.

When I'd maneuvered myself closer to where she waited, she smiled back uncertainly. I lowered myself next to her, leaving the kind of space between us that someone needed when she thought she was sharing a bench with an insane killer.

"How's it going?" Zig-Zag asked, her shaky voice betraying her fear.

"It's very dull here, actually. But I'm fine. I really appreciate your coming." I spoke calmly and soothingly.

"I wasn't sure I wanted to, but now that I'm here, I'm glad I did." She managed another small, slightly more authentic smile.

"I know it's scary to visit someplace like this. I did it once for my job."

"It's ironic, isn't it?" she offered.

"Yes. But you know, they have a whole ward of ex-therapists," I told her.

"Really?"

"No, not really. That was just what we therapists call an icebreaker."

"We other people call it that too." She folded her hands together and glanced down. She was working herself up to something. "Tom? Can I ask you something?"

"Go ahead." So far I was pleased with my I'm-still-just-regular-old-Tom act.

"Do you understand you're crazy? That you killed

George and Ferguson and Dizzy because you're crazy?"

"First of all. I'm not crazy. I've been through some severe trauma, and I'm not the same man you met that day in my office, but I'm not crazy. Secondly, I didn't understand who George really was, so I foolishly resisted him, which eventually led to my defending myself when he attacked me. That was wrong, and I admit it. But Dizzy killed Ferguson. And when I killed Dizzy, she was already dead."

"That doesn't make sense. Don't you see?" She waved her arms as she raised her voice, which attracted the attention of the nearest guard. Surely this mercenary wannabe didn't subdue visitors if they became too rowdy?

"It's just hard to explain," I replied, waving to the guard, who sat back down on his plastic chair in the nearby hallway.

Suddenly, deep inside me, something gave way again, and I was shunted to the side of myself. I could see and hear but it was as though it were happening at a great distance. I couldn't seem to do or say anything. My initiative had been completely replaced by a radical form of passivity. And I was calm. You would've thought I'd be upset or even panicked, but I wasn't. There was a sense of rightness to the experience—that it was natural and appropriate.

Then my mouth opened and Credula spoke.

"Listen carefully, Zig-Zag. I am the same entity that worked through George. I am not Tom. My name is Credula."

"This is really crazy. Can't you hear yourself?" She scuttled away on the bench and held her hands up.

I could. But Credula continued. "Tom is now an

angel. He has made the transition from the physical to the subtle world which is also required of you. George spoke truly to you. You are an angel, and you are needed."

"Stop it, Tom. This is giving me the creeps." She stood, shuddered, and backed away a step.

I remembered what it had felt like to first hear that eerie, inhuman voice. Hearing it now was different. We were members of the same team, and I welcomed him—it—in my head or wherever it was.

"You must fulfill your destiny," Credula told her. "You must become who you are."

"I'm getting out of here," she announced, turning and sprinting away.

Credula was gone then, and I resumed control of my body. "Wait," I called.

The guard glared at me, daring me to chase her and get my ass kicked. I remained seated on the wooden bench and watched her run. Just before she turned a corner and passed out of sight, I saw golden wings sprout from her back and soar over her small, slim body. She was going to be a hell of an angel one of these days.

****

I haven't seen—felt?—Credula again, but it doesn't matter. The important thing is that I don't try to reduce or compress myself in order to fit back into the Tom Dashiel husk that I once inhabited in ignorance.

This is vital. I must be ready when the change time comes. I yearn for the moment when the light will once again carry me airborne. I yearn for the total transformation of our depraved world.

I know who I am.

I know what I know.
I have seen the demon leave the body.

Chapter 19

I woke up at the foot of a limestone cliff, completely bewildered. Where was the institution, the guards? How did I come to be outdoors, somewhere in the woods? Had I blacked out, escaped—was I dreaming? Even with everything else that had happened—or had seemed to happen?—I felt the most lost, the most thoroughly confused at that moment.

Then Dizzy's voice cut through the internal fog. She was dead, I knew, but from somewhere up above me, I distinctly heard her call, "Tom! I don't know if you can hear me or not, but I'll be back soon with help. Hang on!"

I glanced up, my head throbbing with nauseating pain. The rock wall that loomed ahead of me was familiar now. I was back in Fall Creek behind the lime kilns, and suddenly the true memories flooded in.

We had decided to climb our way out—both of us—and I had fallen. Everything else I thought I'd experienced had been generated by my subliminal mind while I'd been unconscious. I'd read of such phenomena, usually in conjunction with illegal drug use, but the textbook descriptions of the experience in no way captured its amazing verisimilitude—the details, the emotional textures, the sense of tangible reality. Consequently, the process of reawakening evoked a surreal disorientation and a momentous sense of loss, even as I knew that Arundel was probably stalking me and might stumble onto me momentarily.

All the feelings, all the sensory input, all the insights and realizations that accompanied my unconscious version of future events—all of this had been instantly transformed, violently yanked from the "it happened" category and tossed into a new "who knows what it means?" circular file. For that matter, if the dream/vision had fooled me so thoroughly, how could I be certain that what I believed to be my current waking reality was authentic? What was actually happening? Was it another convincing dream? Could I trust myself to know—or even find out?

I had to admit that being handed the opportunity to create a new outcome that didn't entail additional murders or a permanent stay in the Napa State Hospital was appealing. On the other hand, I'd survived the fabricated account, more or less. Was I about to die in this one?

"Tom!" Arundel's professor voice bellowed. "Don't be frightened. It's me."

I struggled to my knees, neither of which was functioning properly, and tried to stand. Dizziness and pain pitched me to the rocky ground, where I broke my fall, and possibly my wrist, with a spastic flounce of my left arm.

"I saw you fall," Arundel called from slightly closer. "I only want to help."

Using my good arm, I levered myself onto my back and wriggled toward a grove of acacia trees. If I found a good hiding place, perhaps Dizzy would return with help before he discovered me. I felt blood drip down from the back of my head onto my neck.

This thought triggered an episode of potent déjà vu, and I remembered hiding hadn't worked last time. Should I try something else? Wait a minute, I told myself, there wasn't any last time. I transferred my energy into gathering good-sized rocks, filling my pockets with the only available weapons.

"Ah, there you are," Arundel announced, stepping into the small clearing where I lay. "Are you badly hurt?"

"Yes." My voice was hoarse and shaky.

"Is there anything I can do?" he asked as he strode forward in his ridiculous camouflage outfit.

"Go away," I told him. "Go shopping for clothes." Talking made my head pound more.

"I can't do that, Tom," he replied. "We have something we need to discuss, don't we?"

I managed to sit up, which gave me the capacity to hurl my rocks if I needed to.

Arundel squatted a few feet away, and then a ripple spread across his large pink face, beginning at his chin and working its way up. The new demeanor wasn't Credula's or anyone else's I recognized. Arundel was gone, though. That was clear.

"Hello, Tom," a low smooth voice began. "My name isn't important. What you need to know is that I am the being who acts as the gatekeeper between this world and that which transcends it. As such I hold a meta-perspective in relation to George, and I have consulted others who have access to these higher levels as well. We've arrived at a compromise."

"A compromise?" It was difficult to assimilate any of this.

"Yes. Although the timing involved here is delicate, we are willing to accommodate a schedule change, which will give you more time to accustom yourself to your role. You are simply too important to this operation to squander needlessly."

"What about Credula?"

"I've already spoken with him—or should I say it?—and he is cooperative. You must understand that Credula was constructed to perform required tasks—no more and no less. He has no free will. In that sense, he is neither a person nor a personality."

"And that's a good thing? Someone did this on purpose?"

"Oh, yes. We could never let a human soul kill on our behalf. The karmic retribution would constitute too great a burden."

"Oh."

"Individuals with multiple personalities are in a holy state. Their alters perform vital spiritual tasks for the good of all, although they are usually not aware of this."

My mind was blank, and I simply stared dumbly at Arundel/Whoever. His features implied kindness and warmth, especially his eyes, yet something behind them revealed an unyielding will. It was as if he was one sort of being up to a particular threshold, and then someone much tougher past it.

"True compassion is utterly ruthless," he told me as if he had read my thoughts. "It's 'tough love' times infinity."

"That's counterintuitive," I managed to reply.

"Intuition is capable of evolution. If you become mired in the as-is Tom Dashiel mode, nothing beyond your current understanding will ever make sense to you. That would be a tragedy."

"What's so special about me?"

He smiled a gentle smile. "Right now, nothing. I confess I expected more. However, when you transform, all the qualities of an angel will begin to take root in the fertile manure that sits before me."

"Thanks a lot." I paused and remembered how it felt in my reverie to become angelic. As I formed a question, the entity in Arundel anticipated me again.

"It will not be exactly as you have imagined it," he told me. "Now I must go. George's body will be in hiding for a time, and you will be on your own. Live your life, and do what you are drawn to do. Even in the matter of the life or death of a species, an attachment to outcome is unhealthy. Que sera, sera. Adieu."

"Wait a minute," I tried, but he was already three steps gone. He moved with a casual agility that Arundel himself had never demonstrated.

I lay down again and waited to be rescued, which was about as energetic an activity as I was capable of mustering. I knew I needed to stay alert and not descend into an unconscious state again. I might not wake up this time.

The recent vision/dream returned to the foreground of my consciousness, shouldering aside the new being's information, as well as my pain.

Despite the trauma of the fictional storyline, I was struck again by the lifelike quality of the experience; it had been truly astounding. Except for the initial sensation of being switched off and on, the experience had consistently generated the trappings of reality. The images were just as intense, the colors as bright, and the emotions as deep. This compelling montage, in turn, generated impressions and moods in the same manner that waking life did. Once again, I had to marvel at the sheer inventiveness of the human psyche, much as I had upon first confronting multiple personality disorder.

My head was killing me, but I continued to keep my mind active. I decided to explore what the alternate experience might mean. I asked myself what I could learn from this message from my subconscious? I sometimes interpreted dreams for my clients, or at least steered them toward their own meaning. Could I manage something like that in my current state? I decided to try. What else was there to do at that moment?

Clearly, unconscious fears—my worst fears—were driving the plot of my dream. In the real world, I hadn't yet conjured a truly worst-case scenario—where all the weirdness might end up. A deep part of my psyche decided to enact it for me, revealing what I'd been repressing—stark terror. No, horror. The dream was like a horror film. Even the scene in the hospital for the criminally insane represented a hellacious turn of events. I was mad—floridly psychotic—which was a fear I was in touch with—up to a point. But Credula lived in me? And I ended up believing all the apocalyptic nonsense I spouted in the dream? My subconscious had shifted into overdrive to come up with all of that. I guess I needed a strong jolt to wake up to how deeply I'd been affected by events.

I shuddered as I lay on the rocky ground. For a moment, my physical pain was completely replaced by the flood of fear that raced through me. Then, just as suddenly, the terror and disorientation disappeared. My mind had shut down to protect me. The same subconscious that had produced the dream now protected me from it.

Gradually, my thoughts became more stuporous

until I couldn't focus on anything beyond my physical pain. By the time Dizzy arrived with a park ranger, I was basically an inert, bloody mess, but I was still awake. In a way, it was a relief not to be able to think, but twenty minutes later, when the ambulance guys and the police hiked in, I was thoroughly ready to be hauled off to anywhere that provided major painkillers.

They loaded me onto a stretcher while I told the deputy what had happened to me in general terms. One ambulance guy complained that I was so heavy, it was as if I had rocks in my pocket, which, of course, I still did.

The other one said, "This guy doesn't need rocks to be a motherfucker of a load."

I couldn't argue with either of these assessments. He also added that judging by my pupils and reflexes, he thought I'd been dosed with a hypnogogic drug, which would explain a lot. He told me a concussion alone was unlikely to generate such a vivid dream when I related what I'd endured.

With every shift or jounce on the trail or in the crowded ambulance, my head hurt like hell. I remembered reading about someone who'd suddenly dropped dead two days after a seemingly minor skull injury. I may have weathered Arundel for now, but my survival was still in question, and I was scared.

Chapter 20

Since I didn't pass out again, I was all too present for every bit of the painful examination, wound cleaning, stitching, and bandaging procedures. My doctor was young, and his bedside manner needed work. Mostly he discussed his recent trip to Bali, with particular emphasis on his snorkeling experiences. At one point, a different deputy sauntered into the emergency room cubicle to tell me that Arundel had gotten away and the surveillance cops had been attacked but were okay. For these two minutes, at least, I was able to distract myself from the pain.

My wrist wasn't broken—just sprained—but my right knee—what I thought of as my "good" knee—would probably require surgery at some point. The concussion I'd endured prompted the snorkel-crazed doctor to remand me to an overnight hospital stay for observation. A blood test confirmed I had DMT and some other unidentifiable drug in my system.

"I certainly wouldn't try to rock climb with that amount of hallucinogenic in me," the doctor said. "And it's no wonder your dream felt so real. The combination of head injury and drugs scrambled you so much you could've died. You're lucky, my friend."

"I didn't take any pills or anything," I told him.

"I'm not saying you did, although most addicts would deny it just the way you are. It could've been delivered by someone slipping the drugs into a drink, or even delivered as an aerosol. I've seen this before—as a date rape drug."

"Well, at least I was spared that."

My semiprivate room contained an unpleasant surprise in addition to the usual negatives—fluorescent lighting, sterile decor, antiseptic smell, etc. The unpleasant surprise was named Jack.

Jack was a twenty-eight-year-old patient on a hunger strike for animal rights. He was facing imminent kidney failure, and a court had ordered his hospitalization to ensure he received intravenous fluids. Physically, my roommate was a stick insect, with bones protruding where I hadn't known there were bones. His deep-set dark eyes were surrounded by inky black circles, and his large nose jutted out defiantly as if to dissociate itself from the deteriorating body to which it was attached. Jack's long brown hair was his only non-moribund feature.

His voice was weak and soft, but Jack enjoyed using it. After a half hour of complaining about most everything, an hour treatise on his interdisciplinary major in college—the physics of climatology—and a recitation of his favorite poem, he decided to confide in me.

"This isn't really a protest," Jack told me.

"How's that?"

"I know they won't stop what they're doing because of me. The world doesn't work that way."

"Then what are you doing?" I asked.

"This is an elegant suicide—a way of creating meaning out of a meaningless life."

His explanation was obviously rehearsed, yet I

sensed that he hadn't previously told anyone. What was it about me? Did these people have radar? Was I wearing a sign or something?

"Why tell me?" I finally asked.

"Well, we're in the same boat," Jack answered.

"In the hospital, you mean?"

"Dying."

"I'm not dying."

"Sure you are. Denial is a crutch—toss it away."

"I mean I plan on dying eventually, and it's okay with me, but it's not likely to happen right this minute."

"Aren't you the head-injury guy?" he asked.

"Yes."

"Well?"

"Well what?" I was becoming quite annoyed.

"Serious head injuries are usually fatal," he told me.

"This isn't that serious."

"Sure it is. You're doomed."

"Jack?"

"Yes."

"Shut up."

"Okay."

And he did, too. For a while. Why he wasn't too depleted to talk was a mystery to me. Like an old man who'd given himself permission to say whatever the hell he pleased, Jack ranted relentlessly, only curbing himself when I directly ordered him to. At one point, I wondered if he wasn't part of an observation team—planted as a psychological stressor to test my responses. I decided doctors lacked the requisite imagination to concoct such an elaborate cruelty.

A nurse said I was allowed visitors, but I received none. I was quite disappointed. Where were the friends

I'd always intended to cultivate? Why hadn't Dizzy or Zig-Zag put in appearances? If I'd ever truly needed support—a boost from people close to me—it was now. I hurt and I stewed and I pondered while Jack droned on and on in the background. If I'd been dying, would I die alone, staring at a blank white ceiling while strangers wearing name tags scurried around my bed?

****

My apartment was no better. After the unpleasant night in the hospital, where I later discovered I wasn't allowed visitors, I expected to receive some sort of emotional nourishment from my return to my own space. At the least, I anticipated temporary relief from my bleak mood. A ticker-tape parade would've been fine too. All I encountered was more angst.

Of the five clients I'd stood up during my internment, only two even left messages on my machine to complain. The local newspaper ran a front-page story on me, but of the array of colleagues, friends, and family who surely must've heard or read about the incident by now, only three called—and one of them was a senile aunt who believed I was still five years old. She wanted to know what kind of toy to buy me so I'd feel like her itty-bitty honey-bunny again.

There's nothing like high drama to provide a new perspective on the mundane. My mundane was very mundane. Without the ongoing invasion of all the craziness, I basically ate, slept, read, walked, and saw clients. What kind of life was that? I chose it, I could see now, to try to guarantee nothing drastic could disrupt my supposed peace of mind, which I now perceived to be fear-based. Recent events certainly shattered the long-held myth that I could elude the intensity I feared. Why construct a boring life if it can't even keep you safe? All the tumultuousness—my head injury serving as the final straw—had cracked open the my-life-makes-sense façade. It didn't; it was that simple. I hardly had a life, let alone a sensible one.

So what did I need to do to get one? This was an approach I often employed with confused clients. On a process level, clearly, I needed to summon courage, break my patterns, and attempt something new. In terms of content, I was less sure. Should I actively seek friends, chase Dizzy, join a chess club, ascend to angelhood, or eat out more? I added warning or protecting other devil-named people, buying a sports car, online dating, volunteering at the homeless shelter, and flying to India.

My attraction or repulsion to all of these plans seemed to be based solely on how much they scared me. Thus, eating out was my favorite, followed by purchasing a sports car.

I was struck at this point by how unsophisticated my internal monologue had become. Where was the keen psychological analyst who had aided so many poor souls? Would I continue to uphold the rich Dashiel family tradition of living in my head—identifying myself as my thoughts? It wasn't necessarily my favorite piece of early conditioning, but the syndrome was a cornerstone to my self-esteem and my career.

The surreal feeling that had coalesced in me upon awakening from my dream/vision now returned. Once again I wasn't at all certain what was real, but this time in an internal sense. Was I who I thought I was? My identity now seemed to be an arbitrary scaffold that had been erected in front of God knows who or what. The metaphorical possibilities ranged from a substantial building to a vacant lot. My images of potential vacant lots varied a great deal; I imagined virgin grassland, sandlot baseball fields, and bombed-out rubble. The buildings, on the other hand, were configured in a mélange of styles, and included banks, houses, restaurants, and even public restrooms.

My few insights were like small, random holes in the scaffolding, enabling me to peer through and beyond, yet that uncharted territory ultimately devolved into nothing but a foggy blankness upon which I projected my theories. Perhaps that's who I am—a foggy blank guy. Whoopee.

Chapter 21

I drank myself to sleep that night—the first time in many years—and I woke up feeling as though I'd been beaten with a two-by-four. I was hesitant to brave even the anemic spray of my drought-conscious shower head.

Coffee helped, as did a liberal slathering of Bengay on my knees, wrist, shoulder, and ribs. I smelled like a colossal cough drop, but the chemical warmth was a blissful substitute for the jangling pain. I wished I could immerse my entire head in a bucket of Bengay, but I knew my scalp wound would scream at me. I settled for over-the-counter painkillers.

After an hour of daytime television, jabbing the remote channel changer every few seconds, the phone rang. An unfamiliar voice—growly and uneducated—asked if I was me. I wasn't sure anymore, but I decided to answer yes since I was, at least, probably more me than anyone else was.

"I've got your pal Desdemona. If you don't do exactly as I say, she's dead meat."

"Dead meat?"

"Fuckin' A."

I couldn't think of anything to say.

"Are you there?" he asked.

"Yes."

"So I'm gonna call back later and you're gonna do what I say—right?"

"Right. Except how do I know you really have her?" My brain was returning to active service.

"Hold on," the voice replied.

"This guy isn't George Arundel!" Dizzy blurted out before the phone was yanked from her.

"Satisfied?" the voice asked.

"It's her," I agreed.

He hung up.

Before I could work out any of the implications of the call or even how I felt, the phone rang again.

"Tom? It's George. Zig-Zag's friend is missing. She's frantic. We need your help." His voice actually conveyed emotion; he sounded scared.

"She's been kidnapped."

"By whom?"

"Not you, apparently."

"Not me?" Arundel was puzzled and a bit defensive.

"That's right. That's all I know. Instead of eight billion suspects, there's only seven billion nine hundred and ninety-nine million."

"This is terrible. Was there a ransom demand?" he asked.

"Why would there be? I don't have money."

"I do. Quite a lot. And Zee is like a daughter to me, so her friend has value to me, too."

"The guy said he'd call again later."

"What guy? The kidnapper called you?"

"Yes."

"Why?"

"I don't know. Maybe he couldn't get hold of you—you're on the lam, right? Anyway, I'd better get off the line and call the cops."

"No cops. We can't risk it."

"Wait a minute. What's this 'we' business?" I protested.

"We're in this together, Tom."

"No, we're not."

"We can't let a minor disagreement interfere with the welfare of our friends."

"A minor disagreement? Multiple murders? You think that killing people constitutes a 'minor disagreement,' George?"

"Well, I may or may not have actually killed anyone," he answered.

"What do you mean?"

"Exactly what I said. It's open to question."

"And what does that mean? I'm not in the mood for your games, Arundel."

"It's not a game, Tom, but I don't think arguing would serve either of us. Why don't we talk later, after you receive your next call from the kidnapper? In the meantime, please don't contact the authorities. You could be risking lives before you have all the facts in hand."

"I'll think about it," I answered, and said good-bye.

So there I was in my friendless apartment, still in a great deal of physical pain, with far more new information than I could readily assimilate. Would contacting the police really be dangerous? Should I stay home to receive the next call from the kidnapper? What would he want? Money from Arundel? And what was this business about maybe not killing people? Was George running another scam to manipulate me? What else could it be? As usual, throughout all the craziness, I was accumulating questions a lot faster than I was able to stumble onto answers.

I decided to eat. Then I decided to urinate. Then I scratched my leg. Then I ate again. As an overall strategy, this attention to the physical didn't accomplish much. Finally, I sat on the couch and pondered the situation in greater depth.

Not much of that session was worth reporting, but I did remember I'd promised the police that if Arundel called, I'd let them know. Also, while at the hospital, I'd vowed to myself that I'd only participate further in the whole scary mess in my capacity as a therapist. So how did I respond to rediscovering these pledges? I threw them out the window, plunked down on a kitchen chair, and called Matthew Ferguson.

At first, it was impossible to relinquish a powerful residual connotation of danger stemming from my memories of Ferguson from my vision. Gradually, though, after some preliminary chit-chat, I felt ready to trust him again and poured out a detailed update. His feedback seemed to confirm the wisdom of my decision to seek expert help.

"I'm glad I'm not you," he began, his speaking voice reminding me of his singing voice. "But let me ask you this. You think Arundel is a murderer?"

"Yes."

"Do you think he sincerely cares about the kidnapped woman's well-being?"

"In his own way, yes." I shifted my weight uncomfortably. Even sitting hurt.

"Do you have any idea who the kidnapper might be?"

"No. None at all."

"Do you trust the police?" he asked.

"Yes."

"Have you enjoyed your involvement in this affair?"

"Hell, no. It's been deeply disturbing, terrifying, and…well, sickening."

"Not your favorite feelings, huh?"

"Hardly."

"Well, here's another question," Ferguson announced. "This one might be a little harder to answer. Why are you here?"

"In Santa Cruz?"

"I'm a guru, not a travel agent, Tom. Why are you here on this planet, in that body?"

"Because that's the deal," I answered without much of thought.

"What deal?"

"I mean that's the way it works."

"How do you know?"

I sighed and fidgeted with my hands. "Because that's the way it is."

"How do you know?" he asked again.

"My senses, my brain…books."

"So the world is the way it seems to you?"

"Of course not. I'm not saying I've got everything figured out, but what else have I got to go by?" I was almost whining.

"That's a good question, but I'm going to sidestep it for the moment and ask you this. Why are things the way they are? For what purpose?"

"I don't know." I rose and crossed the room to my beloved recliner. The brief journey hurt. When comfort food wasn't immediately available, comfort seating would have to do.

"Guess," he prompted.

"Maybe there isn't a purpose. Maybe God likes

suffering. Maybe we're here to learn. Maybe it's all a big joke. I really don't know, and to tell you the truth, I'm getting tired of being interrogated." Perhaps I would've been more patient if my head and wrist weren't throbbing so much.

"Good," Ferguson responded. "Now pick one of those maybes—the one you believe the most."

"We're here to learn. That matches my life experience the closest, I guess." I felt calmer now that I was being directed instead of fielding repetitive questions.

"Okay, so what's the curriculum in your situation, and how can you best learn it? That becomes the key question here. Will your studies on the planet be best advanced by calling the police, working with Arundel, or what?"

"How can I know that?" I asked.

"Take your best guess again."

"It's complicated. Calling the cops supports what I've learned about boundaries and taking care of myself in the simple sense. But it doesn't break new ground or truly challenge me. Obviously, partnering up with a psychotic murderer represents the biggest challenge, but that doesn't mean it's necessarily the best thing to do. I know from my work that if people are presented with too great a challenge, their ultimate failure just reinforces their old patterns. You don't challenge the heavyweight boxing champion after you've only taken a few lessons. I don't know. Maybe it ought to be something I haven't thought of yet. Maybe that would be the most instructive."

"Okay, go ahead and create something from scratch," Ferguson suggested.

"Just like that?"

"Sure."

"Well, the first thing that comes to mind is doing both—contacting the police and working with Arundel. But I don't want to be around the guy. At this point I'm afraid he might decide to kill me. And I also don't want to jeopardize anyone else's life."

"So cross that one off."

"Right. Then there's tackling the case myself. I used to be a private investigator, you know."

"I didn't know. What a coincidence!"

"Was that sarcasm?"

Ferguson laughed. "Were you a gumshoe what was one of the gumshoes?" he asked in a heavy 1930s gangster accent.

"Huh?" I had absolutely no idea what that meant.

"Were you good at it?"

"Not particularly. I worked for my dad. But after all my training and experience as a therapist, I've got skills that should help me more now."

"Okay. You're in business. Get busy," he pronounced.

Chapter 22

When I was an investigator, my first step in a new case usually entailed basic online research. I stumbled to my couch, grabbed my laptop off my rattan coffee table, and hoisted it onto my lap. My head and my knee complained loudly at all this movement. I vowed to roost where I was for as long as I could.

I searched for the sort of information I would in a normal investigation—something I should've tried before. Where did Zig-Zag live? Were there any other Arundels—relatives—in the immediate area? Was there an organization listed under Krishnanda's name? I googled the crap out of everything I could think of.

The only new fact I unearthed—and it was hard to find—was that Zig-Zag lived at 207 Cayuga Street, so I hoisted myself up out of the soft cushion, gasped at the pain, and headed over there in my old Volvo. So much for my vow.

It was about six thirty in the evening, and the fog was just beginning to drift in. Cayuga was in the heart of the Seabright neighborhood, about a half mile from a small beach favored by dog lovers. Number 207 was a smallish mustard-yellow Victorian that could easily qualify as a handyman's special in a real estate ad. The paint was flaking off in stocking-like runs, revealing an earlier layer of a clashing color—lavender—and the wooden front steps looked weak with dry rot. The roof displayed three or four layers of gray composition tiles, providing an historical cross-section that reminded me of an archaeological dig, albeit upside-down.

The landscaping, on the other hand, was meticulous and colorful, with flowering shrubs, young trees, and several beds of ornamentals. Someone loved to garden even more than they hated to paint.

A slim young Latino man answered the paneled front door after some loud knocking. "Yeah?"

"Is Zig-Zag home?"

"No. I haven't seen her today."

"Do you mind if I come in and wait for her?" I asked. This was a ploy, of course, to gain access to the interior of the building, where I might discover something useful.

"Who are you? You don't look like any of her friends." He crossed his arms in front of his green T-shirt and glared defiantly. His efforts to appear fierce were unconvincing.

Just then the border collie from the bookstore trotted up from behind the young man and sniffed the cuff of my khaki pants. I recognized her by the diamond pattern on her chest. After a moment, she wagged her bushy tail and kind of yodeled at me. I was stunned.

"Oh, well. If Sadie knows you…." He stepped aside, and the dog and I wandered into the old-fashioned parlor, which was festooned with garlands of bananas hanging from the ceiling.

"We had a party last night," the youth told me. "I've gotta go, but make yourself at home. Zee won't be long if she left her dog here," he added before ambling up creaky stairs.

The bananas were the only evidence of

merrymaking. Otherwise, the high-ceilinged, sheet-rocked room was decorated in a decidedly spare fashion, with only two posters on the walls—satellite photographs of the Middle East—and a mishmash of threadbare furniture and even older lamps. Through an archway, a card table and three wooden folding chairs huddled in a formal dining room. The hallway to my right was completely bare, highlighting well-worn fir flooring.

Finally, I studied my furry hostess. Sadie sat up on her haunches in front of the overstuffed brown sofa on which I perched. She watched me at least as intently as I watched her. My thoughts, under control during my visual exploration of the room, were now a maelstrom.

"Are you a conspirator?" I finally asked.

She cocked her black and white head as if to say she'd gotten most of that, but what was that long word at the end?

I reached out and ruffled the fur on her chest. How could I be angry at such a cute dog? "They made you do it, didn't they?"

They? I rubbed Sadie's head and considered who "they" might be. Arundel and Zig-Zag were definitely in on it. Dizzy? Probably. The bookstore owner might've been hired too, along with the assortment of clients who had so obligingly presented their supposed synchronicities.

Was any part of it true? Was Arundel really a multiple? Were they only capitalizing on the serial murders or were they truly involved in them? Was anyone actually connected to Krishnanda? One of the detectives mentioned that Arundel belonged to a cult.

Wait a minute, I thought, that was in the dream. I

shook my head as if to empty it of the false reality I'd been saddled with. I wondered next if the kidnapping had been real? And why me? Better yet, why, period? What was the point of the hoax?

The scale was boggling, which suggested big money, but there was no obvious fortune to be made. So why bother with all the angels and demons?

I brainstormed possible explanations as I continued to scratch Sadie behind her ears and rub her chest. Her very pink tongue lolled out in canine ecstasy. Did they want to use me to establish an insanity defense for the murders? Worse yet, were they planning to frame me somehow? Did some cult leader order all this for his own twisted reasons? The dreamworld detective wasn't necessarily wrong. Was it a bet or a game between bored rich people? Could my vengeful ex-wife have concocted everything to drive me crazy? Was it all part of a broader conspiracy to discredit Christian dogma or psychotherapy? Maybe the murder victims were faking, too—paid off to disappear for a while. Then that meant the cops were in on it, too. No, I was going too far, I realized, and I decided to catalogue what I knew for sure.

A slew of people had been stabbed to death. I'd been jerked around by a talented cast of assholes. Sadie the dog enjoyed being rubbed. My head hurt. That was about it. It was a depressingly short list.

Sadie licked my hand—I'd stopped petting her— and I returned my attention to the banana-laden parlor. Her tongue was almost as scratchy as a cat's, and her brown eyes gleamed at me in silent connection. I liked her better as a regular dog than a retail clerk/mysterious guide. She was a very sweet creature.

I communed and ruminated while I waited for about

twenty minutes, approaching my feelings but backing off each time before truly reaching them. Then, just after I'd vowed to plunge in and see how I truly felt, a clear high-pitched woman's voice called from the front hallway. I hadn't heard the door open.

"Sarah? Sarah, honey, are you home? There are new developments with Dashiel."

"Come in!" I called.

"Thanks," the middle-aged woman acknowledged as she sidled through the doorway. "Oops," she added as soon as she spied me.

She was an older woman wearing a chic emerald-green pantsuit and a large straw hat, which she removed and held in front of her midsection as if it were a shield. She'd been in Dizzy's women's group, and now I recalled I'd seen her lurking outside the bookstore, as well.

"Sit," I commanded, withdrawing my hand from Sadie's neck ruff. The dog, who was sitting already, lay down in an effort to please. The woman plunked down in a navy-blue Goodwill loveseat across from me. Her movements were disciplined, as if she had been a gymnast or a diver.

"Tell me the truth, or I'm heading straight to the police," I told her.

She tilted her head up and gazed at the ceiling for a moment. Then, as she began speaking, she snapped her head down and stared me in the eye. "All right. I have no choice, do I? Here you go. We're all part of an improvisational acting troupe based in Seattle. Even Sadie here has performed in several movies. We were hired by somebody with more bucks than sense, I think, to do all we've been doing."

"Who?"

"I don't know. Only Tony—I mean George—has contact with him. I don't even know why we're doing it. But the money's good."

"Is Zig-Zag's real name Sarah?" I asked.

"Yes. I'm Jessica, by the way. Sorry for what we've put you through."

"It's a little late for that, isn't it?"

"I suppose so," she admitted.

I considered what she was telling me. It struck me that this so-called confession was being surrendered far too easily. I began investigating an hour ago, and now I knew everything?

"Why are you telling me all this?" I asked.

"You told me you'd go to the police."

"So? Why should that be a big deal to you? Where's the illegal part? Someone's pretending to be a client or a holy man's daughter? Something doesn't make sense here, unless you're leaving something out or lying outright. Murders, perhaps?"

"Oh, no. We didn't sign up for that. What kind of monsters do you think we are? I have had second thoughts about my role lately because of the murders, though."

"How's that?"

"I didn't realize at first that what we're doing might be mixed up with that. For all I know, I might be wanted by the police."

"You might be. Maybe we should go down to the station right now and find out."

"Maybe." Her face gave nothing away. She gazed at me evenly, her pale blue eyes holding steady for several seconds.

It was a classic match-up—an actor versus a therapist. One of us was trained to project fiction, while the other was trained to ferret out the underlying truth. I judged the confrontation to be a stand-off thus far.

"How do I know what you're saying now isn't bullshit, too?" I tried.

"Why should I lie?" She spread her arms out, and I was reminded of the time Arundel did the same. She looked as though she were showing me how long a fish she'd caught. Was this some acting trope for being honest?

"Why is anyone doing this?" I asked with heat. "That's what I want to know. Haven't you even wondered?"

"Of course."

"Then give me some guesses. You've had more time to think about it."

"Revenge, greed, guilt—I'm sure there's a primal emotion in this somewhere. Maybe you're due for an inheritance, and another relative is trying to drive you crazy. Or it could be a psychological experiment some rich buddy of yours is conducting."

"That's it? You don't have any better ideas than that?"

She shrugged. "I've been busy writing a play."

"I should be enraged," I told her. "I'm not, but I should be. You people have seriously disrupted my life. I could certainly sue you in civil court even if I couldn't press charges."

"Whatever you think you need to do…" Her blank expression was back. She looked like an Easter Island statue in a pantsuit.

"Is George—I mean Tony—really a multiple?"

"No."

"How about Dizzy? Is she for real?"

"An actress."

"I'm not sure I buy it," I responded, shaking my sore head. "How can people be so convincing without even having lines to study? I'm not an idiot, you know. I'm a professional who's studied behavior and personality."

"Maybe you wanted to be convinced," Jessica suggested. "Maybe you needed a little excitement in your life. Were you stuck in a rut? That can affect your judgment. And maybe you're a little full of yourself. Who said you were so sharp about people? Yourself?"

"I'll ask the questions here," I snapped, although she'd certainly struck a chord.

"Go ahead. It feels good to get all this off my chest."

Her expression was congruent with her words this time, but what did that mean? I was dealing with very talented people.

"What do you know about this supposed kidnapping?" I asked.

"What supposed kidnapping?"

"Dizzy—or whatever her name really is."

"My God! I don't know anything about it. It wasn't in the plan."

"So you're saying it's real?"

"No. I'm just saying I don't know anything about it. It's possible I'm out of the loop these days. Like I say, I'm working on a play. And I've played a minor role in all this—mostly working behind the scenes. But why would anyone kidnap her?"

I shrugged and continued my interrogation but got no closer to answering that question, or any of the other remaining unknowns. Finally, after a frustrating half hour, I petted Sadie good-bye and limped out. I could only sit around and wait for Zig-Zag for so long.

When was I going to find hard answers?

Chapter 23

So what was real and what wasn't? Back at my apartment, I pondered the question for longer than was probably healthy for someone who already spent too much time in his head. But what else could I do? There was no book to consult, no 800 number to call.

How could anyone function without a secure foundation of basic knowledge, I wondered? How did psychotics do it, for example? They invented their own, I realized—a personal reality that was easier for them to cope with than the consensus version. What were other strategies?

I could give up. I could drive to the airport, fly to Hawaii, and lie on a beach until everybody else lost interest. For a moment, I was tempted. Then I remembered what Ferguson had drawn out of me. Where was the lesson in running? Was my current psychological status so insecure that I had to jet overseas to protect it?

I could also fight fire with fire and launch a counterattack of disinformation or manipulation. This wasn't an appealing notion at all. I knew you couldn't beat people playing their game with their rules. I would be a beginner engaged in a process that disgusted me. No, thanks.

Before I'd generated any more stupid ideas, the phone rang. I took the call in my bedroom, lying sideways on my king-size bed. It was Arundel.

"Hi, Tony," I greeted him.

"Who?"

"Tony. You know—your real name." I wasn't at all sure that Jessica had been telling the truth, but an aggressive approach seemed worth trying.

"I don't remember a Tony," Arundel answered. "And anyway, why would one of my names be more real than another?"

"Look, the cat's out of the bag. You can drop the act."

"Any more cliches up your sleeve, Tom? That's quite a barrage."

"Are you denying it, then?"

"Denying what?"

"That you're an actor named Tony."

He laughed. "Wherever did you hear that?"

"From Jessica—one of the actors in your troupe. I met her over at Sarah's house."

"Who?"

"Sarah—Zig-Zag."

"Tom, I'm getting worried about you. None of this makes much sense."

Clearly, I was getting nowhere. Either Jessica had fabricated her tale or Arundel was truly an imperturbable stage veteran. In either case, I might as well employ another conversational strategy.

"So what can I do for you?" I asked.

"What do you mean?"

"You called me. What do you want?"

"I'd like to discuss our collaboration vis-a-vis the kidnapping."

"Forget it. I'm not even sure there is a kidnapping."

"Why? Did you receive another phone call?"

"No. I just think it's possible the whole thing's a hoax."

"We can't take that chance," Arundel admonished.

"There's that 'we' again." My teeth clenched. Whether he was acting or not, the man was a relentless farthead. Why didn't he just go hide somewhere like a normal fugitive?

"I have business," he told me. "I'll call again." Then he hung up.

I was truly aggravated now. Before I knew what I was doing, I'd thrown my phone across the room, where it knocked over a tall ceramic lamp. As I limped over to pick it up the pieces, I stubbed my toe against the leg of an oak end table. Naturally, I upended it, scattering books, socks, and pistachio nut husks across the blue Mexican throw rug. Next I kicked the nearest object, a philodendron in a green plastic bucket, sending a jolt of pain to my knee. The tall plant tipped over, spilling black potting soil everywhere and damaging numerous leaves that were dry and stiff from weeks of neglect. My knee throbbed mercilessly now, and my head wound screamed.

My long-delayed rage subsided for a moment, and I immediately regretted the damage I'd wreaked on the hapless plant. Apparently, inanimate objects had it coming, though, because a moment later in the living room, I picked up a book of waterfall photographs and hurled it at a wall poster. Anger was in charge again. It felt great.

Therapists don't do things like this. We handle our emotions maturely, I told myself, right before battering the toaster to the floor. Then I lay on my stomach in the hallway, my face buried in the itchy acrylic carpet fibers. As uncomfortable as I was, as much as all my wounds and bruises complained, I wished I never had to get up. I wanted to merge with the carpet—become inanimate—stop thinking and feeling. Nobody lied to carpets. Nobody expected carpets to help them. Carpets had it easy.

****

When I woke up the next morning, I knew something I hadn't known the day before. The old woman was lying about the acting troupe business. In a dream, I'd been reading a novel that had been popular locally a couple of years ago. In *The Monterey Murders*, the main character is tricked by actors into accepting a host of weird spiritual phenomena and is then framed for several murders by a crooked minister. In my gut, I knew the woman had plagiarized this plot in her effort to neutralize my unexpected confrontation. Looking for a quick explanation? How about actors perpetrating a hoax? It's a cheesy, facile plot device. I wished I'd been more lucid the day before. I could've pursued a few more lines of inquiry if I hadn't become sidetracked by the implications of Jessica's story.

For a moment, I was reminded of my ex-wife, who had been fond of these types of mind games. For years, Susan's adept manipulations had kept me guessing, nearly breaking me down before I'd finally become healthy enough to divorce her.

A shower and a huge breakfast helped rejuvenate me, and I found I was actually looking forward to resuming my sessions with my clients later that day. Then the phone rang again. I was becoming conditioned in Pavlovian fashion to hate hearing that sound. The damned thing always seemed to know just when I'd mustered a healthy attitude worth demolishing.

"Hello?" I said.

"This is the guy who said he'd call back. You know who I am?"

"Yeah. We have a mutual friend, right?"

"That's right. Although I'm worried about her."

"What do you want?" I was tired of verbal jousting. I knew I should be more emotional—care more—but even talking to a kidnapper felt mundane. Crisis inflation had rendered it low on the trauma totem pole.

"I want you to take back all that bullshit you told the police. That client of yours didn't kill anyone. I want him out of the goddamn spotlight."

"You want me to lie to the cops?"

"It ain't lying. The guy had nothing to do with the murders."

"He said he did."

"Shut up. Just shut up, asshole. You want to see your friend again?"

"Of course."

"Then quit giving me a hard time. Just call the cops and tell 'em you were wrong—or confused, maybe, 'cuz of the bump on the head. I don't care. That part's up to you. But make it convincing."

"How do you know Arundel didn't do it?" I asked, genuinely curious.

" 'Cuz I did it. And some other asshole is not gonna take the credit!"

"Oh."

"Be a good boy, Dashiel. Do what's right."

"You got it. As soon as we hang up, I'm back on the line to the cops."

So he hung up. I got on the phone to the police. I was hoping that Chief Fred, my important policeman buddy, would decide to handle my call personally. I even asked for him before I remembered that he'd been yet another character in my drug-induced dream. My name was becoming a passport to the stars, though, since I was connected to the real chief anyway.

"How are you feeling?" this gruff-voiced man named Gil Franklin asked.

"Shitty. Listen, I think I got a call from the killer."

I'd decided not to divulge the kidnapping angle since that might endanger the victims—if there really were any.

"He said your main suspect didn't do it—he did— and I think it's quite possible. He was convincing."

"Okay, here's how I want to deal with this. I'm gonna put a detective on, and he'll question you about the phone call from this new guy. When he's done, I'll review what he's got."

"Great. That's all I can ask."

"Actually, it's a lot more than you've got the right to ask. But we're pretty desperate, and you seem like a fairly reliable type. Do you remember talking to me at the hospital?"

"No, actually."

"I'm not surprised. They said you were coming down off something from before you got there, and you were on some heavy-duty painkillers. But I could tell you're a good man, Dashiel."

"Thanks."

"Wait a minute," the chief said hurriedly. "Why do you think this guy called *you*? Why didn't he call us?"

"I don't know. Maybe he saw my name in the

236

newspaper. Maybe he was afraid you'd trace the call."

"Yeah, maybe. There are way too many maybes in this case. All right, I'll be in touch. Stay on the line for Detective Gregory."

"Right."

The remainder of the call was a guided, methodical, redundant reporting of the facts, which I dressed up slightly to influence the police to cooperate with the kidnapper's demand. I enjoyed hanging up first when we were through.

Chapter 24

I'd never realized that listening to my clients' problems could be so soothing. Everything was straightforward—eating disorders, depression, anxiety. I knew all about these small inconveniences, and not only that, they weren't mine. Lost in the lives of others, I idled away the afternoon and early evening. Why had I ever thought my line of work was stressful?

On the way home, still limping slightly as I traversed downtown on foot, my temporary peace of mind was rudely shoved aside. I was abreast of the new movie theater, maneuvering between the two ticket lines, when I heard a loud flapping of wings immediately behind me. I ducked and whirled, startling a young family nearby, but I couldn't find the source. A few tentative steps farther, I heard it again, this time combined with a strange tingling in my shoulders and upper back. With a sense of dread, I twisted my neck and beheld—there was no other word for it—magnificent ghostly-white wings. They shimmered above my shoulders in the fading sunlight—of this world and some other, not quite opaque and not quite translucent. In a moment, they were gone, but I felt myself lifted up onto my toes and then returned to earth.

I was truly freaked out. I stumbled to a nearby wooden bench, and my face fell into my hands. Was this another drug-induced hallucination? If it wasn't, then either my unconscious had finally opted for full psychosis or Arundel was right about my angelic destiny. Both of these options remained unacceptable to me. There was a moment of sensing the proximity of darkness—an abyss—and then I began sobbing. I just couldn't handle it. My body began heaving and shaking as I pulled myself into a smaller and smaller ball. Within the cocoon of my fingers, my mouth grimaced to its limits with each racking sob. My nostrils streamed snot. My gut was a vortex of nausea.

I have no idea how long I suffered on the slatted bench before I felt an insistent tapping on my shoulder, just above where my left wing had been.

"Go away," I mewed.

"Some are called," a woman's silken voice told me.

My head snapped up; I'm sure I was a terrifying sight—tears and mucus liberally smeared over my nasty burn scars. The elderly woman in the white dress didn't flinch or hesitate.

"May I sit with you?" she asked.

I nodded raggedly before feeling overwhelmed and once again hiding my face in my lap.

"You're not going crazy. You're in the midst of a spiritual emergence."

"What?" I grunted.

"Everything's going to be all right. I have experience with this—I do it for a living, actually—and I can see that you are undergoing transformation, not an emotional breakdown."

"Angel?" I croaked.

She laughed. "I'm not an angel. I'm a transpersonal therapist."

"No. Me. Am I turning into an angel? I saw wings."

"Don't worry about that. You're not an angel, but when someone makes a great shift in their spiritual being, there's often some sort of symbolic representation in a vision. Have angels been important in your life lately?"

I nodded.

"You're moving beyond the literal world. Don't let your old, small mind limit your perceptions."

I sat up and examined this woman. She wasn't actually beautiful in the ordinary sense of the word. Her face was too round, and her eyes were too big. She must have been in her late seventies, and she looked all of it. Not only was her skin quite wrinkled, it was leathery and sun-damaged as well. Her smile was sweet but also slightly tentative—she wasn't completely confident she was doing the right thing by talking to me. She wore a white Mexican dress with purple embroidery at the shoulders and green running shoes.

Compassion was etched into her face, as well as a lightness—a very casual air—that I rarely saw in an intelligent adult. Obviously she cared, but my plight certainly hadn't ruined her day, either.

"How can you tell all this about me?" I finally asked.

"I can see your aura. It's quite striking. It's a mix of old and new." She smiled thoroughly.

Some of my despair slid off me. In its place was a freshness—a hint of a powerful new sense of seeing, hearing, and smelling. Seconds later, fear kicked in, and I began to shake again.

"It's okay to be afraid. There's a great deal to grow accustomed to. For a while, the intensity of your experience will be harrowing. Hang in there."

I straightened my posture, although I was still

240

quivering, and wiped my face on my shirt sleeve.

"Do you have a business card?" I asked. "I don't want to take up any more of your time out on the street."

She handed me a teal-colored card that introduced her as Aileen Van Der Voot. I reached into my back pocket and gave her one of my plain Jane cards.

"Tom Dashiel," she read. "I've heard of you. You take on the tough ones, don't you? Should we have our cards shake each other's hands or would you rather we did it ourselves?"

I stuck out my big mitt, and we shook. Her touch was electrifying—but somehow didn't sting.

"Thank you," I told her.

"I have to go now," she announced.

"Okay, bye."

"Good-bye, Tom. Remember what I said."

"Right," I answered woodenly.

After she left, I staggered home and immediately fell asleep. Trauma was tiring.

Chapter 25

I dreamt I was a hunting dog, totally immersed in the moment, reveling in my senses. I woke up to a knock on the door.

"Who is it?" I called from the bedroom doorway, rubbing my knee.

"Paper girl!"

The fellow that delivered my newspaper was in his sixties.

"Try again," I suggested.

"Pizza girl!"

"For breakfast?"

"Egg girl! Get your eggs here!"

I opened the door, and Dizzy beamed at me from my small front porch.

"My hero!" she proclaimed, offering me a bouquet of mixed flowers. "If it hadn't been for you, I guess I'd still be kidnapped."

I accepted the bundle of blue, red, yellow, and purple blooms, and I invited Dizzy in. She hugged the daylights out of me before skipping past. If you ever want to experience an intensely pleasurable few seconds, wait until you've made a big shift spiritually and then get hugged by an enthusiastic, shapely woman. It wasn't fireworks this time; I didn't need them. I was momentarily speechless.

"Nice place," she said. "Is this where you store the

recyclables?"

Numerous empty bottles and newspapers littered the living room. "This is the cleanest room," I told her. "The rest of the house isn't up to these strict standards." I limped stiffly into the kitchen with the flowers.

Dizzy plopped onto my sofa and hugged herself. "I don't recommend being kidnapped, by the way. It's not much fun at all."

"I'll keep that in mind," I told her, returning to the room, which I must admit could've benefitted from extensive tidying.

"Have you talked to Zig-Zag? She's been worried about you," I asked after I'd settled carefully into my well-worn armchair.

"Yeah, I did. She's fine. She's home sleeping."

"With Sadie?" I watched her reaction closely.

"Probably. You can't keep that dog off the bed— I've seen Zee try."

Zip. No hesitancy, no sign of distress, no nothing. That was interesting.

Dizzy was wearing black jeans and an orange T-shirt. She obviously hadn't showered since her ordeal. Her body odor was a combination of sheer rankness and something else that mildly aroused me.

"Tell me more about the kidnapping," I prompted. I didn't need to be thinking with my hormones.

She wrinkled her nose and squeezed her lips together for a moment. "We were somewhere near the ocean. Sometimes I could hear it. And twice a day a train went by—maybe a quarter of a mile away."

I nodded. That would be the cement plant freight that ran along the southern part of town. Combined with the coastal clue, that limited a search to about a three-mile corridor of beach houses and condominiums.

Dizzy continued. "The kidnapper had the worst breath I've ever smelled—I never saw his face—and he fed me hot dogs." She screwed up her features into a truly hideous grimace. "Ugh. Hot dogs! Can you imagine?"

I shook my head. "The cruelty of my fellow humans never fails to amaze me. Was there mustard?"

"Go ahead, laugh. The hot dogs were the worst part. Well, after the fear—I was terrified the whole time."

"How'd he grab you?"

"I was walking on the sidewalk near my house—kind of by the motel next to the taco bar?—and he jumped out of a junky old car wearing a ski mask, waving this huge gun. So I got in the car. From that point on, he kept me blindfolded."

"You're right. That doesn't sound fun at all."

"Uh-uh. I knew you'd think it was Arundel, by the way. That's why I said what I did over the phone."

"That was helpful." I leaned forward and smiled. "I'm glad you're safe."

"Me too. How have you been?"

"Confused, lousy, and in pain. But then last night I had a vision and a good cry, and a therapist told me I'd be okay, and now I am."

"Good deal."

"Have you been to the police?" I asked.

"First thing. The creep dumped me off at Lighthouse Field, and I walked downtown. I didn't tell them about the guy calling you, though, in case that would get you in trouble."

"Thanks."

"They'll probably call you anyway. They

remembered we knew each other from the Fall Creek mess. Listen, I've gotta run."

I stood. "Okay. Thanks for stopping by."

Another monster hug and a peck on the cheek and I was alone again. Alone and hungry.

This time my craving was for more than merely food. I wanted breakfast, but I also wanted contact, learning, love—all that my hermit-like existence had been denying me for so many years. I was both frightened and excited to realize the scope of my hunger. Whatever lid had been nailed on this box of yearnings had been completely pried off. I wanted growth, I wanted sharing—I wanted every one of the human elements absent from my isolated world. I had no idea how to get them, but I knew for certain that staying alone in my apartment wouldn't help. So I mustered myself, dressed, and walked to the Lincoln Street Cafe.

It was an expedition through a jungle of new stimuli. A black Lab barked and growled behind a rusty chain-link fence, noisy birds fought for space in a ripe date palm, the scorched smell of burnt rubber assailed my nose near a deserted street corner. These were so much more urgent and richer than I remembered. If my life consisted of nothing more than the mundane scenarios encountered on a walk, that would be enough.

Of course, life refused to limit itself to this circumscribed script. No sooner had I settled into enjoying the morning, than a new, twisted scenario greeted me at the cafe. My ex-wife Susan sat by herself in all her glory, and I didn't notice her until after I'd been seated two tables away.

She waved her beauty queen wave—I'd always hated that mannerism—and flashed her $20,000 dental work. My sensory acuity vanished; it was as if the world had faded to black and white.

"Susan," I acknowledged from my seat. "I thought you were in North Carolina."

She gestured to the chair across from her, and I dutifully carried my menu and battered bulk over.

"I'm just in town for a visit. How nice to run into you."

If there was ever a poster girl for incongruent speech and facial expression, Susan would be my pick. Her voice was honey; her eyes were loaded howitzers. As usual, when faced with her in the moment, I couldn't imagine why I'd ever been attracted to Susan. I never remembered the massive projection, fantasy, and self-conning that I'd inflicted on myself in my younger days.

"How have you been?" I asked.

"Fantastic. Never better. Jeff sold the company and then promptly dropped dead. You look like shit. Were you in a car wreck?"

"Something like that. I'm sorry about Jeff."

"I'm not. He was a treacherous son of a bitch. Worse than you."

Her glare would've frozen me fifteen years ago. Now I was almost amused. She was an absurd character—someone from a fifth-rate film noir. One second she was all smiles; a second later her mood might swing to its polar opposite, complete with violence.

Physically, Susan was too overweight to be starring in any stylish movies, and her tightly permed blonde hair framed a face that hadn't aged well. What had been cute at twenty-two was now grotesque at forty-four simply because it was essentially the same, reflecting no growth or personal evolution.

Mustering compassion for post-divorce Susan had always been a tough task for me. As I sat and realized the poisonous thought train rumbling through my head, I consciously strove to derail it.

"I guess you just haven't had much luck with marriage, but they say three's a charm. Maybe Mr. Right is going to be next."

"I think I'm going to become a lesbian, actually. Licking pussy is bound to be better than being shat on by macho assholes."

I'd reached the limit of my altruism. Without a word, I rose and walked out. She knew perfectly well how I felt about that kind of language. It was abuse—a subtle variety of violence—and I wasn't willing to subject myself to it. I heard her laughing as I reached the sidewalk.

Breakfast choice number two proved to be much more congenial, and I was pleased to see that the local newspaper carried a story detailing the authorities' search for a new suspect in the serial killings. I did spend most of the meal hiding behind my paper from an ex-client, though, who I assumed would be uncomfortable encountering me since she'd stiffed me for $120. Instead, she stopped by my table and whipped out her checkbook. Life could be good.

Chapter 26

I called Aileen Van Der Voot between clients and made an appointment for the next morning. For once, the rest of the day and evening were relatively uneventful. I watched an old Peter Sellers film on television and caught up on my professional reading. Well, it was just *Psychology Now!*, but it was better than nothing. Someday I might need to know why men who don't love enough often raise sons who love too much.

Aileen's office was very different from mine. For one thing, there were no chairs, tables, or desks—just a light green carpet, large yellow and black Balinese pillows, and a series of black and white photographs of an old man's hands.

"My father," she told me, noticing my curiosity.

"Was there something special about his hands?" I asked.

"No. I've just always been fascinated by hands. You have interesting hands, don't you?"

"Do I? Other than them being rather large, I've never thought so."

She took one of my hands in hers. We were standing just inside the doorway. "Oh, I do. They're such a provocative combination of brawn and subtlety—like a boxer in grad school or a physicist farmer."

"Einstein in overalls. That's not exactly my self-image." I was flustered by my proximity to this older woman, as well as by her words, which could be construed as flirtatious, despite her age. Her tone of voice, though, was matter-of-fact, and her body language further proclaimed her neutrality. It wasn't her fault that the scent of sandalwood turned me on, after all. And if she'd been wearing a conservative suit instead of a diaphanous teal dress, I might not have fantasized at all.

"Do you feel like an experiment gone awry or a small person lost in a big body?" Aileen asked.

"Both. Exactly. How in the world could you know that?" I painfully settled down onto a pillow and stretched out my legs. Her insights had blasted the licentiousness out of me. Perhaps she'd intended just that.

"The way you hold yourself—your posture now and the way you sat on the bench downtown. All that's very revealing if you're trained to pay attention on that level and trust your intuition. Now how can I help you?" She gracefully lowered herself onto a pillow near me and gently smiled.

"Well, I've got one main question," I began. "Why should I be involved in a spiritual transformation?" I asked. "That's what I want to know. I've never focused on it. I mean I don't meditate or anything."

She sat near me and studied my face. Once again, I was struck by the roundness of her countenance. She displayed no right angles or planes, just curves and circles. The overall impression was of softness, but with resilience, like a ball that always regained its shape after being compressed.

"You raise a good question," she replied. "For some, enhanced spirit is a response to a certain kind of stressor—difficulties that appear insoluble."

"It's a rising to the occasion, in other words?"

"Sort of. I don't mean something that brings out the best in you per se, though. It's more like something so traumatic that it breaks down the structures in you that normally inhibit moving up to the next level. So you experience it as misery, not as rising to anything."

"I understand. You get so devastated that you have to change to deal with it."

"Exactly. I wish I'd said it that way to start with. Now tell me about this new perspective you've attained. What's it like?"

"I'm scared almost all the time. Basically, the world looks overwhelmingly beautiful off and on, and my experience is much more direct—less filtered through my mind, I guess."

"That's wonderful."

"I guess. But I still have the same problems facing me that forced the changes. Nothing's really different."

"They may be the same, but you aren't. Are you as anxious about them?"

"No."

"Are you as paralyzed by them?"

"No."

"Then, to you, they're not the same problems now. Meaning only exists in relationship."

"Meaning is exactly what I'm after. What does what happened mean? I don't think I'm going to have peace of mind until I know."

"So as a less-anxious, less-paralyzed guy, are you better equipped to find out about whatever it is?"

"Certainly, but let me tell you about the last few weeks. I want to see if you can make any sense out of it. It's been extraordinary."

"Go ahead. I'm listening."

I told my story as briefly as I could manage. Aileen listened attentively, occasionally asking questions.

"So what do you think?" I asked when I was finally through.

"I think you're a tough nut to crack."

"What do you mean?"

"Look at all the drama it took to goose you into changing. Some people would've been out of personal resources after just a tenth of all that, forcing them to abandon their usual modus operandi much sooner."

"But what does it mean?"

"That's what it means. It's about you, not them. It means you needed something powerful and esoteric, and it showed up right on schedule. The rest of the mystery is just details."

"But there are lives at stake," I protested.

"So?"

"So I need to do something."

"Who put you in charge?"

I thought about that one. Was I caretaking beyond the scope of my actual responsibility? Well, yes. Could I just let it all go? No.

"Look," I replied. "You've got a valid point, but I can't walk away now."

"I'm not suggesting that. I'm suggesting you not identify with a specific role, whether it's mystery-solver or masked avenger, and also that you not be as attached to a particular outcome. These aren't ideas that impel anyone to walk away. On the contrary, they encourage clarity, which, in turn, promotes the generation of solutions, not just in this situation, but in all of life."

"So you're saying that two general principles apply

here, right?"

Aileen nodded.

"One is that over-identifying with a specific role keeps me confused, and the other is kind of the same thing, except it's about caring too much about making things turn out a certain way."

"You got it. What do you think?"

"I think I don't have a choice about attitudes in that realm. I'm set up the way I am."

"Bullshit. If that was ever true, it isn't now." She smiled, but her gaze was steel. "Of course, your making that choice will require a lot of work, but it's worth it."

"Yeah?"

"Yeah." She smiled again, and her eyes were softer now.

I reflected on our conversation thus far, ready to rest a bit. "I've never said 'bullshit' to a client," I told her.

"I do it all the time. I don't mind an honest mistake, but I'm not willing to listen to bullshit."

"How can you be sure you've properly differentiated between the two?"

"Bullshit feels icky."

"That's it?"

"Hey, it works for me."

I glanced at the clock; we were way over the hour. This was either very unprofessional or very generous of Aileen. Without commenting on which it might be, I paid and scheduled another appointment for ten in the morning in two days.

She gave me an Elvis Presley trading card on my way out and told me to study it. I agreed, stuffed the card in my back pocket, and promptly forgot about it. I was seeing a rather eccentric therapist, but I liked it.

Chapter 27

When Arundel called early the next day, I was prepared to deal with him. Not only did I feel immeasurably better physically, my mood had stabilized as well. Whatever else had happened with Aileen, I was now aware of solid ground beneath me. I had a place to stand.

"Hello, Tom?"

"Hi, George. What's up?"

"You sound different. Have you been drinking?"

"No. Would you like to schedule an appointment?"

"What do you mean?"

"I'm a therapist. Do you want my professional help?"

"No, no. I just wanted to congratulate you on securing the freedom of Zee's friend. And it's been determined I didn't kill anyone. I thought you should know."

"Thank you. I appreciate your courtesy."

Arundel was silent. I think he could sense that his Velcro hooks had no counterparts on me, and whatever he had planned was now obsolete.

"Well, I have some things to do," he finally announced.

"Good-bye."

I was pleased with the tenor of the conversation, which embodied a professionalism that had gone AWOL sometime after I was arrested and before I met Credula. The uncentered Tom improvised inexpertly; the post-Aileen Tom operated within a sanctioned structure when it was appropriate—and it worked. The phone call had almost been normal. I felt better, not worse, after communicating with Arundel. It was a revolution.

****

About two hours later, I emerged from the grocery store with two sacks under each arm. This was my first major shopping expedition since my concussion. I was ready to take care of myself again, and I eagerly anticipated the home-cooked meal I'd planned.

As I reached the first row of parked cars, a short man wearing a gray ski mask popped up from behind an old Toyota station wagon, accosted me, and gestured with a large handgun for me to climb into the car. Several women and a teenaged boy witnessed the incident, but none of them intervened or even pulled a phone out of a pocket.

"Can I keep the groceries?" I asked. For once, my adrenals didn't kick in. I was unnaturally calm.

He shook his head and pulled a black scarf out of his pants pocket. I placed the sacks on the asphalt beside me and announced to anyone in range that they could help themselves.

"Shut up," the man told me, his voice calmer than I would've liked. Apparently, what he was up to wasn't particularly stressful for him, which implied a career criminal. Not a good omen. And this wasn't Dizzy's kidnapper's voice. This guy was better educated.

He tied the scarf around my eyes after I'd crammed myself into the backseat of the car, then he handcuffed me to a metal grate between the back and front seats, designed to keep a dog from interfering with the driver.

I probably could've kicked the barrier down, but then we'd have probably crashed. I reasoned that the odds of survival were better if I didn't attempt to escape.

As the man drove for perhaps forty-five minutes, with the radio blaring top-forty country music, I tried to engage him in conversation, but he didn't bite. So I focused on smells, exterior sounds, and turns that might help me determine our destination. It didn't work. After the first few minutes, I was thoroughly confused, as intended. We ran a gauntlet of smells—tar, pine trees, wood smoke, and others. Loud trucks and electric cars whizzed past us from the other side of the road. I heard the chugging of a bulldozer and then the ring of a church bell about ten minutes into the trip.

Wherever we were headed, we negotiated a complex route to get there, turning every half mile or so, it seemed. The only geographical certainty was that judging from our uphill climb, we were somewhere in the Santa Cruz Mountains.

The final stretch was definitely a dirt road, so I wasn't surprised that when we halted and the door next to me opened, I could smell dust and a few wildflowers. I let my kidnapper unlock my handcuffs without resistance, eschewing another escape opportunity. It also might've provided a getting-shot opportunity. I just didn't know enough about what was going on to choose any proactive options.

A hand on my arm and a firm "no" stopped me from removing my blindfold. Then the man tried to pull me out of the car and failed.

"Move it," he growled. I sensed that this was an unnatural tone for him, adopted for effect.

Once I'd clambered out, the same hand grabbed my elbow and guided me a few dozen steps forward, and through a creaky door. As the door was being locked from the outside behind me, I removed my blindfold and surveyed my surroundings. I was in a medium-sized room containing nothing but Japanese-style straw floor mats and Peter Rabbit wallpaper. It was as if the regular inhabitants were five-year-old Zen students.

I paused to breathe, trying to calm down my nervous system's response to being imprisoned, which was more alarming on some level than being held at gunpoint in a parking lot. It helped.

Then I sat down with my back against the wall—specifically, against a cute baby bunny—with my legs stretched out on the floor ahead of me. I worked at cementing in my memory all the data that my not very keen investigative skills had acquired concerning my kidnapper. He was White, about five foot eight, with a medium build. His ski mask was constructed of fabric, while his gun was made of either metal or a durable variety of plastic. He wore jeans, brown hiking boots, and a black sweatshirt. I think he had internal organs, but this was just extrapolation.

For the next half hour, I explored my cell. Four double hung windows—one per wall—were nailed shut and covered with cardboard on the outside. An overhead globe was controlled by a rheostat on the wall beside the only door, which was solid pine, and locked from the outside, of course. Underneath the Japanese-style floor mats was a concrete slab. Also, I determined that Peter Rabbit was a happy bunny, and so were his furry pals.

I was frustrated I knew so little; I resolved to analyze my predicament as well as I could. I felt reasonably sure

I wouldn't be killed. All the murder victims had been stabbed out in the world, and Dizzy had been released unharmed, unless you counted hot dog ingestion as harm. Also, why go to the trouble of keeping his identity concealed if the guy was planning to murder me anyway?

Despite the logic of all this, waiting in the bare room proved to be a particularly challenging context in which to detach from outcome, as Aileen had recommended. Were all the potential futures inherent in my incarceration okay with me? Hell, no.

While I never suffered a full adrenal rush—a response I was growing all too familiar with—I was flooded with dread about what might come next. Torture? Deprivation? Hot dogs? It may sound ridiculous, but the thought of those hot dogs became a symbol of my loss of control. I had planned a meal of quiche, garlic bread, and fruit salad. Would some maniac make me eat something else?

Eventually, Mr. Ski Mask returned, heralded by the rattling of the padlock on the door. I briefly considered hiding and then flinging myself on him before I remembered there was nowhere to hide. And flinging was a bit beyond my physical capability at that point. My knee was still quite aggravated from the cramped car ride, and various other wounded body parts clearly preferred slow, limited movement.

Once inside, my kidnapper kept the gun trained on me and spoke without attempting to disguise his voice, which was vaguely familiar.

"I'm taking my mask off now," he said. "Don't try anything."

My nominal reserve of poise shrank dramatically.

The concept that his anonymity ensured my safety had served as a bigger emotional crutch than I'd realized.

"Don't worry," he said. "This doesn't mean anyone's going to hurt you. The goddamn thing is just itchy, that's all."

In one quick movement, he whipped the fabric over his head and revealed himself. It was the chiropractor from the tower protest crew.

So much had happened since I'd met him. It felt as though we'd been in fourth grade together. What was he doing in my present-tense world? I was mystified. This guy wasn't a psychotic killer, or even particularly abnormal.

He noticed the look on my face. I couldn't remember his name and told him so.

"Emory," he informed me. "And I still owe you a chiropractic adjustment."

"I'll settle for an explanation."

"That comes next and not from me. Now put your hands behind your head. We're going to walk over to the dining hall."

"Dining hall? What is this—a summer camp for serial killers?"

Emory smiled. "You'll see. Now let's move it."

He positioned himself a few feet behind me, gun in hand, and I moved forward on shaky legs. My heart pounded, and adrenaline raced through me now. I was fully terrified. No matter what he'd said, how could Emory let me go now that I knew who he was?

Outside, I found myself on the fringe of a grassy meadow that was surrounded by a redwood forest. Approximately a dozen small cabins similar to the one I stood next to were arranged in a wheel around a larger, barn-like structure. All these wooden buildings were painted white and gleamed in the sun as though they'd just been washed and waxed. There was no sign of anyone else, although well-worn dirt paths crisscrossed the meadow.

We embarked on the widest of these to march to the central hall, and my trepidation grew with each step. I felt as though the hell of the last few weeks was reaching a crescendo, and suddenly hell looked a lot better than whatever was next.

Chapter 28

The interior of the hall was well lit and luxuriously appointed with antique Persian rugs, rosewood paneling, and elegant hand-carved tables against the side walls. Sconces above these cast warm light onto the scenario, and a mammoth crystal chandelier hovered above us.

Familiar faces filled the large room, seated in old church pews facing a small raised stage. Dizzy, Zig-Zag, Jessica, all the environmental protesters, several clients, and the supposedly dying bookstore owner studiously kept their eyes averted as I was led down an aisle between the two rows. A couple of dozen others gawked at me.

Arundel sat in a plain wooden chair on the stage, next to an ornate gilt throne. His eyes were closed, and his face was placid. He wore a brown robe that was cinched at the waist by a silver cord.

Emory directed me to a vacant seat in the front row between two men I didn't know. One wore a policeman's uniform. I seated myself, and Emory strode off. When I swiveled my head to study Dizzy's face, the cop grabbed my ear and pulled my head around before I could.

"Keep your head still and don't try anything," he whispered. "I have a stun gun."

I nodded.

After a moment, I realized everyone in the hall except me was breathing in unison—long, slow, effortless breaths. I tried it but immediately felt nauseated and returned to my own rhythm. When the chanting began, any doubts I may have still harbored were banished. This was a cult. I was in the midst of forty or fifty fanatics, at least one of whom was a murderer.

Who was the guru? Whose throne was it? I reviewed the recent cast of characters in my life who weren't present and decided that Roberta the therapist, Aileen the transpersonal healer, Susan my ex-wife, and Sadie the dog were all extremely unlikely cult leaders. That left Ferguson, whom I could just barely picture perched on a throne. The actual leader was probably a complete stranger.

I was very surprised when a slim, ancient, dark-skinned man in a gleaming white robe slowly hobbled in and lowered himself onto the throne. The cult was led by a dead man—Krishnanda. Who was buried in his tomb, I wondered. I'd seen the man's photograph on the news during his weeklong funeral ceremonies several years back. Were thousands of Hindus visiting his white marble tomb, paying homage to a wax dummy? My mind seized on this issue instead of any of the more intense, all too relevant questions that faced me.

The first thing Krishnanda did was smile at me, and I must admit that receiving his direct attention was a powerful experience. His dark eyes were backless and bottomless—an entrance to a void. It was as if no one was in there, but unlike the vacant quality of catatonia, dementia, or Credula, his eyes conveyed something more, not less, than that which had been replaced. I felt I could fall into him forever.

His mouth indicated that he knew everything. At least that's what it seemed like. I have no idea how a mouth could convey this, but his did. The expression was wise, compassionate, and above all, knowledgeable. Clearly he was a teacher, even if his current curriculum was death.

Despite his obvious frailty, Krishnanda's posture and bearing all the way down to the way he held his fingers was aesthetically perfect—a living work of art.

Overall, his smiling scrutiny hit me as though it were a gale force wind. I actually blew backward in my chair in reaction to his psychic energy or whatever it was. The cop next to me placed a hand on my upper back to stabilize me. Arundel leaned forward in his chair, devilish delight blooming on his face as he watched me.

Then Krishnanda began speaking quickly in a heavily accented voice. It took me a moment to realize he was addressing me.

"Thomas, we need you among us. We need your strength, and we need your love. Most of all we need the power that sleeps inside you. You have passed every test and proved yourself worthy of us. We are also worthy of you. Our work is most important. The world depends on us, although it knows this no more than it knows the other simple truths which are there for all of us to see."

There was a hypnotic quality to the fast rhythm of his speech. The words flowed out and poured over me, washing me in his ideas, his energy. Some part of me knew that if I relaxed my vigilance against him, Krishnanda would conquer and claim me as he had the others in the room.

"I am now going to answer your questions," the old man told me. "I will begin with the ones in your eyes, and later we will address the ones that emerge from your mouth." He paused and then coughed deeply before continuing. "I am not dead, of course. It was necessary for our organization to become less public. This, I know, is only one very small way we have tricked you, although all in all, most of the information presented to you by those you met was accurate. Misrepresenting the truth is a more effective form of deception than transmitting that which is simply fallacious. I do not apologize for what we have done, for it needed doing. The ultimate responsibility for this work will always rest with those who see the most clearly, and I never shirk such tasks, however repugnant. I know, however, of the difficulties you have faced and overcome. It has not been easy for you, nor has it been easy for us. Lying, kidnapping, killing—these are not activities that are inherently spiritual, however necessary they might be in this case. Thus, our members have agreed to mortgage their personal karmic futures for the benefit of all. This is no small thing." He coughed again. "Now I am ready to hear your questions."

I didn't know where to begin, and I was conscious of the audience that was witnessing our exchange. I couldn't see them behind me, but I knew they were there.

"Do you believe I'm an angel?" I finally asked.

"There are no angels. In the realm beyond the physical, there is no hierarchy. We are all equal participants in consciousness when we do not wear bodies. However, as a simple conceptual representation of your potential role in the change…an angel is no less accurate than any other label. That is why we introduced the idea to you."

So a guy sitting on the golden throne says there's no hierarchy. Great. And the rest of his answer was about as clear as mud. What did "no less accurate" mean, anyway?

"Are you going to murder more people?" I asked next, my hostility radiating toward the stage.

"We have no plans to do so. The demonic forces have been sequestered within the bounds of the sacred circle. If further measures will be required, however, we will do whatever is necessary to nurture change."

"How can you possibly justify taking lives?"

"You misunderstand. I am not expressing a point of view, a prediction, a theory, a guess, or anything else that is open to debate. I know it was necessary. I know more surely than you can trust your own senses. This is not braggadocio or arrogance. It is fact. If you say 'I have large feet,' and you do, are you demonstrating arrogance?"

"Knowing the size of my feet and knowing the world's future are two completely different things."

"Not to me. Lifetimes of spiritual study have prepared me to receive information from realms that are not available to you. I am simply an expert in an arena in which you are not. By the same token, I would not question your diagnosis of a patient."

"You should. Psychology is a very inexact science."

"My field is not. Not to me. What other questions can I help you with?"

"Why me? Why isn't my neighbor or a colleague standing here?"

"That is harder to explain. I'll begin at the energetic level. Your configuration fits the pattern of our needs, or, seen the other way around, we are missing that which your being supplies. Of course, energy configurations also manifest in less esoteric levels—in personality, occupation, experience, etc. You are also a necessary cog in the cosmic machine in these terms, although it would require a great deal of time, which we don't have, to explore this in detail. Suffice it to say that I am patiently explaining myself to you because of our discovery of who you are."

"You say you need me, but why do I need you?" I asked. Caught up in Krishnanda's words and energy field, I was aware of nothing else.

"We have a lot to offer you as an individual, which is still what you believe you are. We are a community with all the benefits and strengths of a community. We stand by each other, we love each other. Love is healing—something you need, Tom. I can also help guide you on your unique spiritual path. Do you want to live several thousand more lifetimes, or do you want to move on to the next plane? You cannot accelerate your journey without help. Also, in terms of personal satisfaction, there can be none greater than that which is derived from directly participating in the transformation of the world."

"That's something else I want to know. Just what is this transformed world going to look like? Are we talking about the dead rising up, no more diseases, or just more New Age churches?"

"Let me describe the world after the change. The dead will stay dead, some diseases will remain, but war will gradually fade away. All things exist to serve a purpose, and when the purpose is no longer needed, neither is the phenomenon itself. In other words, war will end because the world will change into a realm that no longer needs war. Spirituality will return as the everyday priority it once was. Science and technology will be demoted, along with personal goals. In greater harmony, the people of the world will cooperate to solve problems such as hunger, pollution, and mental illness. How does that sound?"

"I guess I get the idea."

"Good. I am growing weary—my energy is not what it once was. Perhaps you could direct your remaining inquiries to my assistant." He gestured gracefully at George, who pulled himself erect in his seat and gazed at me expectantly.

"You're like the vice president, huh?"

Arundel nodded. "How may I help you?"

The way he said it, the phrase sounded like even more of a cliché than it was. Perhaps the cult's members asked if they could help each other all day long.

"Are you a multiple?" I asked.

"Yes, but my alters communicate freely with each other. My presentation to you was misleading."

"Is Zig-Zag really Krishnanda's daughter?"

"No."

"My birthmark?" I asked cocking an eyebrow.

"An exaggeration."

"If there really aren't any angels—if they're just a symbol like Krishnanda said—then what about demons? Why kill people with demon names if there aren't any demons?"

"That's a good question," Arundel answered. "Technically, demons don't exist. But the souls of these people were serving darkness, and their names are significant clues to their identities. They are the equivalent of demons. Believe me, their deaths were necessary—vital—to the welfare of everyone on this planet."

"What was the point of the fake kidnapping?" I

asked next. "And who the hell was that guy on the phone?"

"Many of our members are accomplished actors since our organization was founded in Hollywood. As to your first question, there were several reasons for the red herring. One, the police were closing in on me, and we needed to divert their efforts to another suspect. Two, we needed to keep you busy and confused—in overwhelm mode. Otherwise, your old configuration of personality would continue to assert itself, and this would serve no one, least of all you."

"That's not arrogant? Listen to yourself, George. It's dripping off you."

"I am arrogant. I freely admit I'm as full of human foibles as anyone else, and I'm definitely unworthy of my job. Krishnanda, however, is gloriously qualified to make such judgments, and he has, for his own reasons, designated me to be his assistant. I am at least evolved enough not to second-guess an incarnation of God himself."

"Why was someone trying to kill Dizzy when she's part of your cult?"

"No one was. That was something we arranged to draw you closer to her."

"And the weird alters—Credula and the guy in the woods? Are they real?"

"They are. They work through me as Krishnanda commands," he replied.

I glanced at Krishnanda, who appeared to be sleeping. As if he sensed my examination, his intense eyes opened, and he began speaking again without preamble.

"Emory? It's time to escort our guest back to the

nursery. Tom, I want you to think about what you've experienced here."

"I couldn't avoid it if I tried," I told him.

"Good. Emory?"

Krishnanda closed his eyes again, and everyone besides Emory, myself, and Arundel bowed their heads. I departed in a daze, shuffling back to my cell.

Chapter 29

It all boiled down to Krishnanda. Had he legitimately transcended conventional morality? Was his purported prescience sufficiently accurate to warrant extraordinary measures?

I needed to evaluate who this man was, but I was woefully ill-equipped to do so. My only experience of gurus had been Matthew Ferguson and perhaps Aileen Van Der Voot, and they were the equivalent of kittens compared to the Indian's saber-toothed tiger. Anyway, how well had I known Ferguson when only minutes ago I had believed he might be the mystery man occupying the vacant throne?

Certainly, Krishnanda was charismatic and powerful. And a whole array of people, some of whom impressed me as being reasonably substantive, believed in him enough to break the law. On the other hand, how could a holy man endorse murder—no matter the circumstances? That I knew one of the victims and she had been in no way demonic strengthened my resistance.

When I could momentarily shake off Krishnanda's influence, it all sounded as crazy as ever. But the impact of my time with him was profound; I wasn't the same Tom Dashiel I had been an hour ago. This latest version of Tom was much more open to outlandish spiritual possibilities and even seemed to be more comfortable sitting on straw floor mats. Part of me watched myself be different, while another part merely became lost in it. It was an odd sensation. My sense of self had certainly been taking a battering lately.

I didn't know for sure where my ruminating was heading, although I'd like to think I'd have categorically spurned Krishnanda's overtures. As it happened, I didn't get the chance. A tapping at one of the covered windows interrupted my latest internal debate.

"Tom?"

I knew that mellifluous baritone immediately. It was Ferguson.

"I'm here, all right. Be careful. They've got guns."

"Right."

I didn't hear from my rescuer again until he'd popped the hasp loose on the door and swung it open into the fading daylight.

"Ready to go?" he asked, a sturdy stick in his hand. Ferguson was smiling and wearing old denim overalls and brown hiking boots. He looked like a farmer ready to hit the Appalachian trail. I was elated to see him.

"Absolutely," I replied. "Let's get out of here."

I couldn't run—my knee still hurt too much—but he led me at a fast walk toward a narrow trail behind an adjacent building. I could barely tolerate the pain, but I was happy to do so.

"There's a guard at the main gate," he told me. "I parked about a half mile back this way."

"Great. How'd you know they had me?"

As we entered the dimly lit redwood forest, Ferguson explained. "Several witnesses reported the snatch to the police with a description of the victim. It was on the local news. How many huge guys with scarred faces are there? Then I heard that the K-Lovers were having an emergency all-members meeting, and I put two and two together. I've been monitoring the group for a while now; it's clear they're on the verge of something big."

"The K-Lovers, huh? Well, here's a piece of news. Krishnanda is still alive."

"Really? Wow, that explains a lot."

"And he's been ordering his people to kill so-called demons—the serial murders in town."

"Shit," he exclaimed. "Pardon my French."

Dogs howled back at the compound.

"Shit," we both said this time.

I tried to pick up my pace as the baying and barking grew closer, but I just couldn't run properly.

The redwood-dominated ecosystem we were moving through contained very little undergrowth or even other varieties of trees, since redwood droppings distribute a substance that's poisonous to other plants. Unfortunately, this created longer lines of sight that would enable our pursuers to find us sooner.

A crook in the trail aided our cause, but soon after changing directions, an area damaged by fire revealed us again. The transition from fragrant redwood needles to ash and embers was unpleasant. This blackened landscape was Bosch-like in its utter strangeness. I felt we were speed walking on another planet until we entered living forest again.

"I think it'll be close," Ferguson pronounced. "If we have to fight off the dogs, go for either their noses or their balls."

I pictured a pack of rottweilers, Dobermans, or all the other breeds I was afraid of. If we didn't make it to wherever Ferguson had parked, I wasn't optimistic about our chances.

As the silver sports car came into view about fifty yards ahead of us, paws pounded the trail behind us, and I pivoted just in time to see four canines about to catch up to us. Two were small gray terriers, one was a golden retriever, and a portly basset hound brought up the rear, baying with excitement. Ferguson bent down to pet the tail-wagging crew, and all four licked his hand furiously for a moment before we continued.

"I guess the dogs were more for locating us than subduing us," I said.

"Apparently."

The four of them ran ahead, playing with each other. The basset tripped comically over his own ears twice.

"The one with no legs is kind of cute," Ferguson commented. "Maybe we should keep her as a hostage."

"Please. Just get us out of here."

We reached the low-slung sports car, piled in, and Ferguson roared away. Although it was a hard-packed dirt road, he drove at breakneck speeds. Each time we hit a curve, I was positive we were going to flip over, and I braced myself accordingly. I'd never ridden in a car that could do what this one could. We sat a few scant inches above the ground in firm leather seats that transmitted every contour in the road via very stiff shocks. There was a great deal of leg room but a scarcity of headroom, and no back seat at all.

"What is this torpedo?" I asked.

"Lotus. Twin turbos," Ferguson managed to reply while downshifting into yet another hairpin curve. "Don't worry," he added a moment later. "I used to race."

I worried anyway. "Where are we?" I asked a few

moments later.

"Between Boulder Creek and Saratoga, off Skyline Boulevard."

"Don't you think you can slow down now? There's no way they're going to catch us."

"Motorcycles. Crotch rockets. I saw them in the parking lot. If I'd been thinking, I would've disabled them. They're even faster than this thing."

"Oh, God."

Ferguson was right. We reached a paved country road and turned south a few hundred yards ahead of two gaudily painted bikes, which sprinted after us.

"There's a gun in the glovebox," Ferguson told me, accelerating up into the nineties in third gear.

It was a twelve-shot Glock pistol—a nice gun and fully loaded. I felt comforted as I held it in my hand.

We hit 110 on a short straightaway, but the motorcycles still gained on us. The Lotus' handling was rock solid, even as its turbo shrieked at these higher rpm's. Ferguson expertly squeezed everything he could out of the exotic car, but the bikes leaned through the corners more efficiently and were quicker off the mark when the highway straightened.

On the other hand, I reasoned, what could someone guiding a motorcycle at a hundred miles an hour do to you? Shoot a gun? Maybe, but I didn't think so. At least not accurately. Could they cut us off—force us off the road? No. We were a threat to them in that department. So why was I so anxious? Maybe it was the sheer speed, my anticipation of having to use a gun, or just the recent accumulated stress of being kidnapped and escaping. Any of those would do it, I decided. In the meantime, the riders closed in on us.

Ferguson began swerving on the deserted two-lane road to prevent the bikes from passing us, but the strategy seemed hopeless. If he blocked one, the other gained ground. Sooner or later, we would be vulnerable to whatever the motorcyclists were planning.

Maybe the big picture was looking out for us. Certainly, the appearance of a Highway Patrol car at that point was an injection of classical grace into the situation. It was the exact moment in my forty-some-odd years that I most needed the law, and there it was. What were the odds?

The black and white cruiser was heading north, but as soon as the driver passed us, he made a skidding U-turn and gave chase. His car was out of sight behind us in seconds.

"I doubt he'll catch us at these speeds," Ferguson shouted to me. "We can slow down for him, or trust he'll radio ahead and there'll be a roadblock later."

"Roadblock," I called back.

"Right."

Ferguson gunned the motor, and we leapt forward even faster. The bikes receded a bit in the narrow rear window as we roared through a long straightaway at over 140. At that speed, everything but a point directly ahead of us on the horizon was a blur. I couldn't imagine how Ferguson was steering in response to the road. Did he know it well? Were his reflexes superhuman?

Gunshots pulled my attention back into the moment. Realizing they might not get a better chance now that cops were involved, the bikers were firing handguns from behind us. It seemed unlikely they'd hit us, but if a bullet struck the wrong part of the car, we were as good as dead anyway. At 140 miles an hour, even a flat tire would kill us.

Ferguson began swerving again, this time to make us a more difficult target. But as he changed directions coming out of a tight curve, the rear wheels lost traction and we began spinning wildly.

I figured we were in the process of dying, and I was surprised to discover I wasn't afraid. There was a matter-of-fact quality to the mosaic of sensations and impressions, as though I was experiencing them from a place deep enough not to care how it all turned out.

After an eternity, we stopped spinning and found ourselves just off the road, facing the wrong way. The car stalled, and Ferguson couldn't get it to start again. I was dizzy and nauseated but very calm.

The bikes overran us and then revved their way back. I handed the gun to Ferguson, reasoning that anyone with a Glock in his glovebox was bound to be a better marksman than I was. The motorcyclists parked their bikes a good distance from us, dismounted, and drew their pistols.

I was beginning to duck when the cop car came screaming around the curve facing us and jammed on his brakes. Skidding with only a small semblance of control, the highway patrolman shot by the bike riders, who hopped back on their machines and tore off the way we'd come. Apparently, the cop was satisfied with bagging the Lotus. He turned and parked behind us. A minute later, we were out of the car, our hands in the air in response to his drawn gun.

Chapter 30

By the time we convinced the state cop to drive back with us to the Krishnanda compound, the entire cult had cleared out, leaving no obvious evidence to support our story. Ferguson and I remained in handcuffs, locked in the back of the cruiser as Joe Estes, the highway patrolman, explored the property and then returned to report his continued skepticism.

From the driver's seat, he pivoted to face us through a steel grate. His nose led the way. Long and wide, it split his dark brown face into two non-mirror halves. One side sported a heavy-lidded eye, the other seemed almost Asian. And one of his ears was misshapen. He smelled like cigarettes, but not strongly enough to be offensive. All this would've been distracting in circumstances that weren't so dire. As it was, I kept my attention on convincing Joe to pursue the Krishnanda people.

"It's a great story, guys, but I wasn't born yesterday," he said. "We're wasting time here. I'm holding y'all until we get this whole thing sorted out. Now who were those guys on motorcycles, really? Why was there a handgun in your car? Is this a gang thing?"

I felt like screaming. Here we were, sitting around while murderers escaped. I rocked forward, my scowl threatening to pull my whole face down. As the corners of my eyes tightened, a headache began to pound my temples. Before I let loose on our captor, Ferguson spoke up to substitute something more helpful than what I was about to say.

"Do we look like we're in a gang?" Ferguson asked. "And are these handcuffs necessary? This was a traffic infraction—albeit a major one. You've got us locked in here behind a steel barrier. Come on. Have some compassion."

"I don't ordinarily restrain speeders, no matter how fast or reckless they're driving, that's true. Unless it's a DUI, of course. But you've got a firearm, the motorcyclists were brandishing firearms, and Mr. Dashiel here looks like he could be a danger to others."

I guessed this was cop code for "I'm scared of him." Still pissed off, I breathed deeply for a count of eight, and the pain in my temples receded a bit. I knew that reacting to Joe's assertion that I was a violent person wasn't going to get us anywhere, so I pointed out I had merely sat in a passenger seat while everyone else carried on a high-speed chase. And I could scarcely control my height, could I? My mom was big, my dad was big. Did that make them dangerous, too?

"Those are scars from a knife fight, right?" Joe asked, pointing at my face. "You definitely look like you could be in a gang. And it wouldn't be fair to cuff you and leave Mr. Ferguson free."

I gave up. "Good point."

On the way to the highway patrol station south of Santa Cruz, I regrouped and worked at convincing Joe to at least contact my buddy, the Santa Cruz police chief—Gil Franklin. "He'll vouch for me. I'm more or less consulting with the force on the serial killings," I told him. "In fact, I'm the one who steered them to the perp, and he was at the Krishnanda place when I escaped.

Every minute you don't call this in gives this creep a chance to get farther away. These are planners. I'm sure they have an exit strategy."

"Can you corroborate any of this, Mr. Ferguson?"

"Absolutely. All of it. And let me ask you this, Joe. What does your gut tell you? You deal with criminals and liars all day long. Is that truly your sense of who we are?"

"No, not really. I'll call once we get to the station."

"Thank you so much."

****

Once Joe's boss and Chief Franklin had a chance to talk, I video chatted in an upscale conference room with the two of them, an FBI regional supervisor who didn't share his name, and a roomful of unidentified officers. The official debriefing could wait. They needed to know everything as soon as possible that might help them nab the Krishnanda people.

I told them what I knew, as succinctly as I could, and then Ferguson and I waited in the conference room with Joe as our babysitter while the others rushed off to get to work.

"Sorry about the way I acted," the patrolman told us.

"No worries," Ferguson told him. "In your shoes, I'd have done the same thing."

"That's easy for you to say," I told him. "You weren't typecast as some sort of hitman."

"Let me make it up to you," Joe said. "You guys hungry? I could make a pizza run."

"That would be great."

"I'll just check and see who else wants some." He marched out of the room. We could hear him calling out, "Who wants pizza?"

"How are you doing?" Ferguson asked. This was the first time we'd been alone. "How's the life curriculum going?" His voice was gentle, and a half smile graced his lower face.

"It's like a whole semester in a few hours. I don't have to tell you. You were with me back on Skyline Boulevard." I gestured out a window that wasn't there. The room had no windows. Then I turned and aimed my arm in the opposite direction. "I guess north is that way."

"I wasn't in the meeting hall with you, Tom. But I stood near Krishnanda fifteen years ago at his ashram in India. I can only imagine what it must've been like to have him directly focus on you. Even in a group setting, his energy almost made me swoon. On the other hand, I wasn't buying what he was selling, so I was off to another ashram the next day."

"How are you doing?"

"I'm fine. I almost died several times before, so I wasn't worried about that. And the scenario here with the police has been fascinating. Did you notice how everyone yielded to the FBI guy on everything? Even when he called you Chet? And Joe is an interesting character, isn't he? He doesn't match my preconception of a highway patrolman at all."

"Really? You weren't worried about dying?"

"Dying is perfectly safe, Tom. Didn't you notice?"

"Actually, I sort of did."

By now, it was very late. When we paused our conversation briefly, I fell asleep. I awoke to the smell of pizza.

"Good news," Joe announced as he tossed two pizza boxes on the table in front of us.

"Pizza is always good news," Ferguson told him.

"No, I mean they've caught a few people already. No one's talking yet, but they will."

"Who?" I asked in a groggy voice. My tongue was dry and clumsy, and my headache had returned.

"A young gal wouldn't skip town without her dog, and the dog was at her veterinarian, so we nabbed her there when she got the doc to open up after hours."

"Sarah Somebody?"

"Exactly. The one you said lived on Cayuga up in Santa Cruz. Her housemate told us where she'd gone."

I hadn't been hoping Zig-Zag would escape, but nonetheless, a sinking feeling hit my gut. It wasn't disappointment per se. Empathy for her plight? I thought about it for a moment. I just liked her. We'd connected on another level from my brief friendship with Dizzy. And about eighteen levels from Arundel.

In that moment, I sorely hoped George and Krishnanda would pay for their crimes. They were the real villains. No matter how delusional murderers might be, society can't function without holding them responsible for the net effect of their actions.

Joe opened the pizza boxes. He'd gone with onions on one and pepperoni on the other. "And Tom," he continued, "you steered us toward a chiropractor named Emory, and there's only one of those around. He boarded a plane to Milwaukee, and the FBI took him off on the tarmac in San Jose. They realized later that some other cult members might be on the same flight, so a team is waiting to screen everybody on the ground in Wisconsin. They may need you to identify who's who."

"Sure."

"Good work," Ferguson said. "And don't forget your role in this. You agreed to call the Santa Cruz police chief, and that's what got the ball rolling."

"Thanks. I appreciate that." He strode off to get the soft drinks he'd left on his desk. I grabbed an onion-laden pizza slice and stuffed the pointed end into my mouth.

Over the next few hours, as we debriefed in a smaller, less well-appointed room with a polite, extremely thorough detective named Donna, we received periodic updates from our new cop buddy, Joe. He'd thrust the door open from the squad room and call in whatever he'd found out, interrupting an obviously annoyed Donna each time. To her credit, she endured this for our benefit.

Forensic investigation yielded a small vial of liquid at Dizzy's home that later turned out to be a sophisticated designer drug containing DMT, which generated hallucinations and could be dissolved in water. Apparently, Dizzy had drugged me in the Fall Creek woods when I'd used her water bottle. My tumble off the rocks must have disrupted whatever plan they'd concocted.

None of the cult members arrested early on cooperated with the police, but physical evidence at two of their homes linked them to one of the killings. By midday, as we continued to hang around the station—"in case we were needed"—fingerprints on Dizzy's picture frames proved that her real name was Kirala Jenkins. She was wanted in several midwestern states for various scams, including a fraudulent dating service. The Black angel paintings had been crafted by someone else in the cult, whose notoriety subsequently propelled his career upward in the art world.

Over the next few weeks, more members were

corralled, and finally someone I didn't know broke down and spilled the beans about everything. Since the police were through with me by then, I read the details online the same as everyone else.

Arundel committed the murders personally, at Krishnanda's direction, but quite a few cult members participated in the planning and logistics. Charges of first-degree murder, conspiracy to commit murder, kidnapping, criminal conspiracy, and a host of firearm and controlled-substance violations were filed against most of the members in jail, as well as the ones still loose. A nationwide dragnet garnered more fugitives, but Arundel, Dizzy, and Krishnanda were never found.

The press speculated that perhaps the trio had committed suicide, but I'm sure that wasn't their style. I picture them relaxing in hammocks outside a remote cabin in the Rockies, scheming and planning their next campaign to save the world.

Some members of the media propagated the theory that the cult members were merely victims, brainwashed by their evil overlord and thus not responsible for their illegal acts. Fortunately, the authorities didn't see it that way and pressed ahead with prosecutions. Although the trials are just beginning, watched daily by an alarming number of voyeuristic television viewers, it appears that most everyone concerned will do at least some prison time. No one's called me as a witness yet, but obviously they will, so I've spent some time with a dogged prosecutor in preparation for that.

I'll admit I was glad that nothing tied Zig-Zag directly to the murders, lessening her looming sentence. I almost visited her in jail in an attempt to reciprocate her visit to me in the state mental institution. Then I remembered that had never happened, and that she'd held a key role in screwing with my mind.

As for me, I learned from Chief Franklin that one reason I'd been chosen by Krishnanda was simply because they needed a psychotherapist in the cult—someone fully bought into the program—someone who'd fully surrendered to Krishnanda.

He called me to fill me in on what their dealmaking cult member had revealed. "Tom, here's more. As 'the stress of pursuing the cult's goals mounted'—those are his words—our source says that more and more members broke down. I'm not sure what that means exactly. It's probably not a technical term in your world."

"No, but I can imagine how challenging it was trying to conform to the cult's mores when so much of that was likely to have violated a given member's value system."

"Whatever."

I'd lost him.

He continued. "Our guy also says, no offense, that you're the loneliest therapist in town—the one least connected to family and friends—which makes you an ideal recruit. And your last name, of course, is supposed to have an angel ending—you know, the 'iel' in Dashiel. As things moved along, they also liked the way you dealt with all their crazy shit. You stayed confused. You kept going instead of hiding out somewhere—all that."

"Thanks, chief. I appreciate the update." That was the last I heard from him.

In hindsight, the craziest thing about the cult were the lengths they went to in order to manipulate me. It had been overkill on top of overkill. How much money had they spent? How many laws had they broken? How many man hours had been squandered on yours truly? My only explanation is that whatever his other motives had been, Krishnanda must have sincerely believed I was destined to fill some key role in his plans—maybe not in the way he told me, but in some way.

****

These days, I'm pleased to report I spend a lot less time stuck in my head. In the ten months since the mass arrests, I've encountered dozens of excuses to retreat back in there, but for the most part, I've managed to expand the proportion of my waking hours lived in the moment.

I never really liked it up in my mind, anyway. I was just too far out of balance to be able to exercise choice and foray into another way of being. Even merely sampling the alternatives had been beyond my awareness, and far beyond my fear threshold, so I filtered all my experiences ad nauseam, until sensory input was reduced until I felt safe.

Of course, I still wimp out sometimes. But I'm working on it. It helps a lot that, when I can truly focus on the present, I see and hear so clearly that my world transforms into something remarkable. The intensity of this experience triggers fear, but it looks and sounds wonderful as long as I can stand it.

Ironically, after the drug-induced vision, the angel-wing phenomenon, and even my audience with Krishnanda, it was my near-death experience in Ferguson's sports car that emerged as the most transformative episode. There was no dearth of lid-loosening events leading up to the wild ride with Ferguson, but it was my accepting impending death gracefully that popped it off all the way. His racing experience, by the way, consisted of two days of NASCAR summer camp as a teenager.

At any rate, whenever I become anxious now, I remember that at least I'm not spinning in a Lotus at a hundred miles an hour with fanatical gunmen on motorcycles chasing me. And even when I was, it wasn't so bad. Unlike my earlier disfiguring car accident, the recent experience with Ferguson served to open me up, not shut me down.

I can see now that part of my inability to comprehend what happened to me was that I had conceptualized everything in starkly dichotomous terms. The spiritual element of the experience was either fake or real. Arundel was either evil or good. I was either an idiot or a savior. I periodically swung the pendulum of my flawed judgment from one polar extreme to the other, never allowing it to rest in the middle where the truth lay.

I believe now that the crazy and the profound commonly coexist—are even drawn toward one another. I've also realized that accommodating benign intrusions from spirit is a skill I dearly need to learn. Numerous spontaneous synchronicities—meaningful coincidences arranged by the universe, not the cult—had been woven into the K-Lovers' hoax, for example. Spirit, after all, is everywhere, independent of who might be lying to me. I experienced the explicit appearance of the spiritual realm in my life as a problem, then I analyzed it as though it could be a barometric reading on reality. I hope I'm behaving more sensibly now, but someday I'll probably look back on what I'm doing these days and find it just as ridiculous.

I've been studying with Ferguson, trying to expand my understanding of how the world really works, and I see Aileen Van Der Voot once a week, too. Both of them have been extremely helpful in processing the tremendous backlog of feelings that surfaced once the crisis receded. Perhaps I could've worked with a mainstream therapist, but I'm more comfortable with people who understand exactly what I've been through. My consultants help keep me from becoming too serious or self-important, as well. I still wallow shamelessly in these whenever my mood and the opportunity intersect. After all, who doesn't want to be singled out as special by a well-known guru?

My practice is thriving, and my clients have benefited from my adventures as well. With more of me in the room—as a person, not just a therapist—our relationship has become a much more powerful tool. It's quite satisfying.

What else?

I'm scheduled for plastic surgery on my face next month. I'd like to feel more poised in public now that my girlfriend Marcia and I are attending a lot of concerts and shows. I met her on a movie line and was profoundly attracted by her authenticity, long, lithe legs, and our strong sense of mutual attunement.

****

Marcia and I were watching television together the other night when the penguins reappeared on a nature show. The same dopey male was toting his small black rocks to the same fussy female.

"I wonder how she knows which rock is a good one?" Marcia asked.

Entwined with her on my oversized couch, I'd been stroking her long blonde hair and hadn't paid much attention to my old friends. "Beats me," I replied. "Does it matter?"

"I guess not." She kissed me for a long time before finishing her response. "No, it definitely doesn't matter at all," she affirmed.

Have I left anything out?

Oh, yes. Sadie the dog lives with me. I ransomed her from the shelter when it became clear her reputation as a cult dog was hindering her adoption. Ferguson took the basset hound who'd chased us at the Krishnanda compound and spoils him terribly.

Life isn't so bad.

Aw hell, life is good.

A word about the author...

Verlin Darrow is currently a psychotherapist who lives with his psychotherapist wife in the woods near Monterey Bay in northern California. They diagnose each other as necessary. He is the author of *Blood and Wisdom*, *Coattail Karma*, and *Prodigy Quest*. Verlin is a former professional volleyball player, country-western singer/songwriter, import store owner, and assistant guru in a small, benign cult. Before bowing to the need for higher education, a much younger Verlin ran a punch press in a sheet-metal factory, drove a taxi, worked as a night janitor, shoveled asphalt on a road crew, and installed wood floors. He barely missed being blown up by Mt. St. Helens, survived the 1985 Mexico City earthquake (8.0), and (so far) he's successfully weathered his own internal disasters.

For more information, visit verlindarrow.com. To reach the author, email verlindarrow@gmail.

Thank you for purchasing
this publication of The Wild Rose Press, Inc.

For questions or more information
contact us at
info@thewildrosepress.com.

The Wild Rose Press, Inc.
www.thewildrosepress.com